BRIGID
THE GIRL FROM
COUNTY CLARE

Books by Vicky Adin

The Cornish Knot
Portrait of a Man

Brigid The Girl from County Clare
Gwenna The Welsh Confectioner
The Costumier's Gift

The Disenchanted Soldier

The Art of Secrets

BRIGID
THE GIRL FROM COUNTY CLARE

VICKY ADIN

First produced for Vicky Adin in 2015 as a print book and ebook under the title *The Girl from County Clare*, by AM Publishing New Zealand
www.ampublishingnz.com

Cover Image:
Smith & Caughey, Robert Walrond (1859–1932)

To order copies of Vicky Adin's print books:
www.vickyadin.co.nz, www.amazon.com

Ebooks available from www.amazon.com

Dedication

Thanks to the Irish for their stories

PART ONE

The Journey

1

The Leaving

Gravesend, London
Tuesday, 19th October 1886

Brigid's nose wrinkled at the odious mixture of oil, coal and scummy seawater. "Ah, Mammy. What have I done?"

Any enthusiasm she had once felt soon turned to trepidation on the journey from her village in County Clare to the docks of London. She'd been told all sorts of tales about England, as foreign to her as her destination, but she hadn't expected it to be quite so different from her native Ireland.

Bells clanged, engines churned and animals bayed. Hordes of anxious people chattered, sailors shouted and cargo thumped and banged as the crew loaded it. Her ears buzzed from all the noise. She'd never seen so many people and so many buildings in one place. A sudden ear-piercing screech from the steam whistle drowned out every other sound, and Brigid clamped her hands over her ears to ease the pain.

"Breeda!" her cousin Jamie shouted. "Breeda. Do ye hear me?" A head taller than most people, Jamie pushed

1

his way through the throng of passengers and around stacked crates to reach her.

His touch startled her.

"I was calling you, our Breeda."

"I didn't hear you above this frightful din."

"Never mind that now. Come on, come with me." Jamie picked up her small trunk and marched off again. Brigid felt for her great-grandmother's brooch to check she still had it firmly pinned to her petticoat. She treasured it as a good luck charm. Satisfied, she gathered up her bag stuffed with clothes, her rosary, Bible and other precious things and followed him.

It had taken her and Jamie two weeks to get to London. She knew all the reasons why she was here facing the start of her new life, but the reality of the decision was vastly different from the talk. And there'd been plenty of that over the last few years since the potato crop had failed – again.

Brigid had fretted during the idle hours spent waiting to board. Under the command of Captain Sayers, the SS *Dorunda*, a new-style steamship owned by the British India Steam Navigation Company, would take her thousands of miles away from her homeland, across the oceans to Australia. They'd been pushed and shaped into endless queues in order firstly, to pass inspection by the ship's officers and get their tickets stamped, and secondly, for Dr Goodall, the ship's surgeon, to examine their persons. The doctor had placed a long trumpet-shaped object against her chest, with his ear pressed to the other end: checking for infectious diseases, she'd been told. Whatever he hoped to hear she never knew, but thankfully, she and Jamie were both waved on through.

"You're down the back in the single girls' quarters, and I'm up front with the men," Jamie shouted over his shoulder. His muscles bulged as he manoeuvred the trunk through the crush of people and obstacles on deck. Even at eighteen, he wasn't one to be messed with. He'd developed enormous strength through a life of hard farming on stony ground.

"Ah, Jamie. Can't I stay with you?"

"No luck there, Breeda, my love. There's rules. You'll be grand, that you will." His lilting Irish brogue comforted her.

Trapped between the shoulders of the other passengers, she would have had an elbow in her eye if she hadn't moved her head in time. The distance between her and Jamie grew.

"Wait up," she cried and surged forward to grab the tail of his jacket, unsettled by the strangeness around her.

British seamen shouted orders to dozens of brown-skinned sailors wearing strange, brimless black hats, decorated with colourful kerchiefs. Their long cotton tunics, tied with a scarf and worn over baggy trousers, looked stained and unkempt, but the men seemed cheerful enough as they lifted and tossed endless sacks of mail and crates of goods. She hadn't expected to see people who looked so, so … she searched for the word to fit. Exotic, or fanciful, came to mind.

"Keep close, Breeda. We need to get in quick to get ye the best bunk. First in, first served, they said."

As they moved further aft, the crowds thinned out, and Brigid saw families nervously gathered together around their possessions; a woman stood alone, straining her neck to look for someone; a child cried. With no one to bar his way, Jamie led her down the aft ladder into the dimly lit compartment between decks. Blinking to adjust her eyes to the shadowy light, Brigid could see the chamber ran the full width of the ship. What little light seeped in came from the occasional small porthole on either side.

The ceiling rose high enough, but the darkness made it feel low. Bunks stacked two high and two deep lined the outer walls. Jamie slouched his shoulders and bowed his head as he shuffled his way along the central passage. At the far end he spied a set of empty berths – narrow bunks with barely enough space between them for him to stand front on – and shoved Brigid's trunk under the lower bed.

"Oi! You," shouted a woman, appearing out of the shadows. "Yer not supposed to be in here. Yer a man!"

"That I am, for sure, miss." Jamie took his cap off and flashed her a cheeky grin. "And I'm just leaving, ma'am. Only here to help ma cousin with her luggage. Little t'ing that she is couldna manage on her own. I'm sure you understand, a woman as canny as you." He winked at the woman, who laughed and tucked a stray strand of her unruly strawberry-blonde curls behind her ear.

"Gerraway wi' ya, young 'un. You canna flatter me, even if you do have manners."

Jamie kissed Brigid on the cheek and gave her a wink as he disappeared up the ladder.

"Well, lass, looks like we're neighbours. I'm Sally."

A curvy woman dressed in a dark blue full-skirted dress with a rather low-cut neckline scrutinised her. Brigid guessed she would be at least twenty-five years old but couldn't be certain.

"I'm Brigid O'Brien, but they calls me Breeda."

"Well. Glad to meet you, Miss Breeda." She paused.

"I know – Breeda Kneader, Pudding and Pie, kissed the boys and made them ... wild." Laughing at her own joke, she gave Brigid a friendly push in response to the girl's mortified look. "Ease up, a'ways, hen. We've a long way to go together. Just a bit of funning."

Brigid tried a wobbly smile, but couldn't think of anything to say. She took off her bonnet and coat, revealing the deep purple bengaline costume with her own handmade lace collar – a copy of a hand-me-down donated to the convent – and felt indebted to the nuns for her two good dresses and the skills to make them.

"Skinny wee thing, ain't you?" remarked Sally, eyeing Brigid from top to toe. "And that's a lovely bit of lace, an' all. Did you make it?"

"Thank you. Yes, I did."

"Clever you. Wish my hair'd braid as neat as yours."

Brigid patted her dark chignon self-consciously. "I could try and do yours for you sometime, if you'd like. The colour is beautiful. Like molten honey in the sunshine."

"More like scraggly straw!" she guffawed. "We'll see. Get yourself sorted."

Anxious as to how bad the journey would be, Brigid took the advice of a sailor she'd met to claim an upper berth: 'Ye don' wanna be down below 'en people start chuckin' up,' he'd said. 'An' they will, when weather gets rough.'

Sally sat on the edge of the bottom bunk she'd claimed. "Where you from and where you goin' then, lass?"

Brigid unrolled her sleeping mat and blanket, neatly tied her eating utensils together through the holes in the handles and hung them on a hook. "I'm from County Clare in the west of Ireland. I'm going to Brisbane. And you?" After rerolling some of her clothing Brigid shoved her bag hard against the outer wall.

"Sally Forsythe from Dumfriesshire, Scotland, going to Townsville."

The women shook hands, but before anything more could be said, two newcomers wanting to claim the neighbouring berths jiggled past them.

"And who might you two be?" Sally cheerfully greeted the newcomers.

"I'm Annie McKenna," said a shy, thin girl with lank, dark hair and shadows under her eyes.

"And I'm Lettie, from County Derry," announced her look-alike counterpart.

"We're sisters," they said in unison, as they placed their belongings on the adjacent lower bunk.

"Hello, Annie and Lettie. I'll get out the way for a wee bit while you set up." Brigid squeezed around them to give them some space.

The mast, hatchway and ladder took up much of the 'tween deck, and the claustrophobic space was becoming even more cramped. A steady stream of women stumbled down the ladder in search of a bunk and a place to store their belongings. Brigid silently thanked Jamie for insisting she get in early to find a bunk.

Benches of some sort hung from the near-black ceiling space, and Brigid puzzled how they would get them down – and where they were supposed to go. They had little enough room to manoeuvre as it was.

Amidst the clamour, she heard some Irish voices, but most accents she didn't recognise: Scottish ones, maybe, and lots of English. Many a time since leaving home she'd not understood much of what was said. Even the people looked different.

On their journey, Brigid had seen the fashionable families in their stylish clothes and watched the ladies in their finery she'd heard so much about, but while some of the women in this section were dressed like her, in their Sunday best, there were also many still in rough peasant clothing.

"Ow," she squawked as a bag hit her across the back of the head and shoulder. She spun around in time to see a coarsely dressed woman with filthy hands push Annie out of the way.

"I'll have that bunk," she snarled. "You're little enough. Go get yerself a top bunk."

Annie tried to explain she couldn't be parted from her sister, but before she'd finished talking, the woman had shoved the girl's kit from the lower bunk towards her with such force she sent the girl sprawling on the deck. Lettie rushed to Annie's side, muttering something Brigid couldn't hear, but the wide-eyed fear in the girl's face roused Brigid's protective instincts. She leapt to her feet.

"Can I ask ye to be kindly, now?" she said to the woman. "These girls claimed their beds first. I t'ink 'twould be better for ye to find somewhere else."

Her antagonist stood a good head and shoulders taller than her, and Brigid faltered. But reassured by Sally standing beside her, she tilted her head back and faced the newcomer.

"Mind yer own business." The woman turned and glared at Brigid and Sally's determined faces. Immediately, she started wheedling. "I gotta have a lower bunk. It's me legs, you see; I can't climb up, and she's young enough to move to a top 'un," whinged the woman.

Brigid let her breath out slowly, trying to keep her

temper. "That's as maybe, but being a bully about it will get you nowhere."

"Yeah. Now clear off," said Sally. "We don't want the likes of you next to us anyway."

Reverting to her natural bad temper, the woman lowered her head, stuck out her chin and growled, "Who's gonna make me?"

"I am." Sally took a step forward, arms akimbo, her voice menacing. "Do you want to risk taking me on and losing before you start?"

"And me." Brigid's eyes burned with fire. She'd never understood people who were mean or nasty. "But if it makes ye feel better, I'll help you find somewhere," she offered, hoping a bit of kindness would ease the situation.

"Aye. I could do wi' some 'elp. You're a good lass." While the woman spoke sweetly to Brigid, she spat at Sally. "You'll regret this, you will. I'll get you afore the journey's over. That I will."

Wednesday, 6th October 1886

Our journey to the other side of the world began when we piled into Da's cart, me in the front and Jamie in the back, holding on to our stuff for dear life. Behind us, we could see our two families standing in the middle of the road, watching us go. There was little joy in the parting. My sisters stood huddled together, solemn and still.

It had taken many a month to get ready for our leave-taking. Autumn began kindly enough with a just a little more sunlight than normal, and what rain came fell lightly. But by the end of September, the weather got worse. By the time we were ready to leave, the rain had set in.

The damp seeped into everything – even our spirits.

The goodbyes had started weeks before we left. I got excited when friends and neighbours called by to talk, or gave me a small gift – something useful like spoons or linens, woollens or precious, precious thread. But saying goodbye to my two sets of grandparents – Michael and Bridget, and John and Mary – was the hardest part. Well, no, if I'm honest, leaving Ma was the hardest.

Ma had kept busy in the weeks leading up to leaving day. She swept and baked, sewed and knitted, trying to remember everything she considered a mother should tell her daughter. She helped me gather what I'd need on the journey, packed things I could add to my dowry for when I might have my own home. She kept my bedding and clothing dry – draped over the rack above the fire, next to where she hung my Da's and brother John's wet clothing at the end of each day. It fair made the air fuggy with the rising steam and stale smells of peat, straw and pigs.

It was Ma's way of coping, keeping busy. She would sometimes give me a saying to write down, or remind me about one of her recipes handed down from her mother. She repeated what I would need, over and over again, and wouldn't say goodbye, even at the last minute. All she said was, 'Be safe' and pressed the shawl pin that once belonged to her grandmother into my hand and disappeared inside the cottage again. I struggled not to let my tears fall as I said goodbye to my sisters gathered around the door: Norah holding Susan, and Nellie holding the baby Katie, while Máire stood alone – always alone was our Máire. Their tears flowed silently.

Da said nothing as he coaxed the donkey to move along at a faster clip than it usually managed, and we soon reached the main road and turned east towards Ennis. Da couldn't take us any further if he was to get home again before dark.

He shook hands with Jamie and charged him to look after me, but when it came to saying goodbye to me, he just stared, as if memorising my face. Gruffly he said, 'Travel well' and headed off again at a fast trot. He never looked back.

⁖ ⁍

Jamie dumped his bedroll and cloth bag in the dormitory for single men and barely gave the others a nod before heading back up on deck. He'd promised Brigid he would hold his temper and not get into a fight like he used to with the boys at home. The best way to keep out of bother was to have as little to do with anyone as possible, at least until he got to know them better.

People and goods were still being loaded, and with scant room to move, Jamie found a position by the rails towards the stern where he could watch the goings-on.

"Get out of the way, you big oaf," snarled an Ulster voice, as a hand pushed the middle of his back. "You're taking up too much space."

Jamie's fist clenched and he spun around with arm raised, only just pulling up short when he saw the two little girls in tow.

"There's no need for violence, is there?" said a well-dressed young maid to his right.

Jamie found himself gazing into eyes as blue and dark as his own, and at the same level.

"Michael was only trying to make space for me and the girls. You can't mind that, surely?" When she smiled her whole face lit up.

Jamie's clenched fist relaxed. He whipped his cap off and held it against his chest as he flattened himself against the rail. The man forged on past, laden with bags.

"Sorry, miss. Didn't mean no harm. I didn't see you there, that's all. There're so many people, ain't there?" He turned crimson at his foolish attempt at conversation with a total stranger, especially one who made his heart thump a little louder; he looked down at his dirty, scuffed work boots, convinced she would move on by.

"What's your name?" Her voice sounded soft and gentle.

He raised his head and their eyes met again. "Jamie. That is, James O'Brien, miss."

"I'm Maggie O'Neill. I'm sure I'll see you again before we reach Australia."

Michael reappeared and scowled at Jamie. "What's the hold up 'ere, Maggie? Get below and see to the girls."

"Don't boss me around, Michael. I know what needs doing. You go look after yourself and leave me to me own." She turned to Jamie. "And these two are me nieces. Laura is ten and Jane nearly nine. Say hello, girls." The two girls remained silent and peered shyly at him from behind Maggie's skirts. "Don't mind Michael. Too often my brother thinks he owns me."

Jamie stood with his back against the rail, gawping as she disappeared in the crowd, and mulled over what had just happened. He needed to see Breeda.

He pushed his way through the crowds to the aft companionway. A woman who'd not been there earlier stopped him.

"You're not allowed down there, I'm sorry. That's for single ladies only." She stood barring his way and carried on directing people where they needed to go.

He tried to peer over her shoulder and called down to Brigid. "Breeda. Breeda. Are you there, Breeda?"

"Stop that shouting at once, young man."

"Yes, ma'am. Sorry, ma'am ..." Jamie looked sheepish. "Um, who might you be, please? Can ye help me?"

"I'm Miss O'Reilly, the matron responsible for the girls' welfare. And yes, I'll send a message to this Breeda you want to see so badly. Give me her name."

"It's Brigid O'Brien, ma'am. She's my cousin and I'd be grateful to see her. That I would. Thank'ee."

To ease his restlessness while he waited, he paced to and fro, and round and round, until he saw Brigid emerge from below.

"Watch where you're going, yer bleedin' eejit," an Irish voice yelled after him as he crashed into people in his haste to get past, but he didn't pay any heed.

"Breeda, Breeda. You'll never believe it, but I just saw an angel."

"What you blathering about now, Jamie? Angel, what angel?"

"She's as tall as me, wi' pure white skin, and she's going to Australia ... with her brother and his two little girls."

"Ah, well, that's nice, for sure it is. But where else did you think she'd be going if she's on this ship an' all?"

"Ah, don't go teasing me now. You know what I mean."

"Does this angel have a name then?"

"Maggie. Her name's Maggie."

"I'll be happy to look out for this Maggie and be sure to speak nicely when we meet, that I will. Just for you, Jamie. Now, tell me are you settled in your bunk room and have you met any of the other fellas?"

For the whole of his life, Brigid had been the caring one, the mother hen, with a cure-all kiss for a scratch or bruise, and a dock leaf for the stings. She was known as the lucky one because of her gifts, and the plucky one because of her spirit. Jamie settled into telling her what little he'd seen of the ship's quarters, and how he'd not really spoken to anyone, being keen to stay out of trouble.

"But, I t'ink I've got trouble already, our Brid. Maggie's brother Michael hasn't taken to me at all, that he hasn't. Maggie said not to pay him any mind, but when she's not around he might just stir something up. He's littler than me, though, so he'll be no bother."

"Jamie me boy, remember now, you promised. No fighting. This isn't the lads from home now, and you could end up in the brig."

"Aye, I ken." Jamie hung his head and turned his cap around in his hands, and considered how he could keep his promise if provoked.

The loud clanging of bells nearby and the shuddering vibrations shook his body. Someone shouted, "We're moving."

Jamie thrust Brigid in front of him and ushered her along through the crowd until they, too, were on the port side, pressed against the rails, wanting to catch a last glimpse of the home they were leaving. Sailors, braced against hawsers, began to untie the ship and scurried back and forth to loosen and tighten lines as the steam engines powered the ship along the Thames River. Black smoke belched against the grey sky, covering the passengers with smut while the engines roared.

People waving farewell from the dockside shed many a tear, but on the ship there was an unusual calm. The decision to leave had been made a long time ago, along with the painful farewells. This was no time for tears and recrimination – or regrets. If anything, the future looked brighter than the life they had chosen to leave behind.

Brigid stiffened her shoulders, shrugging off a shiver as the gap between the ship and shore widened. Jamie reached for her hand. They had talked about this moment, this point of no return and what to expect, but the tug of loneliness in the pit of his stomach was worse than he had prepared for. It would be harder still for soft-hearted Brigid, who feared the journey across the oceans. Brigid released his hand and bunched her skirt where she'd pinned her great-grandmother's brooch.

"Ah, Jamie." Her voice quivered slightly. "Will you say a prayer with me for those we left behind."

He put his arms around her and nestled her against him while they stared at the receding coastline, and murmured a prayer together. Their life in Ireland was over and the future an unknown commodity only they could shape, without the backing of family and tradition.

Despite promises the rest of the family would follow when the time was right, they both knew she would not see her mother or any of the family again.

Brigid shivered. "Aye, well. Let's look on the bright side. At least we don't have to walk anywhere for quite some time."

He chortled, his moment of introspection passing as his natural exuberance reasserted itself. "'Tis true. But then, we didn't walk as much as I thought we would when we left the village. Those new trains are wonderful t'ings. I liked the clackety-clack sound of the wheels going round, and seeing the countryside pass by faster than I've ever seen anything move before. It were like magic. Now we're on a ship. Ah, Breeda. I'm that excited."

"Still a wee fella at heart, aren't you, boyo?" she teased. "I'm excited too, Jamie, aye, I am, even if a bit on the jittery side."

"Well now, of course. But I'll take care of ye. A poor young t'ing like you can get easily frightened." His eyes sparkled, and while Brigid knew he was teasing, she pretended to be cross.

"That's enough of that talk now, boyo. You're only a matter of months older than me."

"Whisht, now." He looked around to see if anyone had overheard. "I don't want people to know how old I am. I'm the man now."

"That you are, sweet cousin. That you are." She put her hand up to his face and touched his cheek, glad of his company as the life they knew faded into the past.

ℰ   ℭ

Sunday, 10th October 1886

Right from the start of our journey Jamie had whooped and laughed, and waved to all the people who had come out to watch our departure. "I'm off to Australia," he'd called. "I'm on an adventure."

The day after Da had dropped us, we walked south towards Limerick with our baggage getting heavier with every step, hitching a ride when we could, to pick up the train going north-east through Roscrea to Dublin. Jamie talked about the grass, the crops, the animals, the stone walls or the rivers and streams, all the time comparing them with those he'd grown up with. His eyes were full of wonder at the changing scenery the further we moved away from home.

Our journey was not easy. We gave ourselves two weeks to reach London, since we didn't have any idea how long it would take to get anywhere, and there were hours of waiting. Jamie and I slept rough overnight when we could, trying to save our pennies. We couldn't afford a place to stay for both of us; we only had enough for the endless hours on the train, and I could never leave him on his own.

We had a sad farewell to our homeland. For days on end it rained. Drizzle, rain, squalls, and back to drizzle that would rot the crops in the ground. Even when it didn't rain, the sky was grey with heavy cloud. We hadn't seen the sun for days. Every year we hoped the weather would be better, and every year it wasn't.

Not that Jamie cared. He marched along in his tweed jacket and cap, his well-worn leather boots and homespun scarf, whistling all the tunes he could remember with nary a care. Even the weight of the trunk he carried didn't seem to bother him. Sometimes I hummed along with him, but mostly I listened. I had our canvas carry bags on my back – 'twas no more than I usually carried – but I was ever so grateful for the wool coat that reached my knees. I wrapped my shawl around my shoulders, drew my bonnet down over my eyes and tried to keep pace with Jamie.

The train to Dublin gave us shelter and eased the burden of carrying the luggage all the time, but the sitting for hours on end troubled us and we often itched to be on the move. We weren't used to waiting. We were used to walking and working the land, always on our feet and able to sleep well, tired out by the day's work. But we were that restless we couldn't sleep much – well, I couldn't. Jamie didn't do so badly, but everything was so strange. Even our travelling companions were not like the folk at home.

Long after everyone else had gone inside, Brigid remained to watch the scenery change as the ship steamed its way along the River Thames. The buildings grew fewer and less grand, and the villages further apart. Birds screeched overhead looking for dinner in the wake of the ship's propellers, and the air seemed fresher, cleaner – more like Ireland. But once they'd slipped into the Channel, the wind picked up and Brigid felt in need of her shawl.

She squinted into the darkness below deck and shivered, surprised the air was no warmer inside than out – and it stank of unwashed bodies, urine and musty clothes. After the fresh air, the foul odours were nauseating. Some smells were sharp and acidy, smells she couldn't quite identify, that made the back of her jaw ache and her eyes itch.

A few steps along the passageway she realised her mistake. She had come down the wrong ladder into the midsection where family groups sat huddled together. Harried mothers cuddled fractious children and soothed screaming babies, while the men looked forlorn and churlish as they went about the settling. Her appearance raised a head or two amongst the men, and someone shouted something she didn't quite catch, but the laughter that followed gave her an idea of what it might have been. Her heart sank as her stomach churned; instinctively she knew the next fifty-odd days would be a challenge. She made a hasty retreat and headed to the single women's quarters further aft.

As she descended the right ladder this time, Brigid sighed with relief to see Sally chatting to some women nearby.

"Ye look right chilled, lass," said Sally, coming towards her. "Where've you been all this time?"

"Up on deck, thinking … But I got lost and ended up where the families are. And by the look on some of the faces, there are some mightily unhappy folk aboard."

"I'm no' surprised." Sally linked her arm with Brigid's. "It's no' much better in here. I reckoned we'd seen off the worst, but ye should see the two what have taken the berths on the other side of us – not Annie and Lettie – on t'other side." She screwed up her nose and lowered her voice. "Both foreigners. One's a German, fat slob of a woman with nay much English and t'other one's from Denmark. Want a tot? It'll warm ye up."

Amazingly, Sally fished a bottle of gin from within the folds of her skirts and offered it to Brigid, who shook her head.

"Please yourself. But what'cha going to do to fill in time then?" Sally slugged back a mouthful, put the stopper in and pushed the bottle deep into her pocket.

"Hadn't really thought about it," Brigid shrugged, unsure whether to admit she kept a diary or that she had lacework to keep her fingers busy.

"Well, I have. Gotta keep busy or we'll go nuts and end up a-fighting. Someone said there'd be entertainment on deck once we get in open sea. Quoits and draughts, and such. Aye, and music and dancing."

"That'll be fun." Brigid liked to dance. "My sisters and I dance all the reels and jigs."

"That's nice for you." Sally looked sideways at Brigid, but whatever her thoughts, she chose not to voice them. She sat on the lower bunk with her back against the outer wall, her legs stretched out in front of her. "How about you sit 'ere and tell me 'bout yourself." She patted the blanket.

Brigid smiled, glad to find the companionship she longed for in her small corner of this strange new world. Even with Jamie's cheerfulness, she'd missed the friendly chatter of her mother and sisters, or the local women as they crossed to and fro through the village. Back home, there was always gossip to be shared and a story to be told.

She sat at the other end of Sally's bunk. "There's not much to tell," she began. "I come from a little village in the west of County Clare near Miltown Malbay and the Cliffs of Moher."

"I dunno where that is. Never been to Ireland."

"Aye, well. Cloonanaha's a low-lying village, not six miles from the coast. The wind that blows off the Atlantic in wintertime can fair cut through you, like a knife through butter, but it's grand, aye. Green as far as the eye can see, even if the ground's a bit on the stony side. It makes for hard farming, I can tell ye, but there are myths and stories to gladden the heart. I'm the eldest. I have one brother, John, and five younger sisters. Máire's fourteen now, then there's Norah and Nellie, they're still at school. Susan's only three, and the new babby."

"Cor. That's a handful for your mother."

"I know, especially since wee Katie came. But I did my best."

From an early age, when not busy making lace, Brigid had shared the responsibilities of the household with her mother, or helped in the potato fields at harvest time. When she could, she sold her lacework to add some coin to her father's meagre savings.

John, eighteen months her junior, was expected to do as much as any man and worked beside his father, Patrick, on the farm. But times were tough. Most of the crops went to England, leaving little for the locals to put food on the table. There was no more this year than there had been last season, or the season before that, if the truth be told.

"Well, that's no peasant dress you're wearing." Sally fingered the fabric of Brigid's skirt. "That's a right smart outfit. Who taught you to sew?"

Brigid flushed at the compliment. Even though her outfit was at least five years out of date, and without the new-style bustle, which had recently reappeared on the latest fashions, she knew the cut flattered her figure.

"The nuns. I learnt lacemaking and needlework at the convent, and reading and writing, and numbers, at the National School." In fact, she'd shone at school, and the nuns considered her the most skilled traditional lacemaker of all their students. "And Ma's always spinning and weaving and knitting. It's in me blood, I t'ink. I'm hoping to sell my pieces to the ladies in the salon for a shilling or two."

"Well, good luck to ye wi' that one." Sally looked wistful, regretful. She sighed. "What sort of place is this village of yours? Tell me, hen."

Time disappeared as Brigid described her home – or rather what it had once looked like before the bailiffs came. She didn't want to think about that time, right now. Their home had been a large, two-room, whitewashed mud-brick cottage with a flagstone floor and thatched roof. The windows along the front were barely large enough for a man's head, and everyone had to duck to go through the low door. She could still see her mother bent over the peat fire trying to get it to burn properly while the cottage filled with smoke. "Aye, I loved the smell of the broth bubbling away in the big iron kettles that hung above the fire. Putting up wi' the smoke was worth it."

Once she'd started, Brigid happily launched into stories about the constant stream of people who stopped to chat, barter goods or gossip about another neighbour. No occasion was ever too small for a party – one respite in a mountain of gloom – but emigrating … now *that* was a big occasion. They'd had a grand going-away party, they had.

"Granda Michael O'Brien and Granny Bridget, that's Ma's side, they'd come over from Mooghana four mile away, bringing most of Ma's uncles and aunts and cousins with them. Jamie's one of the cousins from Mooghana. Grandpa John O'Brien and Grandma Mary – Da's parents – and his brothers and sisters all live in our village. We're a merry crowd when we get together.

"Ma and me, and the womenfolk cooked up masses of colcannon – mashed potato and cabbage with salt and homemade butter – while the menfolk set out their home-brewed poteen. Powerful strong stuff it can be, too, and as soon as someone pulled out a tin whistle, people were up dancing and jigging till they could dance no more."

"So why you leaving if it's all so grand, then?"

Brigid was a bit taken aback by Sally's tone – not exactly sneering, but something about the scene she'd painted did not sit well with the other woman. Brigid knew only too well why she had to leave. "There wasn't enough to feed everyone."

☒   ☓

The O'Briens were a large family with cousin marrying cousin, generation after generation, her parents included, confusing those who didn't know the people. Whenever the family got together, whatever the reason, the topic of conversation remained the same: The Great Famine of

1845 – always referred to in capital letters – little more than forty years earlier, when far too many had starved to death because of the potato blight. Many of those who survived emigrated to America. They left in their droves, starting the migration of the Irish around the world.

Her Granda Michael and Grandpa John, the remaining cousins of their generation, could talk for hours about the hardships they remembered, the people they knew who had died, the ones who had taken ships across the oceans, and how badly the English treated the Irish.

Brigid would never forget the conversation that started it all – nigh on a year ago, before things turned bad. She could still hear her Granda's voice ringing in her head.

"The landlords are a hard lot, most of 'em," said Granda Michael, reminding them of all the evictions they'd witnessed. The battering rams smashing into homes, destroying everything the families had worked for and built, so they were forced to move on.

"Aye, but it's been worse, now, hasn't it?" Grandpa John had surprised everyone by saying something positive for once. While not as many people were dying of starvation the way they had four decades ago, there were still too many worried where their next meal would come from.

"Aye, that it has," Granda Michael had agreed. "But we've seen better days too, mind."

But not many. Harsh winters, excessive rains and high prices drove many to the brink. Crops sold for profit elsewhere by the English landlords left only the unsaleable and often inedible produce for the locals to live on. That, and whatever else they could grow on stony and infertile ground.

"We have, we have, but still, there's food enough for the moment – when the season doesn't fail us – what with the chickens and the odd pig or two. Mustn't complain, now. Mustn't complain."

The two men had puffed on their pipes and reflected on their problems.

They truly believed that while the potato survived, so would the Irish – but each decade, the blight returned, albeit lesser and more localised, with smaller famines, but damaging nevertheless. The years when the crops were light, the English imported corn of poorer quality at cheaper prices, forcing the local villagers to sell their grain for less and less.

"That may be so, Da," said Patrick, joining his father and father-in-law. "But I've got six girls to wed off. There's no way I can afford the rents for more land. Can I?"

"You're right there, boyo," said Michael, eager for a chance to complain. "The t'ing is, son, we need Lord Finucane and that other fellow to rent us the land, cheap like. We need more land – like we used t' have. And where are the cottages for the boys when they wed? Where're they coming from, I ask ye? Where?"

"Ach, you'll be grand, now Michael," interrupted John. "Your boys will set themselves up right fine, they will. There's plenty of lasses you can find to suit. But aye, I remember when we had enough for everyone. Aye, those days are gone."

A few months later, at another family get-together, the topic on everyone's lips had been the news about a family from a nearby village.

"They're emigrating. To Australia, no less," Granda

Michael had explained. "They got it all planned. They're sending one of the girls out first. There's need for skilled workers, farm labourers and servants – or so the authorities say – and she can go for free. They showed me an advert in the paper, they did, to prove it. Then once she's settled, she sends for the others as remittance passengers or some such. Only have to pay a few shillings each."

Brigid listened in on the conversation, unsure of what it might mean for her family but intrigued by the idea.

"Now, from what I hear," continued Granda Michael, "this Australia place has lots of land and sunshine to grow crops. And the authorities are offering up the chance of getting your own piece of land to farm – and giving people grants to get started. There's job schemes to be had for the young 'uns an' all. And the girls can work in the big houses."

"My, that sounds grand," Brigid had chimed. "But I'd be scairt by so much water, I t'ink ..."

"Scairt?" Patrick interrupted her with a laugh. "You've never been afeard of naught in your life, *mo chailín*. Not even when your cousins tried to scare you, pretending to be banshees."

"Away with ye, Da," she'd said, giving him a friendly push on the shoulder. "That's different. I knew it were them."

"That you did not – you were too little. But you're a brave girl, our Breeda."

Her father soon forgot Brigid as he entered into deeper conversation. "Tell me more about Australia and this emigrating business, then."

In the days that followed, she started to dream of

the possibilities. Maybe the whole family should go. She could sell her lacework, or stitch gowns and jackets with lace insets, while the menfolk worked the land. She imagined what this Australia would look like, with modern buildings and roadways, transport and people, and none of the misty, clammy Irish mist or stony ground. Her ideas grew, but her Da said nothing more about it. Time passed in the daily grind of eking out a living.

Many months later, her father had found her feeding the chickens and collecting the eggs. "Breeda, my girl." He couldn't stand still, his voice faded as he paced away from her and back again. "I've worried about it for a long time now ... but there's just no way around it." He sat on the wooden seat along the wall, clenching and unclenching his fingers. "Ye see ... t'ings is tight. I can't afford to feed ye all. And the babbies must come first. Ye see that, don't ye?"

Her da rested his elbows on his knees and looked sideways at his dark-haired daughter who sat beside him, clutching her basket of eggs. "I have to ask. Will ye wed if I arrange it?"

Brigid hadn't answered. She turned one egg over, then another, and ran her fingers over their shape. All she wanted was to make lace. Captivated by the hypnotic, rhythmical flow of Clones lace as hook and thread looped through her fingers. She could believe she was weaving stories of times gone by and passing them on, creating myths for the future. If only she could go to the big city, she would sell her lace and make enough for them all to live on.

She waited for her father to speak.

"There's a fella over back a-ways that's been talking of wedding his son to expand their holding."

"Ah, no, Da. No. You can't ask that of me. I can't wed someone I don't know."

"Aye, well. I t'ought that might be what you'd say. We'll see, Breeda, we'll see." He pulled his pipe from his jacket pocket and tamped the tobacco down.

Brigid's hands fluttered up and down the handle of the basket, she pulled at her pinafore to wipe her clammy hands, hoping to still her nerves, and watched her father as he lit his pipe. Regardless of her modest efforts, food was getting scarcer, and with less money coming from the harvest, they were headed for desperate straits.

It's not fair, her mind raged. *Her Da and generations before him had farmed this land. They were rightful tenants.* But ever since the blight and the famines, things had never been the same.

But, aye, they'd managed before and manage they would again.

She truly believed it.

Until the bailiffs came.

Her father hadn't been entirely honest; only a matter of weeks later the landlord's lackeys came demanding the rent.

"I've got last month's rent," he told them as he handed over what little he had, "but not the extra you're asking."

The man, wearing a thick black cape to keep the cold at bay, weighed the pouch in his hand. "This'll do for now, but we'll be back. Get it, or you're out."

Each time they came, the amount climbed higher. They took the chickens, the pig and the sheep, until ...

"They've left us nothing," her mother wailed, shivering with the cold and wrapping her shawl around her more tightly. "They even took the grain to make bread from my bowl."

"And if any of you throw your lot in with them," the bailiff growled at the ragged villagers gathered in support, "you'll get what's coming to you too."

Despite the threats from the bailiffs, family and neighbours shared their meagre rations, but there was never enough.

Late one morning the following month, Brigid felt the hairs on her body stand on end when the pitiful sound of women keening reached her ears. She rushed from the fields back to the village to find the bailiffs stripping every house in the village of its food supplies. The women howled. The men, angered beyond control, fought the bailiffs off amidst chaos and confusion. They stormed the walls of the estate, to no avail. No one was home, and no one was listening.

One day – a day that would be etched in her memory forever – the bailiffs returned. They brought the Royal Irish Constabulary and horses and many more men – and the battering ram.

Systematically, they made their way through the village destroying home after home. The pounding shook the earth beneath their feet and echoed in their bones. With each blow a single lament rose and grew as the destruction mounted, until the keening became a continuous, mournful note that carried across the land to the hills and the oceans beyond, to the place of shattered hopes.

Her father tried to comfort her mother, who clutched the tiniest ones to her. Their choices were few, and, to

Brigid at least, their future plans could not and should not include her. She needed to make her own way in life – wed or emigrate. But how could she leave her ma and her sisters? Anguish washed over her like the ever-increasing rings on water after a stone was dropped.

The dream didn't look so grand after all.

"So what happened?" Sally prompted.

For a few hours, sometimes longer if she was busy, Brigid could forget what happened. She could block out the recurring images, muting each vibration echoing in her head and quelling the panic that consumed her. But not often, and not for long.

"The whole village got evicted."

"What! Why?"

"The Land League. They stood up to the landlords, refusing to pay the higher rents. They went on marches and protests. People put up stone fences to block the roads and disobeyed the police and bailiffs. Civil disobedience they called it. We even had a ladies branch – they were the loudest of all, demanding fairness. Lots of people in our village were part of the league, but the authorities banned it back in 1881."

"And ...?"

"The Irish aren't good at taking orders, so they tried other tricks, but the English and the law were against them."

It hadn't always been like that, and it seemed hard to imagine how badly things had got out of hand.

"That's why I'm off to find a new life – to give them hope." A wistful, faraway look crossed Brigid's face. In her heart, she knew they would not follow – not for years anyway – not while her grandparents lived, and maybe not even then. "There'll be more room with me gone, and Norah is good with babbies. She'll be a blessing to Ma, she will."

With a quick shake of her head, she shifted her thoughts back to the present.

Sally had listened to her story without question, but the blank look on the other woman's face suggested Brigid wasn't the only one with a story of suffering to tell.

"What about you, Sally? Do you have family?"

"Nowt to speak of." She shrugged nonchalantly. "Left home when I were younger than you, lassie ... Wonder when they're going ta feed us. I'm fair hungry. I can tell ye."

Brigid, although taken aback by the abrupt change of subject, let it pass. She could do with some food too.

Sailors scurried down the ladders and began shifting people from where they sat. Brusquely, they showed those nearest the ropes tied on the outside walls how to lower the large tables from the roof. Once the tables were in place and the benches positioned along both sides, the corridor became nigh on impassable.

"Grab yer plates and get in line if'n you wants anything to eat," shouted a sailor wearing a stained, once-white apron. "No plate, no mug, no food."

Doing as instructed was easier said than done. The sailors placed large enamel pots and flat pans on tables at one end. Brigid could see steam rising, and her stomach rumbled, but she couldn't move for the crush. People tried to go every which way to retrieve their plate and utensils.

Some of the younger girls scrambled under the tables and stomped down the benches to get to the food first, but the sailors were having none of it.

"Wait yer turn, young 'un," one snarled, and used his metal soup ladle to whack a hand reaching out to grab some bread.

The noise grew louder as the women pushed and shoved, and nothing was going to plan. A sudden deafening rattle of metal spoon against metal pan silenced everyone in an instant.

"You lot on that side – sit. Wait yer turn. You on this side – come f'ward up to 'ere and stand still. Those at the back get in line. Now one at a time, get your plate. Gawd, help me. I gotta do this every time," the cook complained.

Gradually, order returned. Once everyone was standing in line again, the foreign sailors began to serve the food as the crowd shuffled forward in turn. In the crush, Brigid had lost sight of Sally and stood somewhere near the middle. It had been a lesson well learnt and, in future, they would all be better organised. Brigid hoped some might even learn manners from it, but it seemed doubtful. A low rumble of complaint began long before she reached the table to see what was on offer.

The least likely looking woman, dressed in a once-elegant but now timeworn gown, spoke in a surprisingly gentle and cultured voice. "I beg your pardon, sir, but the fare looks rather unappetising. Is this the standard we are to expect?"

Raucous laughter met her question.

"This, my dear lady," mimicked the sailor with the grey apron, "is *better* than what you can expect. Wait till we've been at sea awhile. Ungrateful shrew. At least you're getting your grub cooked for you. Didn't used to be like that, it didn't. And it ain't that long since you lot down 'ere brought your own food to cook, and cleaned up after yourselves. Which, in my 'umble opinion, is how it should have stayed ... Next!"

The exchange did nothing to bolster the spirits of those eating or those who waited. When Brigid's turn came, she was pleasantly surprised. There was plenty of food, and she'd seen worse in her own village.

The sailor ladled a thin soup with a few bits of what looked like a vegetable into her mug, and loaded slices of beef with lashings of gravy, boiled jacket potatoes and a thick slab of bread onto her plate. She made her way along the tables until she saw Sally and managed to squeeze onto the bench next to her.

"We won't starve, at least," mumbled her new friend, chewing on a piece of meat. "But can't say 'tis the tastiest or tenderest meat I've ever had."

"As long as there's broth and praties, I won't mind." Brigid strained her neck to look around the room. "Will we always eat in here, just us women together?"

"Dunno. Probably. Why?"

"It's just I'd like to see Jamie."

"You mean that young fella what carried yer trunk?"

"Aye. That's him."

"Nay, lass. He'll be up the blokes end. They won't let him in here." Sally dismissed Jamie as unimportant. "What you think of them brown-skinned fellas?"

Brigid turned her head to look at two of the workers she'd seen on the wharf and who now helped carry the pots and pans. "I think they look as miserable and unhappy as some of the passengers. Why?"

"Don't know as I trust 'em."

"Trust them, how?"

She shrugged, but Brigid was curious. "Why should we trust them less than some of the lot sharing our quarters?"

"'Cos they're foreign, of course!" Sally sounded astounded she should ask such an obvious question, but Brigid wasn't put out.

"Why does that matter? I don't know anything more about you or Annie and Lettie than them."

"Aye, but least we speak the same language. Not some foreign mumbo-jumbo."

"That's as maybe, but don't mean I can understand everything what's said. They don't bother me, I won't bother them."

"More fool you." Sally pointed her fork at Brigid and waved it in time to her words. "Never trust nobody, I say. That way you'll survive. Watch yourself, lassie. Or you'll find yourself in all sorts of grief."

Their meal finished, the two women joined the throng making their way up on deck. The majority of sailors bustling around and clearly doing all the work were the brown-skinned people she'd seen earlier. They were watched over by a few senior officials dressed in their braided uniforms, who were light-skinned and, Brigid assumed, English. She'd have liked to know where these other people were from but felt too shy to ask.

The line moved forward slowly. Copying the others, Brigid threw her scraps overboard, rinsed her plate and mug in a barrel of once-clean water that now had a floating, greasy scum, and moved on. If she wanted to see clean water, she needed to get to the barrel more speedily next time.

Sally wandered off to chat with some other women, but Brigid couldn't see even one familiar face to speak to. Earlier on, she'd heard more than four hundred passengers were emigrating to the Colonies, so she reasoned it would take time to get to know even a handful of that number.

A hollow feeling in the pit of her stomach seized her. She had yet to learn the skill of speaking to strangers and felt isolated. She'd grown up in a village where everyone knew everyone else, and whilst there were petty squabbles with this one not talking to that one at times, there'd never been a shortage of people to talk to. How would she get on in Brisbane, a place of strangers?

As those unsettling thoughts whirled in her brain, she wrapped her shawl over her head and prepared to watch the last rays of the setting sun glint on the wake.

Friday, 15th October 1886

Our Jamie has the blood for adventure, but I'm not so sure about me any more. I found Dublin too big, and oh, so noisy. There were lots of fine buildings, but near the docks the streets were narrow and filthy. Not dirt from the road, like at home, but filth people had thrown there – and it stank. And the street kids ran wild. Ma would've killed us if we'd behaved like that.

The ferry from Dublin to Liverpool really scared me. It'd seemed large when anchored, but it bobbed around like a cork in the huge waves of the Irish Sea. I couldn't find me balance as I swayed from side to side and crashed into things and it left me all bruised and sore. I felt that bad. Me and several other people spent a lot of time leaning over the rail until the sailors taught us which side of the boat to be on for the wind.

Jamie stuck by my side the whole time, even though he wasn't at all sick. He even handed me a rag to wipe my mouth or fetched water when I needed it. I couldna done it without him. I tried to tell him I was all right, even if I wasn't telling him the whole truth, but I needed to set him easy. I was ever so grateful when we got off the ferry and I could stand on solid ground again. Liverpool was even bigger than Dublin. The docks were huge, with people and carts, and sheds, and ships everywhere. It was all too bewildering, but I hardly saw anything more than rows and rows of houses and the church steeple towering above them before we were herded onto the train.

The rail journey to London, even with the constant noise and breakdowns, long waits and hard seats – if we were lucky to get one at all – was a joy after the ferry. As we rolled on, Jamie kept pointing out the farmland and the villages, which were more like home, but different again. Rows of houses, two rooms high and surrounded by fields with crops and animals lined the track. Stone walls, like ours, and then bigger towns with more buildings, getting bigger the closer we got to London.

I'll never forget London. So big and so grand.

I was greatly relieved to see the ship to Australia was far larger than the ferry, but even so, I'm not so sure I'll make a good sailor.

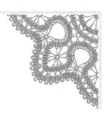

2

Hobnobbing and Fighting

Wednesday, 20th October 1886

Dawn was barely breaking when Brigid struggled from her bunk. The thin, lumpy mattress had offered little comfort, and she'd found the constant vibration and noise echoing through the subsections from the engines unbearable. Give her the silence of a rural night, the owls, the bleat of sheep or the odd snuffle from the pig, any time. And to make matters worse, those who had managed some sleep only added to the noise with their unfamiliar snorts and snores.

She dressed in her stays and petticoats, before wriggling into her best outfit again. The flared, boot-length skirt, with its softly draped overskirt and fitted, lace trimmed jacket, would prove practical for the journey. If she was to make her way in the new world she would need to look the part and less like a peasant girl.

Breakfast of a grey porridge with molasses, dry bread, and tea had been a quiet affair and soon over, thanks to the general air of self-consciousness and exhaustion that sat heavily over the room. Brigid washed her plate in marginally cleaner water, returned her utensils to her bunk and went in search of a quiet spot to write her diary, but people crowded all the open spaces. She despaired of finding anywhere to sit, but eventually a corner of a bench right at the stern offered a tiny area of privacy.

Wednesday, 20th October 1886

I'm that scared by the thought that my life will only exist on paper from now on. No one will read it other than me, and no one will understand or care. And I feel lonely knowing I can only talk to my family by letter. And they'll take so long to reach home the news will no longer matter.

I'm real unsettled knowing Sally's taken against the foreigners, especially the dark-skinned sailors, but I'm not so sure why. It's the natural order of the world for everyone to look down on everyone else. I mean, even at home, the English landlords, with their fancy ways of talking, look down on us poor locals who tenant their cottages, and don't care a bit. But then, my folks and others in the surrounding villages don't trust the gypsy travellers who come every summer – but to me they brought change.

The gypsies came with goods that couldn't be bought anywhere else, and music and dancing. I loved the fairs. I used to go wild about the fabrics and baubles even if I never had the money to buy them, and I joined in the dancing when the fiddler started up. They had adventure in their life that wasn't in mine. I know I wanted some of that excitement, but now, with an unknown world ahead of me, my spirit fails me.

Is that what life will be like, each of us judging everyone we meet, fearful and unable to trust? As sure as sure can be, in this new land we are going to, we'll have to get used to working *alongside people different from ourselves if we are to survive. Dear Lord, give me the courage and wisdom to understand.*

Brigid watched the passengers who walked past her: men in search of their wives or someone to talk to; women in pursuit of their offspring; two women deep in conversation; and a few sailors going about their duty. One couple, the woman obviously distressed, the man trying to comfort her with soft words, hurried by, oblivious to others.

I'm at a crossroads, I think, a place of decision. Somewhere people gather, meet newcomers and move on to a new life with those who fit, to form a community with shared values and ideals. Where will I fit in that greater plan, Lord?

I miss them all at home so much already but I don't know what to write. Ma can only read a few words, and I'm not that close to Máire – she would never understand what I want to say to Ma about being my own woman; my darling Norah's a little touched by the fairies; and Nellie's far too young. As for John, well, he's our father's son and has no time for women's gossip. I love them all, but writing how I feel ...

Dissatisfied, she slipped her diary into her pocket, deciding to find her way about the ship instead. She soon discovered the section reserved for First Class passengers was barred to her. She turned to retrace her steps and walked straight into a young man, impeccably dressed in the latest morning suit with a fashionable collar and cravat held with an elaborate pin.

"Oh. Beg your pardon, sir." She bobbed a polite curtsy.

He removed his top hat, gave a small bow, eyed her from head to toe and smirked. "It is entirely I who should be apologising to you. Forgive my sudden appearance. I didn't mean to startle you."

"That's all right, sir. No harm done. Thank ye. I'll just be on my way, then." Brigid took a step to one side, but he blocked her path.

"No. No. Don't go on my account. Allow me to introduce myself. I am Philip Harrison-Browne, at your service. And who might you be?"

"Honoured to meet you, sir." She bobbed another curtsy. "My name is Brigid O'Brien."

"Nice to meet you, Miss O'Brien." He replaced his hat and adjusted his sleeves. "Would you care to walk with me awhile?"

Flustered now, she stepped aside again. "Oh, no. Thank ye, sir. But I couldn't possibly. It wouldn't be seemly, seeing as you're from First Class an' all."

"I think you should let me be the judge of that." He held his arm out, but she didn't take it.

"Thank ye again, sir, for the honour. But I don't know you, and ..."

"Your modesty does you credit, Miss O'Brien. Very well. Let us say adieu for now. I'm sure we'll meet again." He tipped his hat and stood out of her way to let her pass.

Brigid hurried away, resisting the urge to look over her shoulder to see if he was still watching her.

Moments later, a noise up ahead attracted her attention. She rounded the wall of the saloon to see a crowd forming a circle on the open deck. Men were shouting and waving. Even before Brigid forced her way between them, she knew she would find Jamie in the middle. The sickening thud of flesh on flesh exploded in her ears as she popped up in the front row. Brigid didn't recognise the man Jamie was fighting but took a guess it might be the brother of the girl he was dotty on. Stripped to the waist and a good half-head shorter than Jamie, the man was muscular and in a rage. He was a street fighter too, not short on dirty tricks.

Loud warning shouts came from the men behind Brigid as the fighter threw a sly kick and tripped Jamie. He fell but rolled out of the way just as the man was about to leap on top of him. With his opponent sprawled on the deck, Jamie grabbed him from behind, hauled him to his feet, twisted him around and punched him square on the nose. The man's head snapped back. Blood spurted. He staggered. Jamie grinned, his face gleaming with sweat.

"You've got to help me stop them," begged Brigid of the burly man wearing a cap next to her.

"Why, lassie? They're even enough matched. We could do with some action; summat to talk about."

"You don't know my cousin. He's a clever one and will wear the fella down afore he finishes him off. We've got to stop him. Please?"

The man looked around to see if he could get backup, but the crowd was too engrossed and too fired up to think about interfering. He shook his head at her. "Sorry, lass. It's too risky."

Brigid frowned at the two fighters dancing around each other and sized up the space between them. She dived forward and put herself in front of the other man, but only managed to yell "Stop" in the split second it took for him to push her to one side. At the sight of her, Jamie held back a millisecond too long, which allowed the man to deliver the knockout punches: first to the stomach then an uppercut to the jaw, laying Jamie out flat. The older man spat at his rival, picked up his shirt and disappeared through the crowd.

Shaken, but unhurt, Brigid scrambled across the deck towards the prone Jamie. She knelt beside him and smoothed his hair back from his sweaty forehead to inspect the damage. "I'm sorry, Jamie, I am that, but I just had to stop you doing anything silly."

All around them the crowd booed and jostled while the bookies, eager to pocket the losing bets, were reluctant to hand over any winnings.

She briefly considered who the favourite might be but really didn't care. "I've seen you look worse, boyo. Come on now. Up ye get, Jamie."

Jamie didn't stir. She started to get to her feet, thinking she would try to pull him up to a sitting position, at the same time as a bucket of briny water was thrown over him, wetting her as well. She spluttered from the unexpected deluge. Fire burned in her eyes as she looked up to see one of the foreign sailors standing over her holding the empty pail.

He put it on the deck, placed his hands palm to palm and, with a little bow, apologised. "Forgive me. I obey orders." She followed his eyes to where the steward watched.

Jamie opened his eyes, shut them again against the glare, and groaned.

"Allow, please," the strange man added politely. He stepped forward, grabbed Jamie by the arms, pulled him upright, tossed him over his shoulder and marched off.

Brigid scurried behind, pushing her damp hair out

of her eyes. She didn't see the sailor until he barred her from following Jamie as he was carried down the ladder to the decks below.

"Sorry, miss, you can't go down there. Those are the men's quarters."

"Aye, but he's my cousin. Please? I need to look after him."

"The doctor will do that, miss. 'Twouldn't be safe, believe me." The look on his face brooked no argument.

"Who is that man?" Brigid pointed down the companionway to where she'd last seen Jamie, his head bouncing on the shoulder of the sailor.

"Him? He's a lascar from India, ma'am. Will that be all?" He tipped his cap to indicate the conversation was over.

With no other option, Brigid reluctantly returned to her quarters at the rear of the ship. She'd have to be patient and wait for Jamie to reappear, which wouldn't be until the morrow at least. She prayed he'd be all right and not too mad at her.

Wednesday, 20th October 1886

I'm so out of sorts with that much on my mind. I was right cross after that lascar man threw the water. It might have helped Jamie, but I had to change out of my wet clothes. I know he didn't mean to wet me, but that doesn't change anything. I've had to put on my work clothes while my good ones dry out. I hope they are not ruined; I've got nothing to replace them.

I can see what Sally means about foreign people. He was polite enough, but up close he made me nervous. He shielded his eyes and his face showed nothing. I couldn't tell what he was thinking. Now I'm worried about my things. I hope nobody takes any of them.

I counted the girls in our section and I reckon there's over seventy of us – that's near half our village. To see them all together like this makes me realise I didn't know I'd grown up with so many people, if you add in all the little ones, and the nuns and the others at the school. But I don't know what to make of all these yet.

Some of them are mighty sociable with total strangers. Like Sally – she could talk the hind leg off a donkey. I'm not so good at small talk with people I don't know, but then I'm not as bad as Annie and Lettie who rarely speak to anyone apart from each other. It's like they have a secret language. One will start saying something and the other will finish it. I've never come across the likes of it before. As for the two women in the next bunks, I have as little to do with them as possible. And I haven't seen that Englishwoman again – the one Sally and I sent off.

But what bothers me most is our Jamie. I'm that vexed with him. Why did he have to go acting the maggot so soon and get to milling on our first day? And after he promised me. What am I going to do? I can't mother him all the way to Australia, and goodness knows what will happen to him after that. If he gets to brawling, he'll be in big trouble. Ah, Jamie. You're such a worry.

But he's not the only one worrying me.

That man – Harrison-Browne he said his name was – gives me the fidgets. With all his fancy ways, what does he want with the likes of me? Sally says I should hobnob with him some more so I can get to know the ladies and sell my lace. It seems a bit dishonest to me, and I'm not at all sure I want to ... encourage him. He might get the wrong idea.

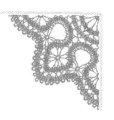

3

Misgivings

Thursday, 21st October 1886

"Breeda!"

At the sound of Jamie's voice, Brigid's hand jerked, marring the page she'd been writing on with a black line. "Now look what you made me do. Eejit."

Not in the least bit interested in the state of her diary, Jamie barely paused. "Bejaysus, Breeda. What you feckin' have to go and do that for?"

She was still angry with him, just as he was clearly angry with her, but that didn't stop her. She checked his black eye and the cuts and grazes on his face. Then she took his hands in hers and turned them over to look at his bruised and bloody knuckles, but seeing the damage was superficial tossed them aside again.

"Don't you be cussin' me, boyo. I did you a favour."

He glared at her furiously, not yet able to let go of his rage. "But I coulda had him, if you'd let me."

"Aye. That you could," she snapped, her Irish accent getting broader as their fight progressed. "I saw the glint in your eye, but where would that have landed you, I ask ye, Jamie. Where? I'll tell you where, you bleedin' eejit.

In the gaol, that's where. And then that angel of yours wouldna wanted nothing more to do with you after laying into her brother. Did you t'ink o' that?"

Jamie, stayed by her words, rubbed his hands back and forth over his head. "Ah, no. I did not. But 'twasn't my fault he came at me ... And mayhap you're right, but the fight was mine, not yours. You shouldna interfered."

"At least this way she'll feel sorry for you and he's the one in trouble. But you should be thanking me - not cussing me. Now go away and leave me be awhile."

Jamie looked at her fondly. "Aye, I probably should bless you. You took an almighty chance coming between us. You could've got a real belting."

"Well, I didn't."

"Ah, you're a brave 'un, our Breeda, and I thank you for that. For thinking of me." He hesitated, his eyes taking in her pose. "You look tired. Are you well?"

"Well enough," she attempted a weak smile. "Don't fret. I'll be grand. Away you go, now."

Still Jamie wavered.

"Go on. Get."

Brigid stared out to sea, her diary neglected in her lap, as the sound of Jamie's footsteps disappeared.

"Excuse me." A soft voice intruded seemingly only moments later, but the sun had moved while Brigid had been daydreaming. "Are you Miss O'Brien?"

Brigid jerked her head up to see a young woman in front of her. "I am that. And who might you be?" Although she had a strong suspicion she was the girl Jamie was so keen on.

"I'm Maggie O'Neill." The young woman started to extend her hand and then withdrew it, clearly uncertain about her reception. "May I speak with you awhile?"

"Take a pew."

"I wanted ... I wish to speak with you about ... um ..." She stopped, her eyes skittered right and left as if she would find the right words written in the air. "It's that brother of mine, you see." The girl's hands shook as she struggled to speak. "I, um, Michael is ... well, I thank you for putting an end to it. And I ... that is ... I'm gae sorry. He shouldna. It won't happen again. I promise."

Brigid sat silently and waited for her to finish, wondering why she'd slipped into local idioms after the polite, rounded voice she'd first used.

"I heard what you did," added Maggie. "It were brave. Aye."

"Where are you from, Miss O'Neill? That's no Irish accent I'm hearing."

"Ah. Noo, it's a wee bit mixed up. I were born in County Antrim, but Faither took us back and fore to Scotland for work so I grew up in both countries." Maggie bent her head and cleared her throat several times. Next time she spoke, her speech had returned to its formal tone. "I must get out of the habit of slipping into dialect when I'm nervous. Forgive me. I should know better."

Brigid instantly distrusted the chameleon-like character of the girl, but she'd promised Jamie to be polite. "Why should you need to know better? What's wrong with the way you speak?"

"My employer, Miss Jenkins - may she rest in peace - always said that if we wanted to get on in the world, we had to speak proper, I mean, correctly." Brigid watched as Maggie took in a deep breath and sighed. "It was so much easier while I was living in England. I was with

45

people who spoke like that all the time, but now I'm finding it too easy to slip back into what is natural."

"So why did you leave then, if everything was so good?" Brigid said, echoing the question Sally had asked earlier. She hadn't intended to be so sharp with the girl and was startled to see Maggie's eyes fill.

"I had no choice." Head bent, she stared at the sandstone-scrubbed deck beneath her feet.

Brigid held her tongue.

Slowly, hesitantly, Maggie started to tell her story. "Faither died some years ago. My brother Michael – and his wife what's passed now – and his two girls lived with our mother. But then Mam fell ill." Maggie lifted her head and looked straight at Brigid, searching for understanding. "It was as if the whole world had turned against me all at the same time."

Before Brigid or Maggie could say anything further Sally strode along the deck towards them. "Ah, there you are. I've been searching the whole ship for you."

Maggie made to leave, but Sally blocked her way. "Oh hello, then. Who might you be, I wonder? Don't think I've come across you before."

"Maggie O'Neill. Please excuse me." She stepped to one side and made her escape.

"What's up with that one?" Sally pursed her lips, watching the girl disappear around the corner.

"We were just talking about family and she got a bit upset."

"No matter. Tell her family's no use to anyone. Come on, lass. There's some deck games going on, and I've got my eye on a sailor."

46

Monday, 25th October 1886

We've settled into a routine of sorts as we've got further from England. The weather's been dry and the sea's calm so far, thank the Lord, and I'm surprised I've not felt at all seasick – others are. But I am finding it mighty warm.

A lot of folk spend more time on deck where it's cooler than below, but the officers say we can't sleep up there, more's the pity. And with so many people on board it's nigh on impossible to find a quiet spot; there's always a body or two hovering around. But there's one thing I can say – there's such hope on board, it's a joy to share. Everyone is expecting Australia to give us a better life.

We've lots of food, mostly meat and praties, but it lacks taste. They're right stingy on the salt, but it's regular as the clock. I think most are eating for something to do, instead of something to enjoy. Some complained at the start, but cook swore his head off at them. The grumbles soon stopped after that and cook's a bit friendlier since. The bread's fresh made, so I'm happy about that.

Sally has taken the upper hand and likes to say what is what. She and I have become friends – you need friends on this ship. It gets mighty lonely at times. I do Sally's hair when I can, but it's got a will of its own with all those curls.

The sisters Annie and Lettie quietly stick together and have so far not upset Sally, but I've not got to know them much. They're an odd pair, who speak little, and we can't hear them when they do.

Then there's Wilhelmina, the German woman who is tall and heavy built and called Minnie. I tried to speak to her once, but she has such very little English that neither of us really knew what the other was saying. Minnie found a few women who spoke her own language and somehow managed to shift the woman from Denmark, who'd taken the top bunk, to another place so she could share with Rosina, one of her newfound fellow countrymen. Since then, Minnie and Rosina have kept to themselves, as much as Sally will let them. She niggles at them all the time about how much room they take up. We've had a bit of music to help cheer us up a little, and most seem happier than they were. I enjoy the dancing.

I wish I could tell Ma I say my daily prayers like I promised. We had church this morning with Father Flanagan. He'll be leading the weekly service and will give us news of what's happening aboard and what to expect up ahead.

The days passed peaceably enough as mothers chattered over the wash barrel or entertained the younger children while the older ones found their own mischief. She wished she could tell some of them salt water was no good for the cloth, but Brigid found honing her skills alongside the other women who did handicraft a daily pleasure.

Agnes and Ester, who shared quarters in the midships with their spouses and children, had formed an early friendship and were soon spending their days together creating or teaching some of the younger women. Brigid liked to help them, glad to pass on her skills.

But to Brigid's mind the pair moaned too much about everything.

"I'm so sick of the sight of water. When are we going to reach land?" grumbled Agnes, her fingers flying as she crocheted.

"We saw land a few days back when we came through them straits. What were they called?" asked Ester, without raising her head from her embroidery.

"Gibraltar," replied Brigid. "And we can't be that far away from the next stop. The ship needs to fill up with coal and water, so I was told."

Agnes snapped her head round to glare at Brigid. "That wasn't what I meant. Seeing it in the distance ain't the same. I wanted to see what the people looked like and how they lived." She stood to adjust her position and flap her skirts to let some air circulate before sitting again. "My, it's hot."

"Aye, 'tis. Clammy like." Ester flapped her hands in front of her highly flushed face and appeared quite put out.

"Maybe we should in sit the shade, it'd be more comfortable," suggested Brigid.

"But the shady side of the ship is the windy side and I hate the wind. No, we'll stay where we are." Agnes was adamant.

Nobody moved; their hooks and needles flashed back and forth unabated until the murmur of voices grew afresh.

Brigid didn't bother to point out that the wind shifted and could blow from any direction, or that the shady side of the ship was dependent on the time of day. Agnes was a creature of habit so nothing would move her, and the other women accepted her decision without dispute.

"So where's we stopping next then, Breeda?" asked Annie, the more vocal of the quiet sisters, to fill a lull in the conversation.

"There's some islands called Galite in the Bay of Tunis, today, then Malta ..." began Brigid.

"I don't like the look of those clouds coming towards us. I've never seen them move so quick," Agnes interrupted, and craned her neck around to see where the dark cloud was coming from.

"I'm starting to feel right queasy an' all," agreed Ester, lifting her head. Like a rabbit coming out of its burrow, she jerked her head left and right to see what dangers might be lurking.

One woman put a hand out to steady herself; another leaned into the next as the ship seesawed through the surging swells. Voices stilled. Nervous eyes scanned the horizon.

"Ooh, I don't like it. Why's it doing that?" Annie's querulous voice didn't help steady anyone's nerves.

"I was told Galite had an eruption last month making the sea swell. Maybe that's got something to do with it?" suggested Brigid, hoping a reason for the extra surge might ease their minds – and hers. The one thing she feared more than being alone was the power of the ocean. It had taken many a fisherman from home to his death.

"How come you know so much, missy?" She guessed Agnes had a nasty side, but until now it hadn't been directed at her.

Everyone turned to stare at Brigid. The hairs on her arms stood on end at the unnecessary hostility.

"I don't know more than what I've been told," she murmured.

"Aye. And why would anyone tell a slip of a girl like you anything?" Another voice joined in – someone she didn't know – an older woman with a dark scowl.

Brigid flushed and tears threatened. Her stomach turned in confusion. She dropped her head and clenched her fists to steady her nerves, feeling the sticky sweat beneath her fingers as blood pounded through her veins. If she was to make a new life, she could not – no, she *would* not – let others stand over her.

"There's no need to be nasty. I've done you no harm. I asked a sailor and he told me."

She gathered up her belongings and, with a brief nod of farewell, gracefully but determinedly made her escape.

Brigid edged her way unsteadily around the bow to the other side of the ship, only to walk headlong into the windstorm. Overhead, the darkened clouds moved closer, swirling and changing shape as they travelled rapidly across the sky. A strange smell of damp metal and salt twitched her nose, and she shivered, despite the humid air.

For the next day and night the seas heaved up and down like lungs gasping for oxygen. The wind howled at a frightening pitch and buffeted those hale enough to attempt to stand on deck. Waves washed over the bow as the ship plunged headlong into the next trough, sending even the hearty below.

The horizon disappeared sickeningly with each nosedive, while sailors strung storm ropes from one end of the ship to the other for people to hang on to – saving more than one life as the ship rolled first to one side, then the other.

Weakened, people took to their bunks, trying to still their rebellious stomachs. The air reeked of vomit and anxiety. Fear spread its insidious wings.

"Our Father who art in heaven ..." began the murmur of numerous voices not far from where Brigid lay. Above it, "Hail Mary, full of grace ... " followed in waves as the familiar chant grew louder. In need of comfort, she added her cry to theirs.

"Hail Mary, Mother of God, pray for us sinners, now and at the hour of our death ..."

Harmoniously, the chant rose and fell. Voices came and went as it was repeated again and again, calming her alarm. Foreign words Brigid didn't understand, but familiar because of their cadence, intermingled with the pulsing rhythm of the prayer.

A woman called out, "Oooh, I can't stand it any longer. Help me."

From nowhere it seemed, Miss O'Reilly, the matron, appeared and moved easily from berth to berth, her soft tone offering succour to those who needed it most.

A soothing male voice started to sing, his strong incantation piercing the thin partitioning. "Hail Queen of Heaven the Ocean Star ..."

Above the din, children cried and begged their mothers for comfort, but if she listened hard, Brigid could still hear the man singing: "... save us from peril and woe."

Nerves stretched and tempers shortened.

"Shut that bleedin' child up afore I kill the little monster," someone yelled through the dividing wall.

"Don't you go threatening my Arthur. It ain't his fault. You lay one finger on him and I'll swing for ya, that I will."

More shouting. Over it all, the prayers and hymns continued accompanied by sounds of crashing and thudding. Anything not tied or weighted down slid haphazardly around, banging into walls, furniture or people, who yelped in pain. Brigid's head thumped louder, she shivered in the clammy, damp air and wished for the salve of sleep.

"Stop that noise. Oh, please. Stop." A girl's voice: begging, rising, sharp.

"Shut yourself up, ya little sniveller."

Shrieks and moans continued. Insults flew. Hysteria flared.

"Stop now. Stop, I say. That's quite enough of that talk." Miss O'Reilly calmly asserted her authority. "We need to support one another during this time. We must wait out the storm and make the most of what strength we have."

Matron soon directed those with hardier stomachs into caring for those incapacitated, and organised the necessary clean-up. Soon the smell of carbolic soap filled the air, replacing one stench with another only slightly more tolerable. Tortured stomachs turned as the acid bit into the back of the throat. Those who couldn't reach the bathrooms on deck or didn't have the strength to hang on to the rail or rope on the way resorted to using the fire buckets, which then had to be emptied. The task was not pleasant, but no one argued with Matron.

Brigid fitted neither camp. She managed to hold her own but couldn't stay on her feet long enough to do anything to help anyone. Yet, thanks to Miss O'Reilly's calm manner and orderliness, the panic soon abated. Voices quieted, and Brigid drifted into an uneasy sleep.

Another day and night passed. The strange Maggie, Jamie and the gentleman from first class haunted her dreams.

And then the weather worsened.

They'd been at sea for nine days. The remaining forty-seven days and nights stretched before them with nightmarish intensity as the terror returned.

Most people tried to avoid the nerve-wracking trek to the toilet and washhouse on the forward deck, but eventually need outstripped dread. Brigid eased herself up the ladder and was instantly buffeted by the howling wind and drenched by the cresting waters. Swallowing the rising bile of panic she edged her way along the rope. The ship suddenly dived under yet another massive wave and she was knocked off balance, landing with a hefty thump.

"Help ... Help ..." she yelled, desperately clinging to the now-slackened rope. Her arms, stretched painfully in their sockets, extended behind her head as her feet slid under the bottom rail and dangled over the edge. "Oh Lord, save me ..." she sobbed. "Oh. Mammy ... Mammy ... help me."

Soaked through and shivering, she gritted her teeth and pulled on the rope with all her strength until her booted feet found traction. Frantically scrabbling backwards away from the edge, with her hands still locked over the rope, she curled into a semi-foetal position. Bits of flying wood from the smashed bathroom and washhouse crashed about her before being swept away by raging water and angry winds. She wrapped an arm over her head for protection and turned the other way.

She screamed. Not more than a few feet away lay a man with blood pouring from his head. She stared at him, fascinated by the way his blood mingled with the seawater, diluted and changed colour as it washed away. She screamed again.

Unable or unwilling to let go of the rope for one second, she twisted and turned until she could pull herself to her knees and manoeuvre into a sitting position, the rope across her lap and her back against the hatchway wall. Bile rose in her throat time and again, until she choked. With her breath coming in rasping gasps, she closed her eyes and waited for her pounding heart to ease.

After a few moments, her head began to clear and her breathing settled. She opened her eyes again and stared at the man, his body bent awkwardly against the bollard that prevented him from being washed overboard. Feebly, she tried to gather her wits but, too afraid to let go of the rope to go to him, she sat motionless, her skirt billowing with the waves that continued to wash over the deck.

Out of the murk, sailors appeared from all directions. Amidst loudly shouted commands and one gruff query to check she was not injured, Brigid lost sight of the man behind the mass of bodies as they took him away. Another pair of sailors, headed in the same direction, nearly tripped over her outstretched legs while carrying a young boy whose leg stuck out at a sickening angle. It was Arthur. She'd seen him a few times hanging around his mother in the women's handicraft group. Poor boy, she thought.

Some time later, the pain in her hands awakened her from her stupor. She eased her grip, waiting for sensation to return to her fingers before she got to her feet and inched her way aft, back along the rope, in search of the relative calm of the single women's quarters below deck. Tears of exhaustion blurred her vision as she struggled to open the door against the wind and the ship's relentless pitching and rolling. She eventually opened the door enough to squeeze through, only to lose her footing and slither and bounce her way down to the bottom of the ladder, landing in a heap.

She was only vaguely aware of the hands that

grasped her and stripped her of her wet clothing. Someone forced a liquid down her throat before the world turned black.

By the time they reached Malta on 29th October, a mere day later, the storm had abated. The sailors were out and about as if nothing had happened, busy loading extra coal and new supplies, and repairing the damage.

Brigid opened her eyes to find Sally seated on the edge of the bed, watching her. "My, you gave us a scare. I thought you were a goner. Truly, I did. How ye feeling now, lass?"

Brigid forced her lips into a semblance of a smile and tried to move. "Ah ... rather stiff and sore, that I am. But I'll live. Was it you who helped me?"

"Aye. Me and the matron. Good ol' stick, that one. Kept everyone in line. Gave you some stuff to help you sleep."

"Oh. Hmm." Her head felt so heavy for a moment she couldn't think what was vexing her. She tried to change her position and groaned with the pain.

"Easy now, hen." Sally helped her to sit up and pushed her coat behind Brigid's back. "There, now. Better?"

Brigid nodded. She covered her face with her hands as memory returned. "I saw a man up there, bleeding heavily from his head. What happened to him? Or was I imagining it?" She rubbed at her temples to ease her head.

Sally didn't pretend. News of the man's death had spread rapidly. "Nay, lass ... you didna imagine it. Wee laddie's name was Niels Pederson from Denmark. Bashed

56

his head in, he did. Reckon he was dead before he hit the deck. Weren't nothing you nor nobody could do about it, so don't you fret none. But better news about young Arthur; his broken leg's been set and he says it dinna hurt much any more. The doc says it'll take some weeks to heal but 'twill mend by the time we've landed."

"Any one else hurt?"

"What, like you? There's a few wi' bruises, but nothing more, but I tell you the last two days has seemed like a lifetime down here. Everyone's that pothered. It'll take days yet for nerves to settle. Oh, I dried your clothes and they're in your bag – they'll need a bit of mending. And that cousin of yours is asking after ye. But Matron sent him away."

"Jamie. Poor boy, I must see him. He'll be that worried."

Brigid tried to stand, but Sally put her hand on her shoulder. "Sit still, lass. I told him ye were fine. Just to give ye a while."

Brigid's bruises developed rainbow hues as the days passed, her muscles stiffened and she ached in every bone. She slept uneasily, and time moved slowly.

Sunday, 31st October 1886

Shut up down here, I don't know what's gone on in the last few days, and I'm that worried.

That girl Maggie Jamie's hankering after be a weird one, and her brother Michael has fair taken against him. I kept my eye on them for more than half a week before the storm and all seemed fine, but I can't be sure all is still well.

Whatever Maggie said to her brother I may never know,

but Jamie and him shook hands and agreed to ignore one another. Long may it stay that way, although I've not seen much of our Jamie since.

The two of them manage to find ways of bumping into each other at every opportunity, even though she's got her poor motherless little nieces to look after. And Jamie behaves more like an excited puppy most of the time, but I can't help worry Maggie is playing a game.

She wants to be friendly with me and I've learnt something about her. I know she's been living away from home, working as a companion maid or some such to a spinster lady in England since she was fourteen. Maggie likes to copy her way of speaking, and says she learnt a few things about how their world worked.

I think Maggie is after a husband who can provide her with those finer things in life she's seen. But what does she want with our Jamie? He's the kindest and most generous-hearted and hard-working soul you could ever wish for, but knows nothing beyond a farming life and labouring with his hands. I can't see it working out between them, but feel helpless.

Then there's that toff from first class. He's been following me, I'm sure of it. We seem to meet up nearly every time I'm up top. He always says hello, wishes me well and goes on his way, but then he seeks me out again when I'm alone and stops to chat or watch me making lace.

And he says such nice things about me. All in a polite and proper manner, but I don't know what to say. I don't know how I should behave around him. I'm all aflutter.

Gradually, life on board returned to its monotonous rhythm as they sailed onwards. The sea became a millpond as the barometer climbed higher with each passing hour. Beads of perspiration shone on every face, and people began to shed as many clothes as modesty allowed. Most simply sat in a semi-trance to conserve energy, in whatever place afforded them shade or a slight breeze.

"Do ya want summat to eat?" asked Sally.

Brigid shook her head.

"Me, neither. I'm that mafted."

"Maybe it'll be cooler tonight."

But it wasn't.

During the storm, meals had become a random event instead of the regimented affair they had got used to, with only bread, biscuits and dried meats readily available – not that many were in a fit state to eat anything. Now the seas were calm and stomachs had returned to normal, mealtimes were restored but most people found it too hot and ate little.

In the end, her need to be out in the fresh air rather than in the stuffy, unbearably hot confines below deck pushed Brigid to get up. Gritting her teeth, she forced one foot after the other up the ladder. By the time she reached the deck, her face was red, her breath came in short gasps and her legs trembled with the effort. She sat down in the shade, happy to watch people while she rested.

Closing her eyes, she listened to the susurration of wind and waves and voices around her. A shadow crossed her face, paused, moved on. She opened one eye to see what had caused it and was startled to find Philip Harrison-Browne standing a few feet away, smiling.

He doffed his hat. "I'm pleased to see you up and around again, Miss O'Brien. I hope you are recovering from your ordeal."

"Aye, I am, thank ye, sir," she murmured. Shielding her eyes from the sun, she looked up at him. "Ah. I'm ... I wasn't ... Forgive my appearance ..." Dressed in a simple cotton skirt and fitted lace-edged blouse, Brigid felt at a disadvantage.

"It's I who should ask for forgiveness – for my intrusion. I just wanted to see how well you were faring. It would be a shame if that pretty smile disappeared." He winked, donned his hat and walked away.

She was at a loss to think what she should make of such behaviour and was about to move somewhere else in case he returned when Maggie found her.

"Oooh, I'm so pleased to find ye at last. I wanted to talk to you. The girls have been a real worry. I came to ask y're advice, but then I heard what happened. You're lucky to be alive, I hear."

"I'll be right as rain again soon enough. What about the girls? Wouldn't Miss O'Reilly or the doctor have been better people to ask?"

"Suppose so." Maggie shrugged affably. "I just didn't think. Laura and Jane were right ill, but they've bounced back since the waves have gone. Even the heat doesna bother them. They're eating an' all now but I can hardly touch a bite."

"Me neither. But the broth is good. And a cup of tea's refreshing, I've found."

Maggie didn't comment, just stared out to sea. Brigid didn't really want to know what Maggie was in a dither about – she needed time to think about 'that man' and focus her energies on getting better – but good manners demanded she ask.

"What is it, Maggie? What's plaguing you?"

The girl shrugged slightly. "There's so much time to

think on this ship and I'm that anxious about what's been and what's to come."

Brigid sighed. It seemed Maggie intended to get something off her chest and had chosen her as the sounding board. "What made you decide to go to Australia?" urged Brigid, hoping to encourage the girl to speak freely.

"Michael."

Brigid sighed again. One-word answers would not get them anywhere. She tried afresh with a more leading question. "What did he have to do with it? Didn't you tell me your ma was sick?"

Maggie nodded and bit her lower lip, surreptitiously wiping her eye. "It's a long story."

"Aye, well, time is the one t'ing we have. How about you start at the beginning?"

Brigid eased herself into a more comfortable position, rested her head against the wall and closed her eyes again.

Maggie's voice was soft as she began her tale. "It all started before Miss Jenkins passed. You remember, I said I worked for Miss Jenkins."

"Aye, I do."

"Well, Michael wrote and said I was to come home. Ma needed me, he said, to look after her. His wife – Eliza – was with child again and couldn't cope with the added strain." Maggie scoffed. "I knew it weren't that. It was more like Ma wouldn't let the woman near her. She didn't like Eliza one little bit. She mighta been little, but that one had a fearsome temper. But, I couldn't leave ... Miss Jenkins was old and frail and slipping from this life. I couldn't just leave her."

Alarmed, Brigid's eyelids shot up when Maggie

gripped her arm. Brigid turned to look at the girl whose eyes bored into hers.

"You must understand. I couldn't leave her alone. She had been good to me and ... I'd ... I'd grown quite fond of her, and ... she ... she didn't have anyone else."

Maggie got up and paced the deck in front of Brigid, getting more agitated by the moment. But she sounded false, too agitated and too intense for Brigid's liking. Loyalty was one thing, but this show of passion was something else.

"Then, about two months later, Miss Jenkins died. For several days, me and the other servants didn't know what to do next, but then this man turns up. He says he's the lawyer handling the estate for the family who wanted to sell up."

Maggie abruptly stopped her pacing and sat next to Brigid. "I didn't even know she had family. They never came to see her when she was alive." Just as suddenly, she was on her feet again. "Anyway, I was dismissed along with the cook and the handyman, but they never gave us any references – because they didn't know us, they said."

She stopped pacing and stared out across the ocean, her knuckles turning white as she gripped the rails. Brigid waited, listening to the cries of the seabirds and watched as one swirled and dived with the current of air. Maggie's thoughts seemed to drift away with the bird as her eyes followed its path high into the sky.

After a moment Brigid spoke. "That hardly sounds fair, I know, but it's not unheard of. What happened next?"

Maggie startled, as if jolted from a dream.

"Oh ... when I finally got home Michael tells me Ma had passed." Her fevered voice raced on. "I was so shocked. He never even bothered to tell me when it happened! I couldn't believe he'd do such a thing, but it was that wife of his, I reckon. Even so, I'll never forgive him. Never. No matter what."

Brigid was disturbed by Maggie's obvious bitterness and animosity towards her brother. Why was she here with Michael if she was that angry with him? As if hearing the unspoken question, Maggie barely paused for breath. "So there I was with no job, no references and my mother gone. I was already grieving, and then the blow of my mother's death on top of everything ..."

By this time, her tears flowed steadily and she mopped at them ineffectually with a lacy handkerchief.

Brigid stood and put her arm around the girl's shoulder to comfort her a little. "I'm right sorry to hear it, that I am."

Maggie gave a weak smile. "I had no time to even think about it before Michael tells me I have to stay and help Eliza. They had the two girls, you see, but they'd lost another and were worried for the new one about to enter the world. So I stayed. We rubbed along well enough, but she ended up treating me more like her maid with all the work I had to do. She was nothing but lazy."

Maggie stopped speaking, and took a few shuddering breaths. Brigid found a clean hanky and gave it to her. Maggie wiped her face and blew her nose, which seemed to restore her a little.

Brigid sat closer. "Go on."

"Not long after she went into labour things started going wrong. I sent for the midwife, but she couldn't come straight away; by the time she got there Eliza was bleeding badly and even the midwife couldn't stop it. We lost them both that night. It was a little boy too. Michael was fair spooked and got oh so angry. He stormed out of the house and didn't come back till the next day."

Brigid's eyes watered and her heart thumped at the sad story. She took back her initial reservations. The girl had certainly had a rough time. She needed a friend.

"That's a rare painful story, Maggie." A moment's silence passed while Brigid thought of something more heartening to say. "But I remember, when things got bad at home, my dear old granny used to say 'we must not dwell on what's done, but look to what's ahead. That way lies hope'. I used to take comfort from her words. Maybe you can too."

"Hope. Yes, that's it. I need hope. That's why ..." Maggie's eyes sparkled with possibility before she dropped her gaze. Dabbing at her nose, she furtively glanced at Brigid from beneath her eyelashes.

Her voice quivered as she took up her story again. "You see, things got more wretched after that. The day after the funeral Michael came home to say he'd booked passages to Australia." She raised her distraught, tear-stained face towards Brigid, her voice stronger, aroused. "I didn't know what to think, and he wouldn't even talk to me about it. Not that I had any idea what I wanted to do, or where I could go. He was the only family I had left ... but then he just said he was the man in the family and I was to do as I was told." She stopped to gulp air into her lungs. "So here I am – nursemaid to his two girls and him bossing me around all the while – with no idea where my life is going any more."

Brigid sympathised. They'd both been forced into emigrating by circumstances beyond their control, but something made Brigid uneasy. Something Jamie told her, about how Maggie had stood up to her brother and how she'd told him not to pay Michael any mind. That he couldn't boss her around. Her initial distrust of the girl resurfaced.

"That's why I wanted to talk with you ... about your Jamie. He's been a right help. He's made me laugh and think better of myself. So I'm hoping you won't mind if he and I get ... um, friendly."

Cunning minx, thought Brigid, trying to get me on side. "Can't say I know you well enough to say, but Jamie is his own man now. If it's what he wants."

Maggie grasped Brigid's hands and came over all smiles. "Oh, thank you. You have no idea how much this means to me. I must go tell him."

Before Brigid could speak, the girl walked briskly away with no sign of the distress she had shown only minutes earlier. Brigid stared after her.

Now what is she playing at?

Tuesday, 2 November 1886

We've been at sea for nearly two weeks, and I no longer feel as fearful as I once did. If I can survive that storm, I can survive anything. I can't imagine anything worse happening, and that gives me hope.

My bruises are healing, but the more I think about what happened during the storm, the more I give thanks to Our Lord for saving me. I could easily have gone over the side. He must have been watching over me and given me the strength to hold on as long as I did. I wonder why He wasn't watching over that young man who was killed when he struck his head. I can still see him lying there beside me. It haunts me that such a young life has been cut short. Why him and not me? The priest did his best and gave him a grand send off, but his young brother was that distraught. I felt very strange as they dropped the body, tied in a canvas bag, over the side. There's something not quite right about it in my mind, but the captain said there was no other choice in this heat.

A bout of whooping cough broke out amongst some of the children. We were told two little ones died, but the women in the single quarters didn't catch it. We said prayers for the wee souls. There are several clergy on board, and plenty of chance for people to clear their minds and hearts with prayer and confession.

The routine of ship life helps break up the long days, but the journey's been something to endure not enjoy, despite some fun times.

Mondays have turned into washdays. Our fresh water is kept for drinking water, so we have to use seawater the sailors scoop up with buckets. But it makes the clothes very stiff and scratchy.

Tuesdays I spend making lace with the other women. We can get into a grand set-to on the worth of the various forms. My crocheted Clones lace and my needlepoint Kenmare lace are finer than most, although there are others like me who can do several different styles. I've watched women stitching the fine-drawn needle-made Limerick lace, while others do the appliqué work of Carrickmacross. One or two can do Mountmellick embroidery with its padded and raised flowers. We all hope to make money from our products amongst the wealthy when we reach Australia.

Wednesdays, the clergy run classes for the older children. I've started helping them to learn to read and write. Thursday is a sad day. I will write a letter home every week, knowing I can't send it, but I'll feel closer to Ma and the others when I do. I miss home so much: the gentle rain, the spongy mosses underfoot, the soft colours, even the smell of the peat fire, but mostly I miss Ma's comforting presence.

Fridays are the oddest of days with little to do that's different, and Saturdays are when we have games; in the evening we often have a singsong.

I don't want to think about my worries with Jamie and Maggie today.

Nor about Mr Harrison-Browne who is becoming persistent.

4

The Art of Coquetry

"Look at that, Jamie." Brigid pointed to an unusual building with domes and spires a half-mile away across a small estuary. "What is it?"

"One of the sailors told me that's the mosque in the Arab section. It's a church of sorts."

The ship's arrival in Port Said had motivated the heat-weary passengers to gather on deck to see this strange place. The breakwater and lighthouse were familiar sights, but not so familiar, or comforting, was the barren desert extending beyond the water's edge as far as the eye could see.

At least a dozen ships lay at anchor midstream in the crowded port, while the shoreline was cluttered with small vessels designed to carry goods and people between ship and shore.

Jamie pointed out various sights. "And this here in front of us is where the English live."

"What, no Irish?" she laughed.

"No. No Irish – least none I've heard of."

Several elegant, two-storey buildings with full-length windows lined the flat area immediately in front of them and stretched inland from the water's edge. They could see people walking around in long white robes, carts drawn by donkeys laden with food and goods, and men from the army in khaki uniforms moving amongst the buildings.

Their conversation came in fits and starts until something new attracted their attention. Otherwise they were content to let their eyes rove.

"The buildings look a lot like those I saw in London. Did the British build them?"

"I suppose so," Jamie shrugged, suddenly restless and looking to and fro over his shoulders.

This had been one of the few times Brigid had seen him without Maggie in tow and while she was enjoying their time together, he was obviously itching to get away.

"You're not really with me any more, are ye, Jamie?"

He had the decency to look shamefaced. "She makes me feel different, our Breeda. Not like a young oaf, but someone who matters."

Her heart sank a little. "Off you go then." If her instincts were anything to go by, he was going to get hurt. "I'll see you another time."

"You're an angel." He kissed the top of her head and sped off.

She watched him go, wondering when Miss Maggie would appear next. She'd taken to 'accidentally' bumping into Brigid at least twice a week to gossip about this and that.

Excitement rose as the passengers chatted about the sights, especially the mosques surrounded by trees and gardens where an oasis was located, but any ideas of going ashore were soon thwarted. The canal was so narrow, ships had little room to pass each other and the vessel was forced to remain at anchor until given the go-ahead to traverse the Suez Canal in convoy later that day. To add to their dismay, the passengers received instructions forbidding them to engage with the locals wanting to sell goods from their small boats.

Reinforcing this command, officers and crew began to move along the rails compelling people to stand back. All the while they shouted at something or someone out of sight below them.

"Get away from the ship," they repeated time and again. "Move away or we'll fire."

"What's going on?" Brigid shuddered at the suggestion someone may be shot.

Polite but firm, the officer explained, "Nothing to alarm you, miss. Just pedlars. Happens every time. Now, can I ask you to move on please, miss?"

"But why ...?" Brigid began.

"Orders, miss. Too risky." He touched his cap and continued his circuit of the deck.

"Move away," he called over the rails. "Move away, I say."

His voice faded as Brigid stared after him, wondering what he meant.

"Enjoying the sights, Miss O'Brien?" Philip Harrison-Browne, attired in a light coloured day suit tipped his panama hat towards her. She was no longer surprised by his arrival. He'd developed the uncanny habit of turning up not long after Sally, Jamie or Maggie had left her alone. To chat, he'd once explained, bored by the pomposity of his fellow First Class passengers.

"I am, thank ye, Mr Harrison-Browne."

"So am I." He winked, smiled directly at her and put his hat on. Every time he hinted at a compliment she blushed but tried to remember what Sally told her:

'Don't begrudge him; it's in his blood. Just flutter your eyelids and give him a pretty little laugh. Not too much, but enough to keep him friendly. Oh, and ask him questions so he does the talking. You'll have him eatin' out of your hand in no time.'

Philip leant his elbow on the rail and looked at her quizzically. "You do know why they won't allow any contact with the shore here, don't you?"

"That I do not. The young officer said it was too risky. What did he mean by that, do ye think?"

"Now, I don't want you to be concerned," he continued, hesitating. "But about a year ago, when this ship sailed this way, it ... well ... some of the passengers contracted cholera ..."

"Cholera!" she squeaked, placing one hand on her breastbone. "But that's ..."

"Steady on." He laid a hand gently on her upper arm, resting it a little too long for her comfort. "The ship is no longer contagious. I know it's upsetting, and even though the disease can be fatal, not everyone got sick, and not all those who got sick died – so don't be frightened." He squeezed her arm reassuringly then put his hand in his pocket. "The ship arrived safely in Australia and made another trip earlier this year without mishap. We're perfectly safe, I assure you. The authorities don't know whether it came from contact with the local people or from contaminated water or food, so they are being especially cautious this time."

"Wouldn't it be fair if we knew what was going on?" Brigid believed in fairness.

Philip looked at her askew. "What? And cause a panic. No. It's best as few people know as possible. I trust you'll not say anything?"

Brigid nodded in agreement, not sure how to keep such news to herself. Sally would spit tacks if she knew. "So why is it that you know?"

"My father makes it his business to know these things." He shrugged, saying no more on the matter. He lifted his hat, flipped his hair back and coughed delicately into his curled fist. "I wonder if you would do me the honour of accepting a little gift."

He withdrew a small burgundy-velour covered notebook from his jacket pocket. "I notice you keep a diary and thought you might like this. It's not much, but I'm sure you will have a use for it."

He handed it to Brigid, who stretched her fingers towards it but didn't take it.

"Oh, no. I couldn't possibly accept anything from a gentleman such as yourself, sir. It wouldn't be proper."

"Who's to know? And why wouldn't it be 'proper'? I'm only giving you some paper."

Tempted by his logic, Brigid took the notebook and smoothed the velour with the palm of her hand. She unclipped the clasp and fingered the fine paper inside. "It's very beautiful. I've not seen anything as fine as this before."

"Yes, beautiful, like its holder. Do take it ... to please me." His voice rose at the end as he cocked his head to the side and raised one eyebrow. "It's a token of appreciation for allowing me to talk to you. You are so refreshing after the dour men of the cloth and simpering maidens and their mothers I'm usually forced to converse with."

She followed Sally's advice and laughed a little, and fluttered her eyelids – not disingenuously, but because she was flustered by the thrill quivering in inexplicable places.

"It's me who should be flattered. I've never spoken with a toff ... sorry, I mean gentleman before. "

He burst out laughing. "Miss Brigid – I may call you Brigid, may I not? I do so enjoy your company."

Suez Canal
Same day

As the sun rose higher so did the temperature. With nothing more to see, and people too spent to do anything beyond stare at the dun-coloured desert and matching houses, most sat around like lumps of lard melting in the heat.

"By God, it's hot!" Like many of the passengers Sally sought the coolest place she could find to sit and wait for the ship to start its traverse of the canal – like all, except Brigid. She paced, sat, stood, paced – restlessly, relentlessly.

"For goodness' sake, lassie," cried Sally. "Will you settle? You're putting me on edge. Either you talk with him or you don't. What harm can ye come to on the ship?"

"Well, nothing, I suppose. It's just ... I don't know. Ah, Sally. Why am I feeling like this?"

"'Tis love, most like," Sally answered cheekily, knowing she'd embarrass her new friend – and she did.

Brigid's face turned into a picture of dismay. "Don't be silly. It's not."

Sally shrugged. "If ye say so, but stop wasting energy. Come sit awhiles – do something useful. How about we make ye another bonnet – ye can wear it when you walk out with him."

"I'm not walking out with him!" Brigid snapped back, but admitted her fingers and mind needed a diversion.

Hours later the call to weigh anchor came at last, and the ship started its slow passage through the canal. Sally and Brigid watched the township fade into the distance. Stone walls lining the waterway helped keep the sand at bay, and for hours on end, the only thing to see was the endless desert, punctuated by strange trees in odd places.

Sometimes a small cluster of buildings broke the barren flatness or an occasional rocky outcrop varied the skyline. An unusual mosque with domes but without spires came into view.

"Look, look," cried a woman. "What are those funny creatures?"

"They're camels," someone replied. "Ships of the desert, they call them, because they can carry a heavy weight and sway from side to side when they walk."

"And they can go days without food and water," added another voice. "They're like pack horses. See, there's a man on the front one, then several carrying goods and another man and a camel at the back."

"They travel from town to town across the desert. How they survive in all those long robes and their 'eads wrapped in those towel things is beyond me."

"Protects them from the sun, they say."

The conversation swayed to and fro around them, but Sally could see Brigid wasn't paying attention. Although the two of them had begun making a new bonnet from the various bits and pieces they had put together, Brigid still denied her reasons had anything to do with Philip.

"Of course it's not because I want to show off to Mr Harrison-Browne – that's your silly idea – it's only because my thread is running out and I need something to do with my hands."

"Whatever you say, hen." Sally wasn't convinced, and apart from Brigid's clearly confused feelings over Philip Harrison-Browne, something else was gnawing at her. "You look as though the worst thing that can happen, already has." Sally joined Brigid at the rails and tried to cheer her up. "Come on, buck up. You can't go round with a face that long, you'll trip over it."

"Sorry, I'm just feeling a bit glum. Can't seem to want to do naught."

"It's the heat, I reckon. Making everyone feel weary, it is, but you think too much. Come on. Leave this for now. Let's find a card game or summat, or some dancing. You like dancing."

"It's too hot."

"Well, they tell me it's hot in Australia all the time, so we better get used to it. Can't go around doing nowt there, can we? We have to work for our living."

"Sure, 'tis true what you say." Brigid paused and looked out across the ship's rail at the never-ending sand and sky. "Sally, do you ever feel there's people watching you?"

"What you on about? There's always someone a-watching someone on this 'ere tub, even if it's just for summat to do. You mean that toff?"

"No. Not him. I know he watches me, and I don't mean like that. I mean creepier – like 'hairs on the back of your neck' type watching you. Like there's someone there behind you, only there isn't."

"You going all fey on me?"

Brigid shook her head. "Not at all. Ah, never mind me. It's just a feeling I get sometimes."

Sally pulled at the loose curls draping over her shoulder. She didn't like hearing Brigid sound so uneasy. It was time for Sally Forsythe to put her ear to the ground and find out what was going on.

Interest in the foreignness of the landscape had rapidly waned in the three days it took to get to Suez, but it became impossible to ignore the daytime heat and the grains of sand swirling in the air, making everything feel gritty. Fortunately, but much to everyone's surprise, the temperature dropped considerably when evening came, and, while the between-decks air was still stuffy, the lack of humidity and the cooler nights made it easier to sleep.

Feeling less tired improved their general frame of mind a little, but boredom and the stress of being confined to a small area surrounded by sea grew. Tempers were readily ruffled and irritability commonplace. To stave off the tedium, most evenings Sally found a card game while Brigid and Philip promenaded around the deck.

"Thank ye kindly, gentlemen," Sally said to loud groans of complaint, as she scooped more ha'pennies from the table. "Anyone up for another hand?"

She dealt to a new set of patsies and called a card. Her skill with cards was the only useful thing her stepfather had given her. He'd taught her how to fleece the most unlikely of suspects to earn more than a bob or two for the coffers, for which she was grateful. What forced her to run away were the beatings and his nightly visits to her bed when her ma was sick. After she died, Sally had taken off. No man was ever going to misuse her like that again. She'd live off her wits and her charm – and a hand of cards – but not her body.

The call went round the table; cards were held, or taken and discarded. Sally was careful not to win too much or too often, so as not to arouse suspicion, but most of the men were too cocksure of their own abilities to think a woman could beat them.

Late at night Sally happily listened to Brigid talking about the events of the evening, either while they lay on their bunks with everyone asleep around them, or while Brigid tried to tame her friend's wilful curls.

"We aren't the only ones out walking," Brigid informed her, pulling the brush through the tangled locks. "The deck gets quite crowded and we often have to weave in and out of other people."

Brigid was so wrapped up in her own excitement she didn't notice Sally said little about her own activities – she instinctively knew Brigid wouldn't approve. Neither would her friend approve of the way she'd dealt with that Englishwoman she and Brigid had confronted on their first day.

Ethel was the woman's name, Sally had discovered. And she was a bully to nearly everyone who crossed her path. Ethel had promised to 'get even' – and had tried. Once she'd tripped Sally when they passed, another time she threw Sally's fork overboard, but mostly she bad-mouthed her, loudly, whenever she saw her. Sally had quietly warned her to be nice or suffer the consequences. Ethel had scoffed, but like most bullies, she didn't like the taste of her own medicine. By the time Sally had finished with her, she was more lamb than bull. Despite nursing a broken finger and screaming blue murder, she never bothered Sally again.

Brigid kept talking even though Sally said nothing in response. "He has such manners, does Mr Harrison-Browne. He is always so charming and doffs his hat, wishing everyone a good evening when he has to step aside to let another pass. And he has this beguiling way of flicking his hair back from his face."

Brigid put the brush down and split Sally's hair into segments, holding it out of the way with hairpins so she could plait the top section first.

"And he does make me laugh with some funny remark about a man with bat wings for ears, or a woman whose hair was piled so high he thought the seagulls would nest in it. I know we shouldn't make fun of people, but he does see life in a different way."

Oh dear, as sure as my name is Sally Forsythe, the girl is going to get hurt before long.

"And I have to thank you," continued Brigid, weaving the side plaits into the top and working her way down. "For your idea of a new bonnet. Indeed, Mr Harrison-Browne even commented on it." Brigid finished plaiting Sally's hair and leaned closer, lowering her voice. "I'm a wee bit bothered, that I am. When he said he mistook the woman with the white skin for a ghost in the moonlight, I came over all shivery. I'm just a-wondering – this feeling of someone behind me all the time – is it a fairy waiting for me, do you t'ink? Is she trying to foretell my doom?"

"No, lass. The fairies canna follow ye across the sea. Dinna fash. It's nothing to worry about."

Two nights later, as they passed through the southern end of the Suez Canal, Sally, Brigid, and Philip stood together to listen to the purser's announcement. Sally didn't feel comfortable with Philip - he was too smug for her tastes. She usually avoided him, but Brigid had insisted she stay.

"Our course will follow the length of the Red Sea as we head towards the Gulf of Aden. The next port of call will be Batavia in the Dutch East Indies, on the 25th of November. Three weeks from now."

"Will we be able to go ashore?" Brigid raised her voice so the officer could hear.

Any hopes the passengers had that the monotony would change were soon dashed. "In Batavia? Sorry, miss. No. Captain's orders. We are only picking up coal."

Sally didn't quite understand Philip's casual shrug and 'see, I told you so' look, but Brigid clearly did.

Still, not to be beaten, Sally turned the disappointing news to her advantage. "All right folks, time we did something to spice things up around here. How about a bit of a party? Now we've all settled down again after that there storm, and the scenery outside isn't up to much, we need some fun to entertain us."

Straightaway the harmonicas, fiddles and accordions came out of hiding, and everyone was ready to play up a storm of their own. But she didn't want any standard free-for-all. This was to be an event, almost a performance; she just had to persuade them to go along with her ideas.

"I've got plans for you too, Miss Breeda," she said, getting into the swing of organising who was doing what.

"Oh no, Sally. I don't play anything, and I'm no good at singing either. Leave me out of it."

"Not singing, naw. But dancing, aye. You're a lovely dancer so surely ye can do some of them Irish jigs. You know them all, and I've found a fella who knows how to play the fiddle for ye. And don't try getting out of it now, Miss Pudding and Pie."

Brigid didn't answer. She shivered and looked sharply around but saw nothing unusual amongst the people behind her.

"What's the matter?"

"Nothing. It's just that feeling again."

"Ach. Don't pay her no mind."

Brigid grabbed Sally's arm. "Who? What are you saying?"

"That feeling you been getting. I've had my eye out, ye see." She tapped the side of her nose to show she'd done some snooping. "It's only Madame Maggie. That one your cousin's keen on. Don't know what she's up to, but."

Sally continued talking about who was doing what, ticking off on her fingers the music, the stories and the songs she had planned. "Are you listening to me?"

"I am that." Brigid stood staring at the spot where she was convinced she'd glimpsed someone. "I was just wondering what she's all about, following me around."

"Slightly crazy, if ye ask me. Those girls she's supposed to be looking after just run wild around the place, 'cept when there's food to be had. And as for that brother of hers ... well, no one has a good word for him. Now, where was I?"

႙ ဣ

Wednesday, 10 November 1886

The three days inching our way along the canal between Port Said and Suez were awful — it was so hot and I found the endless desert right scary — but the days since then as we head into the Gulf seem longer. None of it is gladdening to my mind. Sand and dust. Dust and sand. Towering cliffs, a few buildings ...

Mr Harrison-Browne tries to amuse me with all those wonderful ideas of his, but I don't know what to think. Nothing like that happens to the likes of me. What he talks about is out of my reach, but he makes me feel so special, and important. I get all quivery when he's around.

I've not seen Jamie much at all in the last week. He spends his days either with the menfolk, gambling or else with Maggie, I suspect. Not that I've missed him as much lately. Not since Mr Harrison-Browne has befriended me.

But why would Maggie watch me? She's always hanging around and bothering me with something. I can't believe half of what she says is true. Some of it seemed likely, but Maggie's doing doesn't always match her saying.

At least another week has gone, and we are a week closer to our new home and what that brings us. I both dread it and long for it ...

Brigid shut the notebook with a bang and shoved it deep into her pocket, her latest entry unfinished. She hated this glum feeling that let her deepest worries surface. What would her mother tell her to do, if she could?

Stop that! her brain screamed. Her mother could never help her again.

She thumped both feet firmly on the deck, stood up

and squared her shoulders. She'd made up her mind to stand on her own two feet, proud of her achievements, without constantly worrying about what people thought or said. No longer was there anyone to tell her what to do or when. No one to help her make a decision, no one to guide her – except the Lord. She was her own woman responsible only to herself.

Part of the problem was Mr Harrison-Browne and his advances, but the business with Maggie and Jamie had unsettled her the most. She needed to talk with someone. But who?

Ironically, Brigid was the one Maggie picked to chat to. Or rather Brigid listened while Maggie talked, full of praise for Jamie and complaints about her own family.

"He's such a sweet lad, nothing like my Michael. It's so nice to find someone who cares and treats me right ...

"And those girls are uncontrollable. No wonder Michael wanted me to help. Not that they listen to me. They don't. And he's no help ...

"I don't know how I'd manage on board this boring old boat without Jamie."

And so the story went, over and over. And every time, Brigid tried to work out why, and fretted. What was the girl playing at? Her story – and manner – changed so often Brigid could barely keep up.

Jamie was no better. On the few occasions she managed to find him alone all he could talk about was 'his angel', but she noticed how heavily he drank, and nothing she said made any difference. Where he got the drink she didn't know, and she was sure Maggie was following her between times; that odd feeling of being watched lingered.

She had tackled Maggie about it once.

"I'm far too busy looking after that impossible brother of mine and his children to have the time or interest in what you are doing." Maggie stormed off as if the world owed her something, leaving Brigid to wonder where Jamie fitted into the picture.

Sally was no help either. "I told ye, family cause more problems than they're worth. Ignore them, I say. Put them right out of your mind and live your own life, my girl. It'll be better for ye in the end. Here, try some of this. It helps, I promise." She offered Brigid a swig from the gin bottle, but once more Brigid refused.

She hadn't asked her friend about Philip Harrison-Browne again either. Brigid knew Sally's thoughts, and they didn't help her one little bit.

Sally's musical evening coincided with the crossing of the equator, a celebration in itself with crazy antics dreamt up by the crew. When everyone was on deck, Neptune and his entourage appeared dressed in strange clothing. The children, and some of their parents, screamed with fright. The unfamiliar paganism of the celebrations clashed with her Catholic upbringing. Seeing other women say their prayers, Brigid found respite in her rosary and said her own Hail Mary.

Sally ignored the women's concerns, laughing off the sailors' actions as men behaving like children, and spurred everyone to do their own celebrating. That evening, the concert began as planned. Sweet voices and sad songs brought tears to many an eye, and Brigid's dancing soon had others leaping to their feet. Ignoring the heat, more and more people joined in until a line of dancers jigged to the traditional tunes the fiddlers played. Philip looked to be enjoying the spectacle as much as any of them and clapped in time to the pounding rhythms.

A few jokes and some fairy stories added to the hilarity and a lusty sing-along led by Sally made sure everyone was included – even Annie and Lettie. They had to be the two quietest and most unassuming people on board, but they managed to recite a poem together. Minnie and Rosina, the two German women in the adjacent bunks, sang a Schubert duet with such lilting beauty they silenced the audience.

Next up was Maggie, who sang a rather bawdy song and, much to Brigid's astonishment, Jamie, who was already three sheets to the wind, added his loud voice to the chorus. Brigid could hazard a guess where Jamie had learnt such a song, but as for Maggie – she certainly wouldn't have learnt that from the genteel mistress of the manor she supposedly once worked for.

The moon glowed in the late night sky, with no sign that people were ready for sleep. The rafters rang with the sound of laughter, and joy filled every heart. With Australia now closer than England, and the day and date changing at the same time, their new lives seemed only a hair's breadth away.

Out of breath after the extended dancing, Brigid could barely speak. "Thank you ... Sal. For making me – and the others – do this. You've done wonders. I feel so much better."

Swallowing another mouthful of gin from her nearly empty bottle, Sally wiped her mouth with the back of her hand. "Told you, hen. We needed something to lift our spirits, and there's nothing like a-singing and dancing to do just that. Except 'Mother's Milk' here, of course. Want a drop?" Sally offered Brigid the gin bottle.

"No, ta." Brigid shook her head in amazement. "But I thought they called it 'Mother's Ruin'?"

"Only if you're a mother," she guffawed loudly. "'Tis nourishing milk to me." Never mind how much she drank, Sally always had a good word to say about everyone and everything. With a seemingly endless supply of gin at hand, Sally made a bright and happy companion, but where she got it from was a mystery. "You don't know what you're missing, lass."

"I'll manage," Brigid shouted back above the noise as the musicians started up another round. Soon the spoons came out, adding percussion to the rhythms, and she leapt to her feet again.

Brigid had no idea what the time was when Philip reappeared. He'd been there early in the evening, laughing and clapping along with the rest of them, wearing a singularly amused expression on his face, but then she'd lost sight of him – until now.

"You look delightfully young, Miss Breeda, if exceedingly hot and bothered. Would you care to take a stroll to cool off?"

He'd discarded his hat and cravat, and wore his shirt unbuttoned at the throat. He looked so startlingly handsome it took her breath away. Even so, it still took her a full five seconds of staring into his eyes trying to fathom what he was thinking – intending – before she agreed.

Away from the party, the promenade deck was almost empty. Most of the passengers had retired, others seemed determined to dance, drink and sing the night away. Their voices carried on the night air.

"Better?" he enquired after a few moments.

"Much. Thank you." Brigid's hand rested easily in the crook of his arm as they admired the night sky, both happy to saunter in silence.

At the stern, they stopped to marvel at the phosphorescence on the wake stirred by the ship's propellers. For once, no other moonlight strollers disturbed their solitude. Standing side by side with barely a gap between them, the air shifted with another form of energy.

"I find you utterly alluring, my dear." Philip kept looking over the rail, staring out at the water. "I know I shouldn't ..." He turned his head, took her chin between his fingers and turned her towards him. "And I know it isn't fair to you, given my position – but I can't help myself." He moved closer, his eyes fixated on her lips. He licked his own and sighed. "I ... that is ... you look adorable ... standing there with the moonlight catching your hair ... Oh, my dear ..."

His arms reached around her, enveloping her, his head above hers, looking down into her eyes, at her lips. Unsure, enquiring, Brigid stiffened but, sensitive to the glow of his eyes and his moist, swollen lips, she surrendered to an unknown instinct and closed her eyes. His lips met hers, softly, gently imploring, compelling. Seconds passed. Minutes. A lifetime. He gave her a final squeeze before releasing his hold.

Brigid staggered with the emotion of the moment. She raised her hands to her lips, amazed. "I've ... I've never ..."

"You were wonderful. You *are* wonderful." He took her hands and swung her in an arc. "I've never felt so free."

"Did you just giggle?" asked Bridget, giggling herself.

"I suppose I did. You make me feel ... alive. So ..."

"Oh. Pardon me, sir." The sailor's voice startled them. "I didn't realise anyone was 'ere at this hour. I've just come to check the rigging, sir. If you don't mind."

Pulling his jacket into place, Philip immediately fell into being the gentleman he was. He flipped his hair back. "Not at all, my good chap. We'll leave you to it."

He extended his arm to Brigid, and they made their way around to the other side of the ship until they reached the hatchway leading to Brigid's quarters.

"Until tomorrow." Philip bowed, kissed her hand and departed.

Not until Brigid lay in her bunk, with her heart and mind in turmoil, did she realise she'd not spoken to Jamie all evening. Nor had she seen him or Maggie after her song. A sudden wash of longing swept over her, and she shuddered.

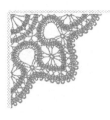

5

Distancing of Heart and Mind

Monday, 22nd November 1886

The passengers' spirits remained high in the days following the equator crossing party, knowing the journey was more than half over. Even so, Philip's daily appearances had a far more uplifting effect on Brigid's state of mind, despite her still being bothered by convention.

"No, I'm not worried about what people think." Philip's response to her continued doubts surprised her. "And neither should you. People may be jealous and gossip, but let them. You are above all that nonsense."

Brigid had never considered herself above anything in her whole life. Philip's constant praise was something she'd not experienced before, and she talked endlessly about it to Sally.

Sally only encouraged it. "If he wants to sweet-talk you, hen, then let him. You might just win him. For goodness' sake girl, the only way we will better ourselves is by being bold. Doing things we never did at home – nor could do, because the old biddies of the town would shame us. There's no one can do that any more. Only we can shame ourselves."

But where this friendship was going and what it

would mean when they reached Brisbane niggled at Brigid's sense of decency. There had never been any question of anything unseemly – not yet, anyway – but why had he chosen her? They only met on deck in the open where people could see them. Men were not allowed into the girls' quarters anyway, and she would never venture into the First Class area, where she might be seen and compared. Not that he'd suggested it.

Brigid enjoyed their conversations as much as his company and open admiration. He was an articulate and knowledgeable man, happy to discuss literature, art, music – topics as distant from Brigid's reality as the moon from the earth.

"Once we reach Brisbane, I shall personally escort you to libraries and galleries, and museums, and you can see for yourself."

She started to believe in the impossible. "That would be grand, that it would. I've never been to any such places in my life."

She treasured the stolen moments of bliss when he stroked her cheek with the back of his finger, or tucked a stray lock of hair behind her ear. But mostly she looked forward to their nighttime strolls when they could hide in the shadows and she would succumb to his embraces, fervently returning his kisses.

He never talked about what he did for money. His father had business connections, he'd said, but beyond that Brigid had no idea what work he did – if any. She could never have imagined anyone not working for a living, before meeting Philip, but he dismissed it as unimportant.

"I'll be going into service when I arrive. How am I going to do all these wonderful things if I'm bound by a mistress?"

"Don't worry your perfect little head about it." He tapped his finger on the tip of her nose and made her laugh. "I'll find a way."

"But I'd like to do more than be a maid one day, I would. I've seen the lacework on ladies' gowns and t'ink I could use my lace like that. I could make clothes for babbies and for the fine ladies, and on linens and such like. I've got all sorts of ideas, I have, aye. But I suppose it's just a dream."

The ship anchored at Batavia on 25th November as expected. Aided by some of the passengers, the vessel loaded over sixty tons of coal, creating dust clouds and covering the men from head to toe, but no extra food or water. Philip reminded her the fear of contamination remained high but, fortunately, the passengers seemed oblivious to the official concerns.

Once they knew nothing of interest would happen, few people paid attention to the port that offered little beyond derricks and ships. But as soon as they headed south-east again towards Australia, people began counting off the days until their journey and ordeal were over.

"I'm getting some ideas about what you and me can do together," whispered Sally one night as they lay in their bunks listening to the sibilant and sonorous sounds of the night.

"Like what?"

"Dunno yet. But I think we'd make a good team."

Below decks was no more pleasant than it had been the first day. People were more comfortable with each other, and the air of distrust had evaporated, but petty jealousies had crept in instead. Those who could afford to bribe the sailors for extra food or clean water, or other 'refreshments', the likes of which Sally enjoyed, had irked the ones without the means. Even Brigid had managed to obtain some soap and fresh water to wash with.

"How's it going to work, anyway?" replied Brigid, peering over her bunk, trying to make Sally out in the dark beneath her. "You're going to Townsville and I'm in service in Brisbane. Can't see me having time to travel."

"You indentured?"

"No. Not really. A girl from home lives there now, and she's with a lady who helps newcomers find employment to tide them over. I have to work a six-month probation at some house or other, but after that I can stay, if they want me, or leave. I don't know what happens if I have to leave."

"Well, then, there's time to come up with something."

Brigid tried to sleep but tossed restlessly while her brain whirled. The accumulated smells of unwashed bodies, grimy clothes and foul breath from the lack of decent food had become loathsome. It was little wonder she preferred to be on deck.

The next day, Philip suggested something uncannily similar to what Sally had said the previous night. "I've an idea that might help your dream along its way."

"What are you talking about?"

"Your lacemaking and sewing skills. I think I can do something with those."

Brigid's pulse quickened. "Can ye tell me how?"

Infuriatingly, he tapped the side of his nose in response. "All in good time."

Thursday Island in the Torres Strait came into view on Monday, 6th December 1886. The ship weighed anchor, and the tender pulled alongside, with the Medical Officer of Health on board. After the outbreak of cholera a year earlier, the authorities now inspected everyone before they landed and before the ship could continue on its way. If any sign of the disease had been found, the ship would have been quarantined where it anchored.

Brigid lined up with the others as Dr Salter made a thorough examination of all the passengers, a process that took many restless hours. Mayhem reigned as hot and irritable parents tried to control their unruly children as they waited.

By late morning, the doctor had found everyone surprisingly well, and gave permission for the two departing passengers to go ashore. Stores were unloaded and the coastal pilot boarded the ship.

With their own destination now only a matter of days away, those remaining stood by the rails, eager to say goodbye. Their laughter and chatter said much about newfound friends who would soon be bidding each other adieu, wondering if they would ever meet again. It seemed to Brigid as if everyone wanted to cram in as much talk as they could, and make promises they couldn't be sure of keeping – anything to allay their sudden nerves.

The *Dorunda* was scheduled to stop at Cooktown, Townsville, Bowen and Mackay on the way to Rockhampton, the last port before Brisbane, where she and Jamie, and the majority of the other passengers, would disembark.

The knowledge that Sally would be leaving in just a few days weighed on Brigid's mind. She would sorely miss the woman, for all her raucous and riotous ways.

Sally was the sort who would find her way amid the mire and come out on top with a smile on her face and a penny in her hand.

"Come on, you must be able to tell me about that idea of yours now?" begged Brigid. "You're leaving in a few days." She'd hoped to prod Sally into telling her something she could think about, at least.

"I know that very well ... but naw. I canna. I have to wait until I see the lay of the land like. Once I'm settled, I'll send you notice. Promise." Sally grinned, putting both hands on Brigid's arms. "I'll not forget you, little one. You've been good for me."

Brigid slid her arms around the other woman's waist and hugged her close. "And you for me."

Easing out of the embrace Sally said, "Now, remember what I told you on our first day on this tub?"

Brigid shook her head.

"I said – don't trust anyone. And I mean it."

"What, not even you?"

Sally laughed mirthlessly. "Especially not me, hen. Not even me, unless I loves ya, that is. Then I'll fend for you with me life. But I'm warning you. Just like what I said about family. They'll hurt you to get what they want. Your Jamie will."

"No. Not our Jamie. He's not like that."

Sally shrugged her shoulders and pulled a face, unconvinced by Brigid's zealous defence.

"If you say so. And make sure *you* con that Mr Philip Harrison-Browne, not the other way around."

"Con? What con? What are you saying? You've been telling me to encourage him, now you're warning me against him."

"Like I said. It takes one to know one. You just watch

when he does that hair thing. He's right out o' sorts when he does it. Be careful."

On the way around the northernmost tip of Queensland, heavy tropical rainstorms made the decks and rails greasy and slippery. By now everyone was used to the dry heat, but this sticky wet cloak was suffocating. The bedding and clothing became damp to the touch. Books curled at the edges, and perspiration ran in rivulets upon faces already flushed pink. After all they had suffered, many found the oppressive air the last straw. Tears flowed and tempers flared, and as the relentless rain continued and the humidity increased they found themselves, often as not, restricted below decks. She hated it. Never mind what the weather was doing, nothing would stop her going topside to escape the rank odours of stale food and sour sweat.

Unwilling to give up their daily promenade, Philip managed to locate an umbrella, much to the amusement – and envy – of the others. While insufficient for the deluges, it did provide protection from the scattered showers.

"I'm used to walking in the rain," Brigid said, wearing a gossamer wool shawl draped over her head and shoulders as they trod carefully along the glistening deck. "And wool is the best for keeping out the damp, but my long coat will be far too heavy for this hot climate. Does it ever get cold here?"

"In the hinterland, so I'm told, but not by the standards you are used to, I wouldn't think. Did you make that shawl?"

"Not this one. My ma wove it from wool she'd spun. It's very fine work and light to wear. But I can spin and weave, aye."

"That will suit my plans perfectly." He kissed her on the cheek, gave her a devilish wink and changed the subject.

Wednesday, 8th December 1886

The ship dropped fourteen passengers off at Cooktown today. I stood and watched them go, even though I didn't know anyone. It helps pass the time. The rain has eased over the last couple of days, and the long breaks between downpours means people are back up on deck again. But today is such a grey day – all steamy and misty. I hope the sun is shining when we get to Brisbane. We said our goodbyes in the rain; I don't want to be welcomed by the rain.

We are expected in Townsville sometime tomorrow. Sally is getting off there, and I shall miss her – but I don't want to think about it just yet.

I've been working on my lace a lot more lately. It's given my hands something to do while I worry about Sally. I've only just found out she can fleece the men at cards. I don't know what to think about that. It's so dishonest, but somehow I can't help feel Sally deserves her winnings. I think life has been tough for her, but I wish I knew what she had in mind for me. I can't see how men who play cards fit with my idea of selling my lace to upper-class ladies and their houses.

But we'll see. I trust Sally. I know whatever she comes up with will be the best for me, and her, together. I trust Philip too – but in a different way. Or at least I think I do. I know Sally doesn't trust him, but I think the way he flicks his hair back is quite sweet.

Whatever the case, I suspect Philip will come up with something that is pleasing to me, but that will be much better

for him. It may turn out to be the same thing, but I can't say for
sure, that I can't.

In need of some time alone to think, Brigid took her
crochet work and sought a quieter spot. Her fingers flew
as she worked the hook in, around, through and out.
Listening to the now familiar sounds of the ship she let
her mind drift.

Suddenly, the hairs on the back of her neck stood
on end. She shivered in a futile attempt to rid herself of
something she'd surely imagined. Even knowing she'd
see dozens of people talking in groups nearby or walking
the decks past her, and possibly even Philip watching her,
she couldn't help looking around just in case anything
unusual was happening.

She lurched the moment she glimpsed the blurred
flash of movement and glint of light from the corner
of her eye. Maggie came into focus brandishing a knife
thrust in Brigid's direction.

The shock was so great Brigid barely noticed the
blade slice through her clothing and graze her leg as
Maggie tripped over her skirts. The weapon slipped from
Maggie's grasp, skimming noisily away, and spun to a
stop further along the deck.

Growling like an enraged animal at finding herself
sprawled across Brigid's lap, Maggie rolled inelegantly
onto the boards at her feet. Brief seconds passed as both
girls stared at one another: Brigid in shocked horror,
Maggie in a white-hot fury. Vaguely aware of people
gathering closer, drawn by the drama, Brigid couldn't
seem to move or speak.

Maggie began to struggle with the tangle of skirt and

petticoats, trying to get to her feet, a crazed expression on her face. Several strands of hair came loose adding to the mad-woman image as she suddenly charged at Brigid, screaming, "Jezebel."

Coming to her senses, Brigid hastily rose, stepping out of harm's way as Maggie came at her, hands clawed ready to strike. The girl spun past and crashed to the deck again, the knife lying within inches of her outstretched fingers. An inhuman sound escaped Maggie's throat when a booted foot kicked the blade out of reach.

"Are ye hurt, Breeda?" Jamie looked anxious and confused. His shadow was cast over the prone Maggie who sobbed uncontrollably.

Brigid shook her head. "No. But what is going on, Jamie?" she asked finding her voice at last.

Jamie stood between them, looking to and fro, as if undecided as to which of the two young women he should go to.

"She's bedevilled with the idea you'll stop me being with her," he shrugged in explanation, bending to help Maggie to her feet.

She rested her chin on his shoulder and wrapped one arm around his neck, while his arm encircled her waist.

Brigid's temper flared. "She's right on that count an' all. What are ye t'inking, ye great clod? You're only eighteen. You canna 'be' with her!"

"You're lying," Maggie snarled, turning to face Brigid. "I told ye, Jamie, she's jealous and wants to keep you for herself. Well you can't have him. He's mine. I tell you. Stick with your own man. You ... you ..." She tightened her grip on Jamie's neck.

"Hush now, *mo chailín*," soothed Jamie. "Shush, I say." Turning to Brigid, he said, "Aye, well. Maybe I shoulda been more honest. I said I was older like. I feel older. And I'm nineteen soon."

"Aye, and like that's going to make any difference."

"I've got to be a man now in this new place with nobody to tell me I can or can't, 'cept what I choose. There's no one telling you what's right when you're walking out with that toff."

Brigid sighed, aware that more people than needed to know were listening. But he was right. He'd not said a word against her and her friendship with Philip. He didn't exactly encourage her, but he'd not criticised either. She wanted the freedom to choose, as much as he did, but she'd always looked out for him, hadn't she? Wasn't that her role?

"That's as maybe, Jamie, and I'm not trying to tell you what to do. Just asking ye to be careful and t'ink on it. Will ye do that for me, at least?"

Jamie nodded silently. Maggie's head, encased in his large hand, rested against his shoulder. Her body trembled, but she stayed quiet, her arms clasped around his waist. By now word had spread. Michael pushed his way through the crowd with Laura and Jane in tow.

"Get your hands off my sister, you *feckin' shoibag*." Grabbing Maggie's arm he wrenched her away from Jamie. "And what do you think you are doing, yer gom head, bringing shame on me like this?" He shook her so violently her head rolled around like a rag doll. "Ye're no' fit to be left with young wans. Now come away."

Clamping her wrist in an iron-like grip, he strode towards the crowd, shoving aside anyone barring his path with his free hand. "Get out o' my way. Move, or you'll be sorry," he growled, jerking the resistant and sobbing Maggie behind him.

As soon as they disappeared from sight, the whispers started. Jamie stared defiantly towards Brigid. A sense of foreboding washed over her. Unwilling to say anything further in front of a crowd of semi-strangers, or provide them with more gossip, Brigid turned on her heel and forced her way through the mass. Choking back the tears threatening to overwhelm her, she didn't see Sally as she surged past.

"Wait, lass," her friend called, quickly catching up. She put her arms around Brigid's shoulder and gave her a quick hug. "Well, then. What a to-do that was an' all. I told you family only causes trouble. Leave him be, lass. Let him make his own mistakes. You've your own life to lead."

Brigid nodded mutely.

"Come on, let's walk a bit until you clear your mind. You can talk later."

Listening while her friend chatted on about this bit of gossip and that bit of news, most of it going over her head, she was grateful. Sally had the knack of turning up just when she was needed most. "Are you hurt, lass?"

Brigid shook her head but glanced down to where Sally was pointing at the slash in her skirt, and noticed a stain of blood. "'Tis nothing much," she answered, even though she could feel the trickle run down her leg.

"That's as maybe, but we should take a look. Do you have another petticoat?"

"Aye. In my carry bag."

The two women made their way down the companionway, blinking to adjust to the darkness. Brigid climbed onto her bunk and reached for her bag behind her pillow. She'd left her best petticoat rolled up in one corner, and it unfolded as she withdrew it. Goose bumps prickled her skin.

She turned the petticoat inside out and around and around, discarding it as she scrabbled in her bag, wildly tossing everything onto the mattress and searching frantically among her possessions.

"What's the matter?" Sally reached out and touched Brigid's shoulder to reassure her. "You look like you've seen a ghost."

"It's gone. I can't find it."

"What's gone?"

"My great-grandmother's brooch. It was here. I'm sure I pinned it to the inside of my petticoat so I wouldn't lose it. But it's not there now." Agitated, tears rolled down Brigid's face. "Where is it? Who could have taken it?"

"Are ye sure?" Sally pulled Brigid's trunk from underneath her berth. "Could you have put it in here?"

Momentarily Brigid's hopes were raised, but she sat back, defeated, with her legs dangling over the side of the bunk. "No. I'm absolutely certain I pinned it to my petticoat. I remember doing it and putting it separate. I've not worn the petticoat since we left London."

Sally opened the trunk nevertheless and both women gasped. Her best dress, another set of work clothes and all Brigid's household linens lay jumbled and tangled inside.

"Someone's been rummaging through here, that's for certain, but that petticoat of yours was still neatly rolled, so whoever looked in here wasn't the one who went through your holdall. Is anything else missing?"

Brigid checked again. Her Bible was still there, and her rosary and prayer book. Her hair comb, a book of poems and the rest of her clothes and eating utensils were all as she expected to find them. And her grandmother's hand-spun shawl, a precious and favoured item. She held it to her face, hoping to get a hint of her grandmother's essence but was disappointed.

She knelt on the floor beside Sally and took everything out of the trunk, one at a time, to make sure. She carefully refolded the linen and clothing, and laid each piece on the bed ready to repack. Another rosary, one her sister had given her just before she left, she found at the bottom of the trunk, lying loose amongst the tableware her grandmothers, many of her aunts and some of the villagers had contributed to her dowry.

Brigid picked up the rosary. "Thank goodness this is still here. My sister made it for me, but I didn't leave it loose like this. I put it inside a little bag Nellie embroidered, but that's missing as well. She's a beautiful seamstress – almost as good as me, even though she's much younger."

Sally struggled to her feet with a groan and clutched her back. "I'll ask around a bit and see if anyone's seen or heard anything."

Brigid nodded. "It's not likely anyone's going to admit to anything, though, is it? It's gone. I just have to accept it, I suppose. But it breaks my heart, Sally. It sure does. I didn't want to leave them behind, but I had no choice, and now my last link with my family has gone too."

She broke down then, laid her arms on the bunk and sobbed for the life she had lost.

The rain had stopped by the time they reached Townsville the next day. The whole ship, crew and passengers, appeared on deck ready to farewell the greatest number

101

disembarking so far. Those left behind created a fearful noise with cornets, fiddles, flutes, tin whistles, spoons and plates, or whooped and hollered at the top of their voices.

Brigid and Jamie stood back from the crowd. Neither wanted to join in the celebration. She'd said her goodbyes to Sally earlier that morning. The two women had wept and promised to keep in touch – although Brigid doubted it, knowing Sally's writing skills were poor. As a going-away gift, she gave Sally some crocheted lace pieces.

"You can sell them if you need money, I won't mind, or they'd make fine collars."

Sally unclasped the thin chain she wore and placed it in Brigid's hand, folding her fingers over her palm.

"It's naw much, I know, but 'tis all I have for now. Goodbye, my dear friend. I shall miss you. But one day I'll turn up when you least expect me, and it'll be all for the good."

They hung on to each other for several moments, trying to control their tears and the urge to never let go. Sally broke their hold first, smoothed her hands down her skirt and, with one last look of longing, picked up her bags and made her way up the companionway as fast as possible.

On deck, Brigid didn't watch her go.

Michael, Maggie and the two girls were also in the number disembarking.

She'd spent hours trying to talk sense into Jamie after yesterday's debacle. "How do you think you can support any wife, and the babbies to follow, until you have a home and a job? Be sensible, Jamie. I'm not saying you can't be with her one day, but you have to be settled first. There's time, our lad."

"No. There isn't. She's leaving. And anyway – who

are you to talk? Walking about with that toff. Is he going to offer for you?"

"Never mind me for now. There must be ways of getting to and from Townsville to Brisbane. Sally and I think we can. Wait a while and maybe you can go see her when you know the lie of the land. See what happens after that."

But Jamie wouldn't listen; he wanted to go with Maggie.

Brigid tried desperately to convince him to stay with her. "She's not the one for you, our Jamie. She's bedevilled. You said so yourself. She needs help. Look at what she did to me? How do you know she won't do something like that to you if you cross her, or worse, to one of the babbies?"

"She'd never. She loves me – and I love her. I should be with her." His voice cracked and he coughed to cover his embarrassment at having spoken so openly.

"Why? Da would tell you love doesn't come into it. It's what brings harmony and property and money to the marriage that counts. There's none of that with her."

"That's as maybe, our Breeda. But we have to make a new life now and p'haps we need new rules to match. Even you should see that – and it could be you need them new rules as much as me."

He'd left her then, and she'd not seen him again until now.

She turned to look up at him, concern written on her face. "Aye, well, Jamie. The time has come, it seems. The captain'll not let you ashore, ye know that."

"Not officially, no. But there are ways."

Brigid's heart sank. "What are you thinking?"

He dropped a soft kiss on the top of her head and disappeared into the crowd before she had time to react.

"Nooo ... Jamie. No. Don't go. I beg you. Don't go."

Pushing and shoving her way after him, she stopped only long enough to ask people if they'd seen him. They all shook their heads, too engrossed in the activities onshore to be interested.

Frantically she searched between decks, except for the single men's quarters and the saloon area, where she was forbidden. She forced her way back and forth along the upper deck again; she even checked the makeshift bathroom, hoping she'd find him somewhere, but didn't.

Drained of energy, she leant against the rail near the stern, her chest heaving from her exertions and, her gut churning with dread, she caught a glimpse of something. From that angle, Brigid couldn't see exactly what was happening at first, but one thing she was sure about as it swung into view: Jamie was hanging onto the side of a net full of mail sacks being bundled ashore.

"Ja ... mie. Jaa ... mieee ..." Her voice was lost in the cacophony. She watched helplessly as he stepped onto the shore, joined the milling crowds and vanished from sight. "Jamie!" she wailed, waving furiously to attract his attention, before sinking to the deck in tears.

Brigid had never cried as many tears as she had in the last few days. As her tears lessened, her resolve grew.

Her worst fear had come to pass. She was alone.

Even Philip couldn't comfort her.

The stopovers to drop passengers at Bowen, Mackay and Rockhampton passed in a blur. After a journey of fifty-six days, the SS *Dorunda* reached Brisbane on Monday 13th December 1886. Brigid stepped off the ship a new woman. Stronger, more determined.

Her new life had begun.

PART TWO

Australia

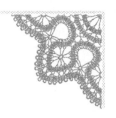

6

Prejudices, Conceptions and Opportunities

Brisbane
December 1886

Philip Harrison-Browne walked into the George Street property as if he'd only stepped out for a few hours, instead of the months it had taken him to go to England and back.

"Hello, son. You look pleased with yourself. Had a good trip?" Harry Browne stood up from behind his 18th-century partners desk to greet his son.

Philip shook his father's outstretched hand and promptly sank into the leather-upholstered captain's chair on the visitors' side. "Not bad, all things considered." Aware that it would annoy his father, he crossed his feet up on the desk.

As expected, his father frowned. "Haven't learnt any respect yet, I see."

Ignoring him, Philip took a cigar from the box, taking time to sniff it before he notched a V into the end with the cutter. Extracting his gold match-safe from his pocket, he lit a match on the striker and held it to the cigar, sucking rapidly to get the tip burning. "Leave off, Pa." After returning the case to his pocket, he rocked back in the chair and blew a couple of smoke rings towards his father. "Don't you want to know what I've been up to?"

Coughing at the fumes, Harrison Browne II, as he preferred to be known, waved his hand to clear the air. "Not really. I know you achieved what I sent you for. I have the paperwork." He shuffled some papers on the desk to one side, opened a ledger and picked up a nib pen. His hand hovered over the inkwell. "What's her name this time?"

"Brigid ... but she's not important – not yet, anyway." He almost felt guilty at dismissing Brigid so airily, when in fact he had much bigger plans for her than he was prepared to admit.

Harry scratched away in the ledger while Philip smoked, contemplating both his surroundings and his companion. His father had certainly developed a taste for the finer things in life over the years. From the original paintings on the wall of his fashionably decorated office to the Turkish rug, Harry lived life well these days. But it hadn't always been like that.

Neither man spoke, each waiting for the other, but after admiring the well-made drapes pulled back from the window, Philip chose to sound out his father now rather than later. "I do have a bit of an idea though, Pa."

"Mm. I'm listening." His father continued calculating figures, dipping the pen in and out of the ink.

Removing his booted feet from the desk, Philip sat forward, eager now to impress his father. "I think it's time to expand. Get some more exotic fabrics and laces, even employ in-house workers."

Within a few moments Harry paused, eyes raised, pen held in mid-air. He put the pen down and sat back in his large swivel chair, folded his hands across his stomach and listened. Philip avoided the details, but described his ideas in depth, creating sweeping pictures from his imagination as to what the store could look like.

"Interesting," his father said, when Philip finished. "Let me think on it." He picked up the pen again, but before he resumed with the figures, he fixed his gaze on his son. "How does this Brigid fit into the picture?"

Usually, Philip didn't care whether or how other people were affected by his schemes, as long as they benefitted him more, but something about Brigid had got under his skin. It didn't make sense, even to him. He dropped his head. "I'm not sure yet. I don't want her knowing too much about it all, at this stage."

Harry raised his eyebrows. "Up to you. We'll talk some more later. Meantime, go and do something useful. You can help Alf catalogue the goods."

Philip ran his fingers through his hair, flicking it back as was his habit whenever he felt uneasy or things weren't going quite his way, like now. He hated not getting his way.

As he hastened down the stairs to talk with Alf, their warehouse manager, he thought about how far his father had come in the last forty years.

At the age of 17, life had handed plain Henry Brown – without the 'e' – a tough blow. Despite his innocence, he'd been transported for seven years, accused of stealing medicine for his sickly widowed mother.

Once in Sydney, Harry was put to work in the stores, thanks to the legacy of Commander Arthur Philips, the first Governor of New South Wales. His idea was to use prisoners who could read and write to help run the new colony, so they could learn to do something useful with their life. Harry became a model, if shrewd, prisoner, and a good dealer, well liked by most people he came in contact with. Four years later, in 1842, he received his ticket of leave.

The bell tinkled above the door as Philip entered the warehouse.

"G'day, young guv'ner," said Alf. The pair shook hands. "I've received the first bolts of cloth from the ship already. What other sort of stock should I expect?"

Alf, himself a former convict, had been Harry's right-hand man ever since Harry had first arrived in Brisbane, at the age of twenty-four, with his Certificate of Freedom in his hands and big plans.

"I managed to get my hands on a lovely array of textiles and designs that are the pinnacle of fashion." Philip described some of the men's suiting and the ladies fabrics, as well as the hats and accessories he had purchased while in England. He watched Alf as he laid a couple of rolls of the new fabric on the counter to inspect the quality.

Once free of the army's constant surveillance, Harry found employment with Mr Wicklow, a wealthy general merchant who provided the ever-increasing numbers of free settlers arriving in Sydney with their much-needed household goods.

Harry had been a quick learner and mastered his trade well, thanks to his mentor. After rising to head of the drapery department, and wanting to learn the skills to run his own business, Harry even attended evening classes at the Sydney Mechanics' School of Arts.

"Will we be needing new shelving or display cabinets,

do you think, Alf? Especially for the new range of gloves."

In those early years in Brisbane, Alf had the local know-how and practical skills that Harry lacked, but Harry had the ideas. Together, he and Alf set about establishing a mercantile business, just like the one Mr Wicklow had started in Sydney, only better – a place with class and style. To match that image, and wanting to put his past behind him now he was a free man, plain Henry Brown became known as Harrison Browne II. Taking his first small step to independence.

Alf rubbed his chin and thought about Philip's question. "I think we can manage for now. I'll move some of the existing ones around and see if that works first."

He and Alf continued discussing the layout and the inventory, labelling, pricing, and stacking as they went.

Later in the afternoon, Philip rolled down his sleeves and retrieved his jacket, preparing to finish up for the day. "Before I go, Alf, I'd like your opinion. I've had an idea to branch out a bit. I've spoken to my father about it, but I'd be keen to know what you think."

For the next few minutes, Alf listened to what Philip had to say about new departments and more staff, nodding now and then, just like his father had. "Well, maybe. Not sure it's summat your pa would want to do. But let me think on it."

He had hoped to pique Alf's interest enough so that he would talk to Harry and promote the idea on his behalf, but Alf was too clever. He knew Harry's ways too well to accept 'the boy's' word. He'd just have to wait for the two of them to talk and decide whether to allow his idea to flourish or not.

Angry and frustrated, Philip went in search of a drink and some company. Normally after a long sea voyage, he would head to the obscurity of the Dunsmore Arms – a rather tired old pub about to be replaced, if the rumours were true – where he could get drunk with impunity. But today he was too keyed up for that and set out to find some old school friends, hoping they, at least, would back his ideas.

Hands in pockets, hat fashionably tilted to one side, he stood on the footpath and looked up and down George Street. He had two choices: turn right and go to the Transcontinental Hotel, situated just around the corner from where his old school once stood in Roma Street; or turn left and go to The Queensland Club. The club overlooked the splendid Botanical Gardens, and while both buildings were only two years old and both offered congenial surroundings, only one was suited to business.

He turned left.

The original Queensland Club had burnt to the ground back in 1870, and it had taken a long time to get another building under way, but the benefit was now his. The new club, opened in 1884 on the corner of Alice Street, was far superior, with accommodation and facilities second to none. Many a deal had been made while seated in the studded leather wing chairs, a fine whisky in one hand and a cigar in the other.

No sooner had he walked through the club doors than Hugh Paterson and Sam Barton greeted him.

"Oh, look who's returned." Hugh stretched his hand out in welcome. Like Philip, Hugh had been born in Brisbane; unlike Philip, Hugh's parents were both free settlers.

While Philip had been accepted into the Brisbane Grammar School at the age of eight, when it opened in 1869, it had been a touch-and-go argument whether Hugh should go there or to boarding school in England. The friends were both glad Brisbane had won the day.

"You're just in time. Join us for dinner, why don't you?" Sam, another friend from school, shook hands, and the trio settled at a table.

In this new town, money and influence were bestowed upon those who would never have passed muster in the old country. Who you knew was as important as ever, but their background was no longer critical. The sons of ex-convicts and the sons of bankers could mingle side by side, based only on aspirations and acquisitions. What made the difference was their standing in the business world.

Philip flicked the napkin onto his lap. "I can't tell you how much I've been looking forward to a good feed. I'm sick of salt beef, badly cooked fish – when they could catch any – and potatoes."

He had succeeded quite well at school, mostly at business and mathematics, and he'd mastered enough of the arts, languages, literature and music, to give him a way with the ladies. His knowledge of the finer things in life proved a suitable fit to his business acumen, and his natural charm did the rest. Although, he had to admit, adopting Harrison Browne as his surname was proving a distinct advantage. He liked being Mr Philip Harrison-Browne instead of simply being Philip Browne, an unknown.

The waiter appeared with the wine and took Philip's order. "I'll have the crab entrée, the roast pigeon with oyster stuffing and fresh fruit salad with vanilla ice cream to finish. Thank you."

While the others gave their orders, Philip poured the excellent red wine into three glasses.

"A toast: To friendship and prosperity."

Hugh and Sam raised their glasses. "Hear, hear!"

Hugh's family were bankers and always happy to talk investment. Harry was friendly with Hugh's father after years of doing business together, but knew little of Sam's family, except when his mother visited their store.

Sam's grandfather had been an ex-convict, but generations later his family were now successful and wealthy graziers. Of the three, Sam was the only one who had boarded at school.

"You know what, old chap," said Hugh, after Philip had regaled them with his latest stories of his trip to England, a journey he'd done most years since he'd turned twenty-one. "I've never been on a ship, nor has Sam here, and every now and then I wonder what it would be like, but you don't do much to inspire a body into taking the risk."

"Sorry to disappoint you, mate, but what do you want? Stories of great adventures, pirates and good times – or the truth?"

Hugh shrugged. "I'd like the chance for some adventure – and to see new places – instead of being at the bank every day with my father watching over my shoulder."

Sam chuckled. "Don't include me in your notions. I get enough excitement on the station, thanks. If the stock or the dogs don't cause problems, the wildlife certainly will. Try sleeping out in the bush sometime if you want adventure. I come down here for a rest."

The young men snorted at Sam's stories of snakes, crocs in the river, dingoes and whatever other creepy-crawlies he could come up with to amuse them.

Hugh ordered another round of drinks from the

passing waiter. "So tell me, what little filly took your fancy this time?"

Philip, feigning innocence, laughed. "Well, let's see now. There was one ... or maybe two ..." He amused them with a racy story about the girls of London but avoided any mention of Brigid.

"Oh, come on. You must have seen someone who was more interesting."

"No one worth talking about." Philip flicked his hair back from his face and avoided the question.

After his time spent in England, he appreciated he lived a privileged life in Brisbane. The English treated him with a certain kind of respect when he visited the warehouses and factories because he had money to spend, but his was a lowly standing in that community. He would never be invited to socialise with any of the owners, being left to the whims of the managers. The girls he met were not the type to take home to his mother either. Was Brigid? Probably not.

Even while telling his story, matching Hugh's raunchy jokes with smuttier ones of his own, Philip dreamed of his plans coming to fruition. Maybe Hugh and Sam could help him. You needed friends you could trust when it came to expansion such as he envisaged: someone like Alf.

"Sometimes I wish ..."

"Wish what, old man?" urged Hugh.

"Oh nothing. Just thinking about a conversation with my father."

A thrill rippled through him every time he remembered the stories his father told him of his younger years. These days, there were times Philip would hardly give credit to those tales, if Alf hadn't confirmed them.

Harry had become strangely risk-averse.

In those early days, when Harry first arrived in Brisbane back in 1845, there had been little call for Sydney-type merchants. To get started he'd opened a pawnshop and sometimes found he needed to take on items that didn't quite have the provenance to match, simply to get established.

"You mean stolen?" A youthful, wide-eyed Philip had asked. "Cor."

Harry had been careful, of course. He had no intention of getting caught out by the law and ending up back in prison. The pawnshop had been a genuine business dealing fairly with those in need. He never double-dealt his own kind, but thanks to contacts in Sydney he began receiving items with a similar dicey provenance. He didn't so much break the rules as bend them a little to his advantage.

The business began to change for the better when Mr Wicklow sent Harry a shipment of goods, damaged on their journey, which he considered unsuitable for sale in his Sydney store. Alf had repaired the furniture and household goods, while Harry cleaned the hats and gloves, and trimmed the best of the water-damaged fabrics and suiting, and sold them as 'direct from Sydney'.

In his day, Harry could bluff his way around any problem. If there were stains on the manchester or drapery, he offered an extra length of haberdashery or a pair of gloves as recompense. He bought low and sold high. His reputation as a merchant grew until demand exceeded supply. Mr Wicklow put Harry in touch with suppliers in England. Word spread. Eventually the pawnshop was closed in favour of Harrison Browne Drapers, purveyors of high quality goods. It had taken two decades, but he'd achieved his goal.

Now, twenty years later, Philip was the one seeking expansion.

"Do you want me to tell your father you spend as much time with the tarts as you do on business?" Sam asked teasingly, dragging Philip back to the present. "Would he keep you home, then?"

"Don't be daft. As long as I do the trade, he doesn't care what I get up to."

But Harry cared about his business. Queensland welcomed its first free settlers in 1842, a mere three years after the transportation of convicts ceased and the penal colony at Moreton Bay closed. Brisbane had been nowhere near as grand as Sydney in those early days and struggled to get established. It had been a rough, raw town, but the numbers kept growing and, more importantly, free settlers with their wives and families began arriving in ever-increasing numbers.

A few years later, many of those transported were considered free men, with a Certificate of Freedom to prove it. Even prisoners serving a life sentence received a ticket of leave. By 1850, the majority of the population lived their lives with impunity and opportunity. Harry was only too pleased to help kit out both ex-convicts and newcomers with the items they needed.

Philip had never told his friends any of these stories. These days his father was an honest, respectable citizen of high standing in the community and would never stoop to bend the rules again. He'd made his point, and his money.

Now Philip wanted his turn.

He wanted someone like Alf – Harry's go-to for all problems – someone who would back him up through thick and thin. He listened as Hugh and Sam discussed investments, livestock prices and shares – topics he found boring.

"Enough of this business talk. There's got to be something more exciting in life."

"Such as?"

Philip shrugged. "I dunno. Anything." Should he mention his plans? His idea was in want of roots, or maybe wings, he wasn't sure which, but since neither his father nor Alf had given him the confidence to think it would work, his mind gnawed away at all the problems.

Even though Hugh prompted him, he changed the subject, again. "Don't mind me. Just feeling a bit undone by the journey, I suppose. Let me tell you about a night I had."

As the evening wore on, the three friends became more raucous as Philip's make-believe stories of his conquests with the women grew. Some of the older members peered around the wings of their chairs at the noisy trio. The steward was even obliged to ask them to lower their voices.

"Shush now, Hugh," warned Sam. "You'll get us thrown out of here if you're not careful – and I want to stay here, even if you don't."

"What's your problem, Mr Goody Two-shoes?"

"You're making too much noise, Hugh. Whisper when you speak."

Hugh rolled his head to one side and pointed a wagging finger at Sam. "How would we manage without your guiding hand? Trip over your big foot, I suppose."

"More likely your big mouth," quipped Philip. "Now, are we going to stay here and get drunk or see if there are any pretty ladies about?"

Bets were taken as to which of them would find a suitable 'lady' friend first, but since they were already three-quarters cut, they chose to stay and finish the job.

Unexpectedly, Hugh leaned forward, teetered and put a hand on the table to steady himself. Blood-shot eyes glared at Philip. "What you are hiding?"

Philip was nowhere near as drunk as Hugh, but his friend's acuity sharpened his wits. "I'm not hiding anything."

Sam, the least affected of them, also looked at him with an amused expression. "Hiding might not be the right word. But there's something you haven't told us."

Philip flipped his hair back, poured another drink and eyed Sam cautiously. Hugh was more like him, a bit of a gambler, who wanted more from life than their fathers could give them. Sam seemed content to live amongst the cattle and the dust. But Philip trusted Sam. He was steadier.

Maybe he should give them something to speculate on. "I'm thinking of branching out on my own." He paused, wondering how much more to say. "Unfortunately, Pa has other ideas."

Hugh snorted. "I'm not surprised. Your dad's got you wrapped around his little finger."

Philip bristled. Hugh had voiced exactly how he felt: controlled by his father, always having to ask for permission to do anything yet sent on interminable errands like a toady. He had no intention of admitting it – not even to those he considered friends. Some things were too private.

"Not really." Philip tried for nonchalance, sipped his drink and lit a cigarette. "I've been biding my time, learning the ropes, but I think I'm ready to try my hand at something new."

"About time, I say," said Sam. "You always did have great ideas when we were at school."

He was right. Even as a youngster Philip had an outstanding ability to see an opportunity, and an uncanny knack of appealing to people's sense of greed. They got something from the arrangement, but he always kept the best part of the deal for himself.

"I could be interested in investing in what you've got planned," Sam added.

Hiding his elation, Philip drew on his cigarette, carefully flicking the ash into the crystal ashtray. "Would you? I'd like that. Can we talk in more detail? When it's convenient, of course." He hoped the right mix of enquiry and intensity showed in his voice. He wouldn't want to rush things, but then if he doubted Sam's purpose or ability, he might lose him altogether – and he had to get someone to listen to him. "How long are you in town?"

"I'm here for two more nights. Let's talk in the light of day." Sam nodded towards Hugh, who had fallen asleep. "Right now I think we'd better get him up to bed. Are you staying here tonight?"

"Ah, no. I'm off home. I'll need to speak with Mother in the morning. I've been away for months. She's expecting me." Family was important to Sam, so Philip was happy to pander to his whims if it would help his cause.

"Fair enough," replied Sam, smiling. "Can't disappoint our lovely mothers, now, can we? I'm in business meetings for my father most of the day. How about we meet here, say four o'clock? We can talk and have dinner to follow."

"Excellent!"

Between them, they roused Hugh sufficiently to guide him up the grand staircase and into his room.

Philip bade Sam a good evening and elected to walk the three miles home to the Browne house in Spring Hill.

He had a lot to think about.

૪૦ ૯૪

Brisbane
December 1886

"Are you Brid-get O Bryn?" The man standing at the entrance to the Immigration Depot spoke slowly and deliberately.

Brigid had carefully dressed in her best outfit, which showed off her handmade lace on the collar and V-inset, a complete contrast to his shirtsleeves, baggy trousers and wide-brimmed hat. She spoke politely, emphasising the correct pronunciation. "I am Brigid O'Brien, that I am."

He looked her up and down, finally fixing his eyes on hers. "I don't care what yer name is. You're to come wi' me."

Brigid had spent a miserable eighteen hours in the draughty, dilapidated old building waiting for word of the ship's arrival to reach her new employer. To her mind, the dingy, dirty facilities were worse than on the ship, and the food rations were limited to day-old bread and chewy dried meat. Now it seemed this ill-tempered man was here to fetch her. All in all, the welcome had not turned out to be as reassuring as she had wanted, despite the sunshine.

Uncertain who the man was, and confused by his attire, she wasn't going to be put off by his surly manner. In an attempt to quell her nervousness, she held her back ramrod straight and stared back at him. "And who might you be?" she demanded.

After surviving her worst fears and losing all she valued, she'd willed herself to begin this new life on her own terms, confident in her ability. How she'd come to that decision had been a painful battle. It warred against everything she'd been brought up with, but since she'd reached rock bottom already, there seemed only one way to go.

"Name's Collins," he drawled. "Lady Fiona's fetch-and-carry man. You comin' or not?"

"Pleased to meet you, Mr Collins. Can you help me with my trunk, please?"

He looked from her to the trunk sitting on the verandah and back again and made some sort of noise Brigid took to mean displeasure. When she made no move, he reached forward, pulled the trunk towards him and, turning around, hoisted it upon his back. He headed off down the steps towards the wagon without waiting for her.

Brigid picked up her carry bag, draped her coat over her arm and followed.

The dray was no different to those she'd seen in Ireland, with two large wheels in the middle and pulled by a horse as unkempt as its driver, but she judged it to be a little longer. The bench seat up front was hard and unsprung – as they invariably were.

As the dray made its way along busy Queen Street, her eyes followed a smart-looking gig as it passed by. One day she hoped she'd be able to travel in a vehicle like that, with a lovely padded seat and a canopy to shield her from the sun. Thinking about the way the sun beat down on her despite the early hour, she was glad she'd worn her large-brimmed hat, rather than her bonnet, after all.

"So what do you do, Mr Collins?" Brigid turned her head to and fro trying to take in all the surprisingly fine buildings with footpaths and verandahs lining both sides of the street. She hadn't expected Brisbane to be so built up. In her mind, she was coming to a small town like Ennis, but these buildings were grander, newer, yet somehow different from anything she'd seen at home.

"What I'm told." The driver clicked his tongue at the horse and steadily steered it around another wagon parked outside the general store.

Rather taken aback by his abrupt manner, Brigid tried a different approach. "Can ye tell me what I should know, now I'm here? There are a lot more buildings than I ever imagined. What else should I expect?"

The single-storey homes she saw were mostly built of wood, whereas the public buildings were stone or brick.

The man shook the reins over the back of his horse. "Heat and flies and hard work."

Brigid was already aware of the flies – they'd buzzed around her constantly all through the previous day and last evening. As she waved her hand to keep them from settling, she decided they were just as annoying this morning. "Surely life must be better than that?" Brigid used her bright and cheery voice. "Isn't that what we're told. A land of opportunity?"

The horse plodded its way along the street, passed by multi-passenger coaches, four-person broughams, and two-seater phaetons, drawn by various numbers of horses that clip-clopped their way about their business. Dust rose from their hooves. People came and went from doorways, and energy filled the air.

"For some, maybe," the driver grunted, settling back into silence.

Brigid began to feel sweat on her forehead and down her spine, thanks to the steamy air; even the gentle breeze was hot. The cool shade beneath the curved iron roofs of the verandahs, which provided protection from the sun on most of the houses, beckoned her. She imagined sitting somewhere like that doing her lacework.

Soon they passed down an avenue of tall trees with peeling bark. Their sparse leaves fluttered in the air, but they provided little shade and even less respite from the heat. In the distance, she could see palm trees like those they'd seen in Port Said. Everywhere she looked, the place seemed strange in many ways, yet familiar at the same time.

A few turns later and up a steep hill, Mr Collins pulled the horse to a stop under one of the large trees lining the street. "This is it, miss." He climbed down from the wagon, lifted her trunk from the back and put it on the ground by the picket gate leading to the front garden. By then Brigid was standing on the footpath wondering what would happen next.

"Whose place is this?" She gazed up at the large two-storey, three-bay house with an upstairs balcony adorned with ornate iron lacework and balustrade.

"Dunno the lady meself. 'Twas told her name was Browne."

He climbed back onto the wagon and picked up the reins.

"What do I do?" she called out, when she saw he intended leaving her on the side of the road.

"How would I know? Try knocking on the door." He flapped the reins over the horse's back. "Get along, now," he clucked and the animal plodded off down the street.

A short flight of steps led to the front door recessed under the verandah that ran along the front and side of the house. Brigid left her trunk where Collins had dropped it, hoping she'd find someone who could help her carry it, and walked up the path. Standing a few feet from the front door she considered using the rear entrance, but not seeing any way of getting round the back she walked up the steps and gave the knocker a sharp rat-a-tat.

A few moments later, a matronly woman dressed in black opened the door. Her eyes were small but sharp. She inspected Brigid from head to foot in a second.

"I'm Bri ..." Her voice caught in the back of her throat, and she put her gloved fist up to her mouth while she cleared it. "Pardon me," she said, remembering the training the nuns had given her about how to speak and introduce herself. "I'm Brigid O'Brien. I believe Mrs Browne is expecting me."

The unexpected transformation that came over the woman when she smiled put Brigid at ease. "Come in, girl. Come in. It's good to see you arrived safe and sound. I'm Mavis Johnson. Now, where are your things?"

Brigid stepped across the threshold into the hallway that smelt of beeswax and fresh-cut flowers. Adjusting her eyes to the darkened space, she placed her carry bag on the floor and rolled her coat up on top of it. A hallstand, two upright chairs and a narrow table with a vase of assorted flowers and greenery filled the foyer next to the staircase leading to the upper floor.

"I'll get my Jack to bring your trunk in, but right now Mrs Browne is looking forward to meeting you."

Mavis led the way down a wide, wood-lined passageway and into the kitchen at the back. A tall, upright woman wearing a full apron, and the sleeves of her cotton blouse rolled up, was kneading dough.

While the cooler air at the front of the house had been refreshing, the heat in the kitchen nearly threw Brigid off balance, even with the door and window thrown wide open. The woman wiped her forehead with her arm and, watching Brigid from the corner of her eye, carried on kneading.

"So you're Brigid. I hope your journey wasn't too arduous. I know they can be, and they are all terribly tedious." She paused to thump the dough on the table a couple of times, generously sprinkled more flour around, picked up the rolling pin and began to flatten the dough. "Mavis will show you to your room. Get yourself changed – there's a uniform for you – and come back here when you're ready. You've a lot to learn about life in Australia. It's greatly different from home." She straightened up once the circle of pastry was large enough to fit the pie dish Brigid had spied on the table among piles of fruits and vegetables. "That's beautiful lace on your jacket. Did you make it?"

Brigid stood mutely watching and listening, taking in the details of the compact yet highly functional kitchen. The large central table served as the workspace, and some delicious aromas she couldn't quite place were coming from something in the modern oven.

"Lost your tongue, missy?" nudged Mavis.

"Ah, no. Sorry, ma'am," said Brigid blinking rapidly. "I was distracted, but aye, I made the lace ... Thank ye for asking. Um, pardon me if I speak out of turn, but ... are you Mrs Browne?" Brigid couldn't understand the order of the place. Mavis was hovering behind her doing nothing, while the lady of the house seemed to be doing all the work.

Mavis and Beatrice Browne chuckled at Brigid's confusion. "Were you expecting some sort of lady? If you were, you'll be mighty disappointed. This isn't like the home country, lass. We all started out in this mess together, and we'll work it out as we go along. I like to make my own pastry, that's all. Mavis is the cook here, but I like cooking when I'm in the mood, and have time. Jack looks after the garden, that's Mr Johnson, but there's still plenty to do. Now run along and put something lighter on before you melt away."

"Don't you fret none," Mavis encouraged as they trudged up the wooden staircase at the back of the house. "Mrs B is a generous and easy-going employer. Back home she'd not been one of the upper class and she isn't here either, but the master, he likes her to have help so she has free time to do ladylike things around town. Helps the business, he says. There's only the two of them most of the time, until the young master comes home." She stopped at the far end of the narrow corridor. "This one's yours."

Brigid gasped as Mavis opened the door to her room. The attic rooms at the back of the house were small, painted white. With a heavy white cotton coverlet on the single wire-framed bed, the room shimmered with light. The other furnishings were sparse – a washstand with a pitcher and ewer set, and a chamber pot, a dresser and a chair – and the white muslin curtains framing the sash window overlooking the rear garden utterly thrilled Brigid. "I've never been in such a room like this," she admitted. "It's beautiful."

Mavis agreed. "You're a lucky girl. There's your outfit, hanging behind the door. Don't be long."

As soon as Mavis had closed the door behind her, Brigid spun around with her arms extended and her skirt swinging, thinking she would burst with joy.

The uniform she was expected to wear was far too big. She had to roll the waistband of the light blue skirt so she wouldn't trip over the hem, and the matching long-sleeved, collared blouse would need a lot more pin-tucking to make it fit well. Brigid tied the strings of the full white apron tightly around the front, which at least helped pull in the excess fabric. After she'd hung up her best dress and folded the rest of her clothes neatly into the drawers of the dresser, she made her way downstairs again.

"Is that a bit cooler?" Mrs Browne greeted her. "I like to keep up with the fashions, but we have to be practical. It's too hot for the fabrics and styles we knew back home. Oh dear, it's a bit big, isn't it. But my, that colour suits you. Your eyes are so blue now."

Brigid flushed at the compliment. "I can take it in to fit."

"Clever girl. Mavis will find you a needle and thread." Mrs Browne finished her pastry and went to wash her hands under the pump over the sink in the scullery. "Mavis, you can fill the pie now. And we'll have a lettuce salad and some baked tomatoes to go with it, and don't forget Mr Browne's potatoes."

"Very good, Mrs B. And how about some tapioca for pudding?"

"Excellent. Thank you, Mavis. Now Brigid, follow me."

The rest of the morning disappeared in a whirl of instructions as Mrs Browne marched her through the downstairs – the parlour, the dining room, the conservatory and then the garden. She was introduced to the herb and vegetable patch, the fruit trees and on past the flowerbeds and shade trees to the stables at the back. Brigid could hardly take all of it in – there was so much to look at.

"What shall I call you, ma'am?" Brigid scurried along behind her long-striding employer, who continued rattling off descriptions and explanations. "It's just I've never heard people use first names before, 'cept they be family or the same class."

"I can't stand ceremony, but my husband insists that we maintain some sort of standards. You'd better call me Mrs Browne. Although Mrs Johnson does shorten it to Mrs B when we're working together. You can too – if there's just us, mind. Don't let Mr Browne hear you."

They re-entered the house, past the scullery and straight into the kitchen.

"Right, Mavis, I'm sure you have tasks for the girl while you get luncheon ready. Mr Browne will not be joining me today, so I'll eat in the conservatory."

Beatrice Browne strode off along the corridor. At the same time, footsteps could be heard bounding down the stairs. Shortly after, voices travelled along the hallway to where they worked, but they couldn't discern any words.

"Sounds like the young master is home," said Mavis. "I didn't hear him come in last night. Must have been real late, but his mama will be pleased to see him. She has a real soft spot for him. Pop along and ask if he is wanting luncheon. My hands are wet." Mavis carried on chopping the vegetables while Brigid hovered in the doorway looking hesitant. "Go on, girl. Get a move on."

Brigid tiptoed along the hallway on edge about interrupting their conversation. The voices had moved into the parlour, and she tentatively knocked on the open door. To her left, a man stood with his back to her, his arm resting on the mantelpiece. Mrs Browne sat facing her in the wing chair on the other side of the fireplace.

"Yes, what is it?"

"Pardon me, ma'am. Mrs Johnson wants to know if the gentleman is staying for luncheon," she muttered in a voice barely above a whisper.

"Come closer, girl, and speak up."

Brigid took two steps into the room, bobbed an awkward curtsy and, keeping her eyes glued to the pattern on the rug, repeated the question. "Ah, yes. Philip, this is our new maid. Do be nice to her. Now, are you staying for luncheon?"

At the mention of his name, Brigid's heart began to thump so loudly she could hear the echo in her ears. She raised her head slightly, her mouth partly open. Surely, it couldn't be the same Philip. Life wouldn't be that cruel.

He turned, tugged his jacket into place and swept a lock of hair back from his face, the way she'd seen him do so many times. She stared at that heartbreakingly familiar face, and her dreams shattered in the seconds it took for him to recognise her. The fleeting expression was wiped from his face in an instant.

Time seemed to stand still between them until he tipped an almost imperceptible nod in her direction.

He turned to his mother. "Thank you. Yes, Mama, I shall stay."

"Very well." Looking back towards Brigid, who had dropped her gaze once more, Mrs Browne sent a message back to the kitchen.

"Please tell Mrs Johnson to set the table for two. We shall eat in the dining room after all."

Brigid bobbed again and fled.

She spent the rest of the day in a state of anxiety. Fortunately, Mavis was too busy to notice her helper was distracted. Brigid managed to complete all the tasks asked of her without dropping or burning anything and was thankful she'd not been told to serve at luncheon. The chore of doing the dishes in the scullery gave her plenty of time to think.

She couldn't just leave – she had nowhere to go and knew no one, let alone had any money – but how could she stay in the same house as Philip, now he'd discovered her here as a maid? She crossed herself several times in the course of the afternoon when the notion she might have to wait on him, as well as his mother and father, entered her mind. Holy Mother of God! What should she do?

Days passed and she began to relax a little. She was yet to meet the distinguished Mr Browne and she hadn't seen Philip again either. Her chores were mundane and kept her in the back reaches of the house. Later in the week, when she was putting the scraps out and collecting fresh vegetables from the garden, she heard her name being called.

"Brigid."

She looked around trying to work out where the whispered call came from but couldn't see anything.

"Brigid." Philip's voice reached her. "I'm behind the hedge. No, don't look. Just carry on what you're doing and listen. I don't want my mother to know about you yet."

"Why are you talking to me at all? Go away and leave me be." Her hands were shaking; she wasn't sure whether anger or despair was the cause of her distress – whichever, the situation was ridiculous.

"I was so surprised to see you, I didn't know what to say. I'm sorry I pretended I didn't know you."

She finished emptying the scrap tin and started to pick some peas and beans, placing them in the open basket. "You don't need to pretend no more. You're the young master and that's all there is to it." Moving to another garden bed, she knelt to dig up a few onions and two large beetroot.

"But don't you want to do all those things we talked about?"

Briefly, she let herself imagine the impossible. "Aye, I do." Her voice was barely audible. She shook her head, stood up and dusted off the front of her apron. "But it just can't be, so don't think on it no more."

Picking up the now heavily laden basket, she added two ripe tomatoes to the stack and started to walk towards the house.

"Don't you believe it. I still have plans for you, Miss Brigid." Philip's voice sounded full of promise, just as it had on the ship. But now the situation was hopeless.

Tempted to turn around to look at him, she saw Mrs Browne watching her from the conservatory window. She blanched but kept walking, increasing her stride to get into the house and out of sight as fast as possible.

7

Mixing It Up

Townsville
December 1886

Sally was drawn to the clink of glass and hum of voices coming from the two-storey building on the corner of Wickham Street and The Strand. She'd turned her nose up at the miserable accommodation the Immigration Scheme was offering, and was in need of a job and a place to live. She'd wait for no man to tell her how to live her life, and being a barmaid seemed as good an option as any. At least, that was one thing she knew how to do. She learnt some tricks on the streets of Glasgow after she'd escaped the clutches of her stepfather.

Entering the high-ceilinged foyer, she ducked into the cloakroom, glad of the chance to remove her heavy mantle in the stifling heat. Hiding her carry bags behind the other coats, she pulled out an array of grooming effects from her reticule. She redid her hair until it looked full and flattering, nestling her fair curls softly around her face and puffing them out under her hat. A dash of rose water and a tiny amount of rouge rubbed high on her cheekbone and on her lips to emphasise the whiteness of her skin and she looked glowing with health. The happy-go-lucky servant girl of the ship disappeared and was replaced by a striking woman who knew what she wanted.

Despite the heat, she'd hidden her best outfit under her cape prior to leaving the ship and while the hem was a bit grubby, thanks to the condition of the streets, she knew they wouldn't be looking at her feet. The rich red empress stripe brocade with a fitted bodice and not quite demure V-neck suited her – and, after all, first impressions counted.

From the entranceway, she could see the public bar to her right, and extending along the length of the building to her left was the gentlemen's lounge. She headed left. With a beaming smile plastered on her face, she pushed the door open. She faltered slightly before letting it close behind her, swallowed, squared her shoulders and strode purposefully into the bar. It was do or die.

She tilted her head to the man on her left, leaning against the bar, whose eyes followed her, and to the man on her right sitting in the tub chair, his newspaper lowered so he could watch her progress. A few steps further and she spied an opportunity – a man was rising from his chair with an empty glass in his hand.

"Can I fetch a refresher for you, sir?" she said cheerily, placing a gentle hand on his shoulder to encourage him to sit down. Two others sitting at the table with him looked back and forth from her to their companion.

One of them gave a low whistle. "You lucky devil, Ted. Order us another round while you're at it."

The room fell quiet; the man behind the bar stopped what he was doing, wiped his hands and threw the towel over his shoulder.

"Mrs McKendrick!" he called in a loud voice. "You might like to come and see something in the Gentlemen's Lounge."

"Now," said Sally, her heart thumping wildly as she gauged the impact she'd made on the clientele. "What would you gentlemen like?" After taking their orders she approached the counter to be greeted by an impressive woman with dark hair and bright, knowing eyes, in a well-cut black dress. She and Sally faced each other, each sizing the other up before either spoke.

Sally decided to take the initiative. She extended her hand. "Hello, I'm Sally."

Mrs Emily McKendrick hesitated. She accepted the outstretched hand and after a quick shake, let it go again.

"I've just arrived off the ship, and when I saw how busy you were, I thought I'd call in and lend a hand. You don't mind, do you? After all, I've got nothing better to do today, and these gentlemen are in need of refreshment." Sally flashed her brightest smile, turned to the barman and repeated the drinks order.

By this time, all eyes were on her and Mrs McKendrick, who was scrutinising the newcomer. "I'll give you today to prove your worth," she said at length.

An immediate ruckus followed her announcement. Arms were raised in the air to attract Sally's attention and shouts came from all corners of the room.

"Over here, miss. I'll have another."

"Sally," cried one man who had been close enough to overhear her name. "Sally, love, I've got an order for you."

Some of the men started to bang their glasses on the table, demanding Sally serve them first. To avoid a riot until she could take everyone's orders, she started to sing snippets of folk songs she'd learnt as a child. 'The Skye

Boat Song' proved a great start, although she knew she'd have to pick up the pace the more they drank. 'Ye Banks and Braes', 'The Scottish Soldier' and 'Loch Lomond' all worked their magic as she made her way around the room, taking orders from some, encouraging others to go to the bar themselves, and getting still others to join in singing the chorus.

By the end of the afternoon, the lounge was packed. Word had spread of the new serving lass. Mrs McKendrick had come out from the kitchen to help serve – leaving the cook and scullery maid to manage as best they could to keep the patrons fed – and still more people tried to get into the crowded space. Reluctantly, Mrs McKendrick was forced to shut the lounge room doors. She sent some of the new arrivals around to the public bar and suggested to the more inebriated that they return to their wives and families.

Sally found the heat wearisome. Her feet were sore, her shoes pinched and she knew the underarm of her gown would be stained with sweat. She was flagging, but she kept a smile on her face and continued her friendly banter while she waited for a cue from the mistress. Had she proved her worth, or would she be thrown out? It had to work. It just had to.

Gradually, as dark fell, the bar quietened and settled to a restful murmur. During the lull, Mrs McKendrick, who'd gone back to the kitchen to make sure there were enough pies for dinner, returned to the lounge bar. She poured two glasses of brandy and invited Sally to join her at a small table by the window. "Seems you've made an impression on the customers. Not sure I care for your approach – bit too uppity for my liking. Now, I am grateful for the extra sales, but ..."

Sally jumped in before the woman had finished her sentence, in case what she had to say wasn't what Sally wanted to hear. "Thank ye, Mrs McKendrick. I'm only glad to help. What would you like me to do next?"

The woman lowered her brows. "Who said I wanted you to do anything at all?"

"Well, no one exactly, but I can see you're a canny businesswoman." Beneath the table, Sally pleated the fabric of her skirt between her fingers. "And since I'm in need of a job, I think we can benefit each other."

Up close, Mrs McKendrick appeared younger than her plain dress indicated. She had an upright posture with a good figure, despite a little plumpness. The harsh Australian sun had weathered her skin bronze, and worry lines creased the area around her eyes, but her physical appearance wasn't what struck Sally, it was her intensity. She had a genial smile, when she bestowed it, and an ever-changing face as thoughts and emotions flitted across her mind. But her eyes – dark, sparkling orbs, warm and perceptive – were her most captivating feature.

"Can you cook?"

Unsurprised by the question, Sally instinctively knew Emily McKendrick would not easily concede, but neither was she a fool. "Not as good as you, I'd guess, seeing as what comes out the kitchen. But, aye, I can a little. But I'm thinking it's not me cooking that will make you money."

Emily McKendrick threw back her head and laughed – a deep, rich sound. She raised her glass. "You're a woman after my own spirit."

Sally touched her glass against the other and took a sip, carefully resisting the urge to down the amber liquid in one go. She watched and waited while Emily supped.

"I think I agree with you – we could profit one another. You're hired – for now. But no shenanigans. You can sing, you can serve drinks, you can flirt, but if I catch you with a man in your room, you're gone. Do you understand me?"

"Yes, Mrs McKendrick. And thank you ever so much." No way would any man find his way into Sally's bedroom, not until she had a ring on her finger, and even that, she doubted. If it happened, it would be on her terms.

"Twenty-one shillings a week. Room and all found. Deal?"

"Deal. And I promise, no men." Sally tilted her head and looked out of the corner of her eye with a coquettish smile. "But there's no harm in using a bit of persuasion now and then to get them going, is there?"

"None whatsoever."

The two women drained their glasses and went about their tasks. She saw no need to tell Mrs McKendrick her plans to make a little extra money on the side.

Several weeks later, towards the end of January, Sally was settling into her new life, even if she still struggled with the weather. The heat rose to unbearable temperatures at times, and the clammy, humid conditions made everything sticky. The rain turned out to be something to welcome. Although short-lived, it came in downpours, washed the dust away, made the air smell fresh and cooled the temperature for a while – until the sun came out again. She now understood the importance of the verandahs and shades – and the value of appropriate clothing. Never had what she'd worn meant so much. Her memories mostly consisted of the times she'd been numb with cold.

Dressed only in her chemise and standing by the open window hoping to catch a breeze off the ocean, Sally began to hatch a plan, one that had taken root while sitting under the shade of the large Moreton Bay fig tree with Emily McKendrick on Christmas Day.

The Christmas Day meal had been an unusual affair. Mrs McKendrick had turned on a feast for staff and customers alike, who had nowhere else to go. Sally could honestly say the day was better than anything she expected and the first Christmas she had celebrated since she was a wee child and her mother was still alive.

The laden table nearly groaned with the weight of food, most of which she couldn't name and had no idea what it tasted like. The first course was a local fish called barramundi, served with oysters and crab. Grilled parrot and roasted wild duck followed, and the meal ended with a magnificent flaming plum pudding, packed full of dried fruits, the likes of which she had never eaten, even in Scotland. But the day had been far too hot to enjoy so much food, and the pudding sat heavy in her stomach.

The exotic and refreshing fruits, like pawpaw, quince, pineapple and guava, became Sally's new favourite treats. She'd been amazed they could be used fresh in salads as well as cooked in sauces and pies – not that Sally wanted to learn anything about cooking – but she surely enjoyed eating.

After the heavy meal, many guests drifted off to find a place to sleep the afternoon away, while Sally and

Emily sat in the shade and talked. Their conversation was still tentative after only two weeks of getting to know one another and still on a mistress–servant relationship, but since Mrs McKendrick had no complaints and Sally was wise enough to keep her tongue in check, a rapport was developing.

"My father owns the hotel," Emily told her. "He has two others in Brisbane and Sydney, but sent me here to Townsville to learn the trade. Luckily, Walter doesn't mind the licence being in my name."

Walter McKendrick was exactly the sort of husband Sally wanted: one who did as he was told. Well-spoken, good with the customers and extremely affable, he was content with his status, as long as he had the visible public role. Equally happy with the arrangement, Emily managed the books, the kitchen and the staff, but she had ideas for the future.

The hotel was grand by Australian country town standards and far better than the rough drinking pubs found elsewhere. They had accommodation, often held public meetings and entertainment, and welcomed the gentlemen of the town, but Emily had seen what could be done in the cities.

"I'm much in need of better-trained staff who know how to set well-dressed tables, with quality furnishings to match. But none of that is available here in Townsville," Emily bemoaned as she languidly waved a palm frond in front of her face. "I do so admire that lace you're wearing. Quality like that is hard to come by."

Sally had fashioned the lace Brigid had given her to sit as a high collar at the back of her neck and extend in a small V down the yoke. The open lace was lighter and cooler to wear than the throat-wrapping collars that trapped the heat, but still retained decorum and style – much as she'd like to abandon both. But Emily's comment had set Sally thinking.

Sally reluctantly moved away from the window and began putting on her corsets and petticoats. She looked at the two gowns she had to choose between and knew there was an answer there somewhere.

Many of the fashionable, upper-class ladies who had emigrated from the grand houses of England remained steadfast in their determination to wear only the latest and best that Europe could offer, regardless of its unsuitability to the climate. High collars, long sleeves, tight corsets under fitted jackets, and petticoats with bustles and trains were all the rage, but Australia was a different place and, in Sally's opinion, needed more practical fabrics.

A few of the women who worked for a living had started to abandon the heavy fabrics and restrictive undergarments, but unfortunately only servants and farmers' wives had adopted anything remotely sensible. Sally often had pretty, yet practical ideas pop into her head, seemingly from nowhere, but she had no clue how to go about putting the ideas into action. What she did know was she needed Brigid's sewing skills.

If Emily McKendrick wanted to push an advantage with high-class, quality surroundings and furnishings, then maybe Sally's little plan might take shape after all. She had promised Brigid to come up with something, and that something seemed tantalisingly close, if only Sally could work out a way of getting the two of them together.

Meanwhile, Sally donned her sweat-inducing dress and prepared to meet and greet the lunchtime crowds.

ಭ ಚ

Townsville
January 1887

"Ah, Maggie, what more do you want from me?"

Life had not become the warm, encouraging place Jamie had hoped for since he jumped ship in Townsville all those weeks ago. He'd fully intended to get Maggie and the two girls away from Michael, but it turned out Michael's hold over Maggie was stronger than Jamie's.

"I want you to be getting a real nice job that'll provide a decent home instead of all them dirty jobs you're picking up here and there. I've enough of that with Michael. He's nowt but a labourer and always will be. But I expect you to do better."

Michael had come to Townsville with work already waiting for him with the railway company serving the goldfields further north, but Jamie had found it nearly impossible to get work that wasn't short-term. In the last two weeks of 1886 and early in 1887, he'd managed a bit of butchering, some carting and fencing, but nothing of a permanent nature where he could settle down and make an offer for Maggie's hand. They'd had many an argument about where she was prepared to live.

"That's hardly fair now, Maggie. I'm a farmer. That's all I know. If you'd come farming with me we could build a life together. You know that, but I can't help it if the heat and dust make me manky, can I?"

Maggie and the girls were living in a small, two-room

142

miner's cottage at the end of a long, narrow lane on the outskirts of town, with little in the way of comfort. She hated it but had no other option. At least there were a few neighbours within sight.

Despite his offer to marry her, Maggie had point blank refused to move anywhere where she might encounter snakes and crocodiles, or those black people she heard about. She needed people around her to feel safe, not living in the middle of nowhere in the outback. He tried to reassure her, and while Maggie admitted the few local women she'd seen around town dressed in Western clothes were less intimidating than she'd expected, she'd still kept her distance.

"Scram, now. I can't be bothered with ye no more. Not till you come to your senses. Go now, I say, or I'll tell Michael."

"You don't mean that, our Maggie, and you know it. It's just the heat talking. I'll take the girls for a walk. Keep them out of your hair. You go rest awhile."

Michael had threatened to kill Jamie if he ever saw him again, which meant Jamie only visited when Michael was away working. Often disappointed after his talks with Maggie, Laura and Jane usually saved the day. They had grown fond of him and he of them. When he could, he would walk with them to or from school, although he found a number of times Maggie had kept them home so she had company.

"Come on, girls."

The youngsters squealed with delight as the three of them headed off to the beach.

"Be good now," warned Maggie. "And wear your hats," she shouted, as they disappeared from sight.

Jamie loved sporting with the little girls, feeling

young and carefree again, much like back home with his brothers and sisters and cousins. It gave him comfort and strength. He was growing to like this vast country, so different from his own, but sometimes he felt lonelier than he cared to admit.

Every time his mind drifted to those times back home, he thought of Brigid and wished things could be different. He missed her terribly, but he couldn't work out what hold Maggie had that tied him to her against all sense and logic. Whatever it was, he knew he couldn't leave.

He was now delivering ice blocks for those new-fangled ice chests – he'd never have believed it possible if he hadn't seen them with his own eyes – and hoped it would become a permanent position. At least that way he could live in the township, which would please Maggie – and working with the ice was proving a bonus in these steamy conditions. He'd ask if there were any broken bits he could have as a gift to Maggie. That might improve her temper. He strode off down the road whistling tunes from home, happier than he'd been for a while.

A sudden storm swept through the town in the third week of January, uprooting shrubs, ripping branches off trees and damaging buildings in its path. Jamie found it strange that it had gone as quickly as it arrived, coming from a land where storms were the norm and could rage for days.

For those who had lived in Townsville longer, heavy rainfall and strong winds were common. Even so, Jamie couldn't get over the way everyone continued their daily routines as if nothing had happened. Teams of people cleared up the mess, repaired the damage and life went on.

Fortunately, no one was injured, but Jamie worried about how Maggie and the girls coped. He dared not visit because Laura had told him Michael was home again. He'd have to bide his time and wait until the girls gave him the all clear.

The scorching, clammy heat returned, and Jamie found he was busier than ever. He soon learnt the knack of handling the large blocks of ice, and his strength proved a real asset in lifting the heavy slabs.

One of his regular customers was the butchery and meatworks he'd done a few shifts for over the Christmas period when the regular staff took a day or two off. The works were expanding and needed to keep the meat fresh while waiting for shipment. While the refrigeration business was developing at a rapid pace, Townsville had yet to catch up with the latest technology. In the meantime, ice blocks did the job. Coffee shops, hotels and other eating places demanded ice to chill their coffee and tea, make ice cream and fruit ices, and to keep drinks cold. Jamie was busy.

Back home, Jamie had never heard of chilled drinks or ices; the towns and villages he lived near were too poor and remote for things like that to reach their lips. He knew what ginger beer was. His ma had made it at home. But it tasted nothing like the new Schweppes brand, and he'd never tasted anything like their sweet lemonade and fizzy tonic water either. But these days Jamie was far more interested in what the Castlemaine Brewery in Brisbane had to offer, or the local Townsville Brewery that had started up earlier in the year in competition. He'd developed quite a fondness for the beer he could buy on tap at the pubs.

The elegant, upmarket Queens Hotel was not one of his regular drinking places. He felt quite out of place whenever he had to deliver their ice order. The publican was a Mrs Emily McKendrick. Even that was a surprise. He didn't know women could be publicans. To his mind, the women who frequented pubs were of the class his Ma and Pa had warned him against, but Mrs McKendrick was a refined, well-dressed lady who spoke kindly. She also had a reputation for being a great cook, if you could afford to eat in her establishment. He couldn't, but sometimes she rewarded him with a pie.

"It's yesterday's," she explained the first time she gave him a homemade oyster pie. "I don't usually have any left over. The oyster is a favourite, but the storm kept the customers away, so there's one to spare. You're welcome to it."

Jamie mumbled his thanks as he gingerly transferred the steamy pie from one hand to the other, blowing on it to cool it down. He had no idea what oyster tasted like. They were another new delicacy he'd heard about, but after one bite he decided the taste was much to his liking.

After a few times delivering the ice, Mrs McKendrick asked him to change his routine. "Can you call in the mornings, instead of the evenings, please, Jamie? I'd prefer to have the ice fresh to start the day. It tends to melt quickly when the door to the ice chest is opened all the time."

Jamie didn't care. As long as he had a job and was paid for it, the time of day made little difference to him. He was delivering the ice as usual, a few days before the end of January when a young woman came out through the kitchen door. She was dressed in a lightweight sprigged cotton dress and a large hat, and carried a parasol, which she opened as soon as she stepped into the sunlight. Jamie couldn't see her face, but something about her seemed familiar.

He had left the bullock wagon blocking the lane and her path so he turned around and headed back to the vehicle. "Sorry, miss. I'll just move the wagon out of your way." He climbed up to the driver's seat, took up the reins and moved the animals forward. As he twisted around to see if she had enough room, she looked up at him, tilting the parasol behind her head. Recognition simultaneously leapt into their eyes and they both spoke as one.

"Miss Sally?"

"Jamie O'Brien, is that you?" Sally smiled, lighting her face with a glow of health and ease. "Well, fancy seeing you here."

Seeing Sally come out of the hotel dressed in fashionable clothing befuddled Jamie. She obviously wasn't a kitchen maid, but then ... Suddenly, he didn't want to think about what else she might be.

"What are you doing here?" he asked rather too brusquely, trying to cover his discomfort.

"Now, I dinna think that's the way to greet someone – do you? Especially someone who's a friend of your wee cousin an' all."

Jamie climbed down from the wagon again and stood a few paces away.

"Are you turning a wee bit pink there, me lad?"

Even more flustered, Jamie stammered. "I, um. Well, that is ..."

"Whisht, Jamie. It's me you're talking to. I won't eat you. Have you heard from Brigid then?"

He pushed his hat to the back of his head and wiped his sweaty hands on his trousers. He knew removing his hat for a lady would be more polite, but the sun was too strong and he still wasn't sure Sally was a lady. "No. I haven't," he admitted. "I don't know where to find her."

"And she won't have a clue where you are then, either, will she, you dunderhead."

Jamie swallowed the retort that came to mind. He couldn't let his temper get the better of him yet. "What about you? Have you had a letter?"

"Aye, I have," Sally teased.

A surge of longing filled his veins. "How is she? Is she well? Where is she?"

"Hold your horses, lad. One thing at a time. Once I got settled ..."

Sally stopped talking as soon as Jamie's eyes wandered between her and the building behind him, his unspoken questions written on his face. "Is it Brigid you want to know about? Or are you more keen to know what I'm doing living in the hotel?"

Abashed, Jamie lowered his head. It looked like Sally was being her usual outspoken self again. They'd not had much to do with one another on the ship, since Jamie considered Sally had too much to say to Brigid about Maggie.

"Brigid," he mumbled. "Tell me about our Brigid. Please?"

Satisfied with his response, Sally continued her story. "I sent a telegram back to the immigration people asking them to let her know where I was. I got a letter from her just after Christmas. She's working as a maid in a nice area of Brisbane for an important man about town who runs the drapery store. Big it is, she says. Two floors of

148

goods the like of which she's not seen ever."

"Aye, she'd be as happy as a pig in muck if she could work in a place like that."

Sally stared at Jamie, trying to decide whether she should get to know him better and tell him about her plans, or to dismiss him and let him go his way. Jamie shuffled his feet under her gaze waiting for her to say something more.

"She asked after you. Even after what you did to her, she still cares enough to ask about you. I'm trying to make up my mind if *I'll* forgive you."

"Oh, Miss Sally. I am right sorry it had to be the way it was. I can't explain what made me do it, but I know I'd do it again if I had to. But our Brigid is that special to me I'd do anything ye ask to make things right. I would ..." Jamie was almost gabbling, the words were coming out of his mouth so fast.

Sally raised her hand to stop him talking. "All right. You're forgiven – for now. But if you do anything to hurt her again, you'll have to deal with me."

At that point, Mr McKendrick emerged. "What's the hold-up, lad? I heard the wagon pull up ages ago and I've been waiting." He looked between the two of them, assessing what was going on. "Sally, do you know this man? He's not bothering you, is he?"

"No, Mr McKendrick. He's no bother. I do know him a little. He was on the same ship as me coming out, with his cousin, who's my friend. We were just catching up. Sorry to hold you up. I'll be on my way and get those things Mrs McKendrick wanted."

"Very well, then. As long as he's not being a nuisance. Come along, lad. Bring that ice in."

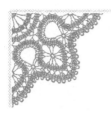

8

Truths Spoken and Unspoken

Brisbane
January 1887

"You've had plenty of time to think on it. What do you think I should do?" asked Philip.

Towards the end of January, as arranged before they had each gone their own way – Sam home to the station for Christmas, and Philip swallowed up in the labyrinthine network of Harrison Browne Drapers – the two young men met up again.

A month earlier, they had talked through Philip's ideas for expansion. Philip wanted to spread his wings and he'd suggested to his father that they add a dressmaking and handmade lace department. Exactly where Brigid fitted into the picture he was still working out, but there were options. He could present her as a descendant from the Irish aristocracy, or of French descent, but first he needed to create an air of mystique around her that would attract bees to the honey pot. He'd also suggested that he be allowed to open a second branch, maybe in a smaller town like Townsville, or even in New Zealand, to test the waters. His father had refused.

Sam had wanted to think the concept through ahead of making any decisions. He'd even suggested Hugh could run some figures, but Philip was reluctant to involve Hugh so early in the discussion. They'd separated without having reached any conclusions.

Now, sitting in the private bar of the Grosvenor Hotel hoping to avoid anyone they might know, Sam sipped his beer. "As I see it, you've two choices. Listen to your father, work in the store, climb your way into his shoes as he expects, and everything will be handed to you on a platter. Or, ignore your father, take this girl on, which means moving elsewhere, and start from scratch. Is that about the nub of the issue?"

Philip ran his fingers through his hair, flicking it back from his face. Things weren't going how he wanted. "Put that way it doesn't sound much of a choice. But Father is driving me to distraction." He thumped the arm of the chair with the flat of his hand. "He just won't listen to reason." He didn't tell Sam his father considered the scheme unjust and a misuse of power. The cold anger in his father's voice echoed in his brain: 'I'll not allow you or anyone in my employ to exploit anyone.'

His father's comments were unjustified – that wasn't what he was doing. He'd make him pay for doubting him, one day.

Sam crossed one leg over the other and relaxed into the chair. "Don't despair just yet. I understand how you feel, but you do need to think rationally about it all. I'll ask you again – what's this girl to you?"

Philip had turned the question over in his mind a lot since Sam had first asked it back in December. Brigid stirred up feelings he couldn't explain: not ones of lust – he knew them only too well – but ones of discontent.

He'd been inspired by her spirit. For all her timidity and meek acceptance of her place in life's pecking order, she had grit – and freedom. But she was young enough and naive enough to be putty in his hands.

She'd never told him why she left her family and her country, but to his mind it took courage, whatever the reasons. And now she'd made the break, she was in charge of her own destiny. He wanted that freedom – freedom to do what he wanted without asking permission. But to do that he needed the courage of his convictions, like she had – and maybe being around her would show him how.

"Nothing like what you are hinting at," Philip laughed. "I'm intrigued. For all her humble background, she has a spark about her that I think could prove an invaluable asset if only I could just tap into it."

"If you say so, but let's talk about the logistics. I've done a few numbers."

For the next couple of hours, the two of them discussed Philip's options. Harrison Browne was an established drapery business with a warehouse in George Street and a shop in Queen Street. For some reason, best known only to his parents, his mother had no hand in the business and rarely set foot in the store either. Yet, what it lacked, in Philip's opinion, was a woman's touch.

Never mind what Philip suggested, his father had rejected all his ideas, especially those for Brigid. "Foolish boy. You'd be found out in a moment. There is no Irish aristocracy to speak of – it's British. And as for being French! No one would fall for that ruse."

The barb had hurt and he'd smarted for some time, but he would never let his father see how it affected him.

"At least your father listened to your ideas," said Sam.

"Not for long. And I should have known better than to ask Alf to help me, and even Mother was a letdown."

His mother had been loyal to her husband and supported him regardless of how much she sympathised with her son. But her reasoning baffled Philip.

"I can't understand Mother's logic that Brigid's background would be a deterrent to the influential ladies and would lose us trade when they found out – and they would, according to her. But I don't agree. That's the trick – making sure they didn't know."

"You are dreaming. Just because you're smitten with her doesn't mean everyone else will be," Sam reluctantly pointed out. "And your mother has a point. The girl has a lot going against her: she's Irish and Catholic, uneducated beyond the basics and works as a domestic. There's no way the matriarchs of this town will let a girl with a background like that flourish."

"But that doesn't make sense. And she's more schooled than that. Believe me." Philip swallowed his brandy in one mouthful and ordered another. "Mother is always going on about how much better and fairer it is here, and how she has standing in the community because of her ability rather than who her family were." Philip got to his feet and paced around the table. "Shouldn't Brigid be given the same chance to prove she can be more than what she was born to? Shouldn't I?"

"Hey, don't shout at me. I'm just pointing out the obvious. I happen to agree with you – after all, that's how our family got its chances – but ... what's the odds your mother is afraid you want to be more involved with this girl than you're letting on?"

Philip stared at his friend as the idea sunk in. Had his mother seen him talking to Brigid? Maybe Sam was right. He sat down again. "I'd like you to meet her," he blurted. "Then I think you'll see what I'm talking about." He trusted Sam's judgment of character. His astuteness had been proved right more than once.

"That could prove a bit tricky. Isn't she going to be suspicious, and where do you suggest? Hardly in surroundings like this." Sam waved his hand around the room. The hotel was a male bastion for drinking. "And we can't take her anywhere friends of our mothers might see her."

Philip sat forward, as if to speak, leant back and flicked his hair. He sat up again. "What if we met her at the market, or at the park? It would seem a casual meeting of people who are previously acquainted."

Sam sighed. "All right. If that's what you want."

On Friday, Philip watched Brigid leave the house heading for the markets in Roma Street. She was carrying a basket full of produce to sell and, he was sure, a list of goods to buy. As soon as she was out of sight, he fetched his horse and rode to the club.

"Come on, Sam. She's on her way. If we hurry we'll meet her in the street before she gets lost among the stalls."

Sam looked up. After a full day of billowing clouds scudding across the leaden sky that threatened rain, the air throbbed and the wind was keen. "We should be all right this morning, but when that lot falls, we'll know about it. It's going to be a whopper of a storm."

Philip never doubted Sam's predictions. He and his family relied heavily on being able to read the weather for the safety of their stock. "Well, let's hope it holds off until we're back."

Leaving his horse there, Philip hurried with Sam along George Street, up Anne and into Albert Street in time to see Brigid approaching.

"There she is," he nudged Sam. "She hasn't seen us yet. Let's hurry."

Brigid walked along with a jaunty gait, taking in everything that was going on around her.

"She's a looker, I'll give you that. No wonder your mother thinks you have an ulterior motive."

Philip looked sideways at Sam, nonplussed by his remark. True, Brigid's black hair made her skin appear almost translucent and her eyes sparkled like the blue of the ocean; she was a tiny wisp of a creature too, but Philip had seen more beautiful women. In fact, he'd always considered her friend Sally from the ship was the more physically striking of the two, but Brigid had something else, something that drew people to her.

"I'm glad you see something in her already, but wait until you speak with her, then you'll know what I mean."

The gap between Brigid and the two men narrowed, but she didn't notice them until Philip spoke.

"Good morning, Miss Brigid." He raised his hat, and immediately she lowered her gaze as her skin tinged pink.

"Morning, Master Philip."

He wished Mavis had never told her to call him that. "Surely there's no need for you to call me master?"

But to his dismay, she unwittingly added to his woes. "'Tis only proper, while I work for Mrs Browne."

Philip hadn't told Sam where she worked, and he hoped it wouldn't mar Sam's opinion of her.

"Anyway, none of that matters," Philip cut in. "I'd like you to meet a friend of mine. This is Sam Barton.

Sam, I'd like to introduce you to Miss Brigid O'Brien."

Sam lifted his hat. "A pleasure."

Brigid bobbed a small curtsy, only looking him when he asked, "How are you finding Brisbane?"

"It's a wonder. It truly is. I love coming to the markets and seeing so many strange fruits, and there's ever so much produce. Never seen anything like it in my life."

Sam chuckled at her enthusiasm. "I'm glad you are finding it to your liking."

"Oh, that I am, sir. That I am."

Philip watched the interplay between the two and was sure he detected that spark he'd told Sam about, but it wasn't only coming from Brigid.

"Shall we walk with you awhile, Brigid? You can show us the ways of the market."

This time, the colour infusing Brigid's face was not embarrassment, at least he hoped not, but a keenness to share her joy. "The big business goes on under the tin roof, but I like the smaller stalls scattered around the outside. It reminds me of home."

As Sam had predicted, when the rain came it thundered down. Raindrops bounced off the ground; puddles turned into pools that grew into lakes.

Philip arrived home late afternoon, an hour or so after the rain started. It irked him he'd not had time to talk further about his plans – or Brigid – but Sam reckoned he would end up stranded at the club if he didn't leave.

"What about you?" Philip asked. "Would you like to come and stay at my house? I'm sure my mother wouldn't mind."

156

"No, thank you for your offer. I won't bother your mother. I'll be quite warm and dry here."

Mavis Johnson met Philip at the door and helped him strip off his wet jacket and shoes. "Oh my, you're near soaked through. Lucky you're home when you are. That's some storm brewing out there. Here, I'll take these. You go and get changed, and bring me them wet things to dry."

She bustled off to the kitchen carrying his shoes, muttering about how much damage the rain would do to the vegetable garden.

Situated high on the hill, the Browne property usually had a sweeping view of central Brisbane and the curving river that was the lifeblood of the town. From where Philip stood at the upstairs window he'd opened, he could barely make out the river through the rain, but he could hear the tumbling and roaring of the water as it gushed along kerbs, around trees, over hills and down the streets to the river. Wilder. Faster. The wind roared, keening like an old woman at a wake.

Dusk fell early. The drapes billowed in the wind.

In many ways, the storm matched Philip's mood. Possibilities and opportunities were building inside him, preparing him to sweep away obstacles in his path. He laughed at the clap of thunder.

The meeting between Brigid and Sam had gone better than he'd hoped. She was fresh, unaffected and warm-hearted, totally unaware of her appeal – and Sam was captivated.

Even though his father said his plan took advantage of Brigid's naivety – exploitation, to put it bluntly, he'd said – and he'd have nothing to do with it, Philip couldn't agree. Brigid would get paid for her work and, after all, they were in the business of making a profit. Just because Brigid wouldn't get the credit was neither here nor there. Workers worked, owners profited.

On the ship, it had all seemed so simple. Once he'd created a fascination about her, he was certain her skills with the needle would do the rest. He'd imagined how Brigid would create high-end, one-off pieces that would sell for a fortune. He could see all the fashionable ladies flocking to the store to get their own special lace design, but since Brigid would only be able to make so many in a set time frame, the rarity of each design would make each one even more valuable and sought after. He could sense the money rolling in.

He even expanded the idea to include dressing some of the finer homes with embroidered napery, and lace-bedecked bedding and window hangings – all handmade by Brigid. He was certain she would fall for the idea as soon as he mentioned it. He didn't think it would be hard to persuade Sam to come in with him either.

"Philip? Are you there, Philip?" His mother's anxious voice calling from the bottom of the stairs interrupted his thoughts.

"Yes, Mama. Coming."

At the sight of her distressed face staring up at him, he quickened his pace. "What's the matter?" He took her hand and putting his arm around her, escorted her into the sitting room where the lamps had already been lit. "Come and sit down. I'll get Mavis to get you something. You don't look at all well."

This behaviour was so unlike his mother, he was ruffled. He was used to her being in charge and taking care of everyone else.

"No, no. Don't bother Mavis and I'm fine, really. It's

just I'm worried about your father. I've seen the water rise like this before. You were too young to remember, but we had a flash flood back in '63, which took everything in its path. The damage was enormous. I'm worried it will happen again. We've a lot more to lose now. Have you seen him?"

He immediately felt guilty for not showing up at the warehouse or the shop. "Father? No, not today. I had a meeting with Sam Barton."

His mother pulled a handkerchief from her sleeve and patted her brow, surreptitiously dabbing at her eyes and nose. "Oh, well," she sighed. "We'll just have to wait for him to return, I suppose."

Outside, the rain beat heavily upon the roof, and water gushed noisily over the guttering. Philip needed to shout to be heard. "I'm sure he'll find somewhere to shelter. Don't fret, Mama."

Despite his reassurances and the sultriness in the air, his mother began to shiver.

"Mavis!" he bellowed down the hallway. "Mavis. Bring Mother's shawl, quickly."

He knelt in front of his mother sitting in her favourite chair by the window. Her head was turned to watch the relentless downpour, and he saw her bite her bottom lip. He picked up her hand, surprised to find it cold, and rubbed it between his hands.

"Mavis!" he bellowed again.

"Don't shout, please, Philip. It hurts my head." Beatrice spoke absently.

Mavis trundled in, clutching a lightweight wool shawl. "I'm here. I'm here. No need to shout, young master. Now, what's amiss?"

At Mavis's touch, Beatrice gave her a small nod and

159

put her hands up to pull the shawl more tightly around her shoulders, but didn't speak. Philip looked at the shawl, thinking the one he'd seen Brigid wear was much finer. He knew he was on to a good thing. Why couldn't anyone else see it?

"Mother seems inordinately concerned about my father in this weather. I've tried to assure her he will be all right and will find shelter, but I don't think she believes me."

Mavis put her finger to her lips and indicated Philip should follow her. "I'll just get you a nice warm cuppa, Mrs B," she said kindly, patting her mistress's shoulder.

On her way to the kitchen, she tut-tutted. "I hope you're right, young master. I hope you're right. But if this rain keeps up I don't like to think what'll happen. There was a big flood way back when you was a nipper. Your father spent two days at the warehouse lifting stock and sandbagging walls and doors, trying to divert the water. All to no avail, the stock loss was huge."

Philip surveyed the familiar kitchen as Mavis bustled about, filling the kettle and waiting for it to boil. It had been a favourite haunt of his growing up. The place had changed little over time and had been his mother's domain as much as Mavis's.

She chatted on. "Water's no respecter of things in its way. When he finally came home that time, he was exhausted and took sick soon after. He spent weeks in bed unable to move 'cos of the fever. She'll be worried it'll happen again, no doubt. And your father's that much older now. Not so strong, either."

She set out a tray with a cloth, a fine china cup and saucer, and a plate with a slice of her fresh-baked madeira cake, along with a cake fork. She put another slice on a

160

separate plate and handed it to Philip. "Here, get this inside you while you can. Devil only knows how long we'll be cooped up here."

He took a bite and memories of childhood filled the room: the warmth, the laughter, the people ... The people! Of course, that was what was missing. He stopped eating and put his plate on the table just as Mavis was filling the teapot.

"Where's Brigid?" He didn't think he wanted to know the answer. The last time he'd seen her was at the market, but Mavis wasn't to know anything about that.

The look on Mavis's face said it all. She was troubled. "She hasn't returned from the market."

If the image of his father stranded in the elements hadn't galvanised him to action, the idea Brigid might be exposed to the storm's wildness did. A timely flash of lightning and a window-shaking clap of thunder made him jump, but more opportunely, it greatly alarmed the two women – Mavis squealed and his mother howled. He could hear her from the other room.

He dashed along the corridor and into the sitting room. "Don't be alarmed, Mama. You are quite safe here." Deciding it wise not to mention Brigid, he soothed his mother. "But to put your mind at rest I shall go and seek out Father. I'll bring him home, if I can, or stay and help if I'm needed. I'll send a message as soon as I can." He knelt down and gave his mother an awkward hug before retreating.

"No. Philip. No." Beatrice was on her feet and running after him. She grabbed his arm. "I couldn't stand it if I lost both of you. I'm sure you are right – your father will take shelter. Stay here, son, where I know you're safe. Please. Philip, please."

Gently taking her hand off his arm, he led her back to her chair. "I will be safe, I promise. I will take Meg and ride the long way down. You know how sure-footed shire horses are, and I'll take care to avoid the flow path. I can see where it is going."

He dropped a kiss on top of his mother's head and leapt up the stairs two at a time. Grabbing his large felt hat and heavy oilskin from the wardrobe he hurried back downstairs to the kitchen. From the scullery he snatched his long riding boots, and once fully attired strode off across the back garden to the stables.

ℬ ℭ

Wednesday, 26th January 1887

The sheeting rain came as a shock. Nothing had prepared Brigid for such a heavy downpour. Used to the soft Irish mists that hovered over the countryside for long periods, or the screeching winds and sharp rain that lashed the west coast of Ireland, she had not known anything like this. A booming roar turned her dismay to foreboding.

"Run!" a woman yelled, causing panic. "Run. Quick. The water's coming."

Brigid soon lost her basket as she was swept along in the crush of people trying to salvage their produce and wares and find shelter. A woman fell and became trapped under her table. Brigid stopped to help and was nearly trampled by the billowing throng. She had barely caught her breath before being driven forward again.

"Get out of the way, girl," a man shouted, pushing at her.

She had no idea in which direction she was being pushed, but it took all her strength to stay on her feet. Above the storm's turbulence, voices shouted, calling out for people they couldn't find. Mud oozed underfoot, people lurched and skidded as they tried to escape the confines of the marketplace. Shrieks and wails rang in her ears – "Help me, God. Help." Was that her own voice she recognised? And still the relentless push persisted. Her bonnet fell back and her hair tumbled over her shoulders, sticking to her face as the wind tossed it about.

After what seemed an eternity the crowd started to thin out, with people running in different directions. Brigid found she was no longer trapped between the shoulders of the people around her. Her sodden skirts weighed heavy against her legs, and she tripped and fell several times. A foot kicked her and once someone stood on her hand, but it sank into the mud and suffered less damage than it might otherwise have. Another time a hand under her armpit dragged her upright. "There you go, girl. You'll be right now," said a woman.

Each time she struggled to her feet, the mud clinging to her clothing sapped her strength further.

Freeing herself from the worst of the mêlée, Brigid followed a group of people running upstream as a river of water came rushing down the street. She was gasping for air and knew she had to catch her breath. A side alley offered brief shelter. Slumping down on a stack of crates, she pulled her knees up to her chest and untangled the choking ribbons of her bonnet. The wind howled even more forcefully through the narrow space while the water raced past, ballooning against the side of the building and redirecting a rising flow of water towards her. Her ears ached and her teeth tingled. Hot, burning tears streamed down her face. "Jesus, Mary and Joseph. Are You up there, God? Are You trying to kill me? Is that what You want? I mean to say, I don't want to sound ungrateful or anyt'ing, but it does seem to me that You're making me life a tad difficult lately."

Now she'd started talking, exhaustion turned to outrage. It had been a long day, and night was falling. She wiped her nose with her damp sleeve, leaving her tears to mingle with the rain.

"First, You led me away from me home, and all that I loved, and sent me on a journey. Now I'll not complain about that if that is Your will. But the storm You sent at sea nearly killed me, and now You send another my way. Am I being punished for something, because if I am, I don't know what it is. And I don't t'ink I'm ready to die just yet."

Comforted by her conversation, she got to her feet. She'd not talked out loud to God before, at least not like that. She'd always said her prayers, of course, and she'd asked for things sometimes – silently, in her head, hoping He'd hear her – little things of small consequence, but never out loud and never demanding answers.

"Am I supposed to learn something from it, God? Is that it? Whichever it is, I wish You'd show me the way because I'm getting mighty weary."

A blazing flash of lightning lit up the opposite end of the alley from where she'd entered, followed by a clap of thunder so intense she screamed. She put her hands over her ears to stop them ringing. Was that a sign?

She ran to the end of the alleyway and into another street. She looked left and right but could see nothing to help her. She had no idea which way to turn. She knew she should try to find her way back up Spring Hill to the

Browne house but couldn't begin to guess where to start.

She turned right.

Overhead, the sky was a solid charcoal without a hint of light. Water ran in rivulets in every direction, following the slightest slope of the land, gathering momentum as it went. There were fewer people in this area, and they wouldn't have noticed her anyway. They were too engrossed saving themselves and what possessions they could.

She trudged endlessly against the raging wind and merciless rain, in a maze of alleyways, until she completely lost track of how many times she'd turned, or which way. Through the murk she couldn't see where she had come from or any landmark that would guide her to shelter – and safety.

"So much for showing me the way," she muttered heavenward and turned yet another corner. Her feet were immediately submerged in water well over her ankles and she could feel the torrent pulling at her legs.

As far as she could see, the ground in all directions was covered in rapidly rising water. She sensed she was near the river, the air smelt of sludge and dead animals, and something else she couldn't place. Grease? Tar?

A heavy object banged into her leg and sped on by, the hem of her skirt was snared and tore away as she struggled to hold her footing. The surge was fast moving, gathering trees, fences, small animals, household goods and anything else in its path small enough to be ripped from its place.

Frightened she might be swept away too, she scuttled back into the lane ahead of the rising water following her. She ran. Higgledy-piggledy, up streets, down lanes.

Her breath came in heaving gulps; her legs throbbed.

She lost track of time.

Exhausted, she dragged her feet along. Instinct was all that kept her upright as the desire to lie down became overpowering. "Don't. Stop," she repeated with every step. The mantra circled her mind as awareness of her surroundings faded.

"Briig ... id." Was someone calling her name?

"Briig ... id." It sounded like her brother. What did John want her to do now?

She was so terribly tired.

"Briig ... id." The call came again.

Her eyes fluttered open. A hazy shape wavered.

They closed again.

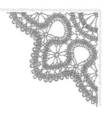

9

Love, Fear and Death

Townsville
March 1887

Months had passed since Sally had first stumbled across Jamie outside the hotel that day in January. She could laugh now at his disapproving face, but it had annoyed her at the time. She'd had enough of men thinking they could control her. But then, he really was quite young. At least he was a hard worker, she'd give him that.

Despite herself, Sally was drawn to Jamie's freshness and honesty. She still judged him an idiot to have left Brigid for that irrational woman but admired his certainty he was doing the right thing. And he loved those two little girls. Who'd have believed it? A big bloke like him being soppy over a couple of brats. She tried not to think about it – but there were days when her thoughts wouldn't leave her alone.

For days after their meeting, the papers had been full of the storm that hit Townsville.

But what had scared them both were the reports about the severity of the storm as it travelled south and hit Brisbane. The flash flood had been one of the most damaging the town had seen, with houses floating away and bridges demolished. With no knowledge of the landscape in Brisbane, they couldn't imagine where Brigid fitted but prayed she was safe. They'd not had a letter in a long while.

Jamie came nearly every day from then on, either to deliver the ice or more often to see if she'd heard from Brigid. The papers continued to talk of the clean-up and the damage the flooding had wreaked upon the business district, but still they heard nothing.

Emily McKendrick had proved to be a good employer – even a friend – and she'd had few enough of those in her life. The bar was thriving and Emily encouraged her ideas, but so far Sally had not found a way of asking if Brigid could be included in her schemes. She didn't know why it seemed so important that Brigid join her in Townsville and they become a team. It didn't even make sense. They were as opposite as could be, with different goals.

Brigid was a talented seamstress and lacemaker, but humble and caring. Someone would take advantage of her one day if she wasn't careful. Someone like that Philip Harrison-Browne. She was too compassionate and too trusting for her own good. Much to her own surprise – and anyone else who knew her, if they'd been able to read her deepest thoughts – Sally was worried.

Unlike Brigid, she wasn't clever at anything except beguiling people. Oh, yes, she was entertaining. She could make men laugh. She could fleece them at cards and have them come back for more, but she was a loner, even if something was missing. No one would take advantage of her or rip her off. She certainly didn't want to be considered a do-gooder.

But when Jamie turned up at her door with Maggie, she had little choice. "What the hell am I supposed to do with *her?*" she berated Jamie as he carried the bruised and battered woman into the hotel kitchen.

"Michael's been having another go. Can you care for her until she's strong enough to decide what to do next? And the little ones? I can't leave them on their own." Jamie's eyes looked at her beseechingly.

"Why not? I was left to fend for myself at their age." Sally remembered only too well the days when her ma was sick and she had to find food, or beg or steal medicine, and avoid a beating from her stepfather.

"Aye. So was I, but at least I had family or neighbours around who would keep an eye on me. Did you not have that?"

Sally barely moved her head. No, she hadn't. "Ah, all right, then. Let them stay. But don't expect too much care and attention. And goodness knows what Mrs McKendrick will say when she finds out."

Emily had been torn. "It's bad for business to have children hanging around the hotel. The men come here to escape all that. But I can't see them on the streets, neither, so keep them out of sight and quiet. Else they'll have to go."

Sally hated every minute Maggie spent recuperating in her room, but the girls were angels compared with what they'd been on the ship. Whatever had tamed them was a benefit, in the circumstances, but she didn't like to see them so subdued. They reminded her too much of herself.

At least Maggie wasn't as changeable as she had been before, but her moroseness affected them all. The girls took her food, which she barely touched, but their appetites were healthy enough, and they willingly helped in the kitchen in return. Even Emily seemed taken with them, coaxing a smile occasionally as she gave them a treat. And Sally was glad when, two days later, Maggie announced she was leaving. No thank you or kiss my foot, she just took the girls by the hand and was gone.

"Hmph! How's that for gratitude."

"Don't judge her too harshly, Sally. That is one very troubled woman doing her best. She'll crack one day."

How Emily could see any good in her was beyond Sally's understanding, but Maggie wasn't her problem any longer.

Her problem was the increasing advances of one of Emily's big-spending regulars. Her skin crept whenever he touched her. The same shivery feeling she'd lived with for so long, the one she hoped she'd escaped by coming to Australia to start living again. He'd put his hand on her back, her arm, or tip her chin so she would look at him every time he came to the bar. He laughed and teased, and told his companions what a beauty she was and a wonderful asset. He was ebullient and public with his praise and attentions, but his whispered requests to join her in her room were becoming insistent – and threatening.

To add to the problem, he was a well-respected man about town. He entertained and was entertained by the leaders of the community. He attended all the soirées, receptions and dinner functions. He was a hard-nosed businessman – and he always got his way.

She'd beaten him at cards – more than once – and he'd not forgotten or forgiven. After the last time, he threatened to expose her if she didn't meet his request.

"Aw, now you wouldn't want me to lose my job, would you? Mrs McKendrick is very particular about what goes on in her establishment. She's made it plain, she has. No men upstairs."

"I'll set you up somewhere discreet if that is what you want."

"You flatter me, Mr Carruthers, but I'm just a small-town girl working for a living. I'm not grand enough to be a mistress. Let me get you a drink." She extricated herself from the conversation.

But the next time he returned, he tried again. "You won't have to work any more. A woman like you shouldn't have to work." He smiled, raised his glass, laughed; pretended they were having a casual, but amusing interchange.

"But I like my work. I like singing, and being charming to you and your friends, and entertaining you all. There are others more suited to what you have in mind." She hoped he couldn't sense her fear or revulsion.

The smile never left his face, but his eyes hardened. "You thought you could cheat me and play me for a fool. Nobody does that to me, especially not publicly. It's time for you to pay."

Keeping up the play of a friendly chat, she rested her hand on his shoulder. "No, Mr Carruthers. You've got it all wrong. I'm sorry you lost, but it was just a card game. I didn't take your money. I didn't cheat you at all."

He laughed again, held her upper arm between his thumb and forefinger, and squeezed the soft part. She gritted her teeth against the pain and tried to keep the smile on her face.

"I don't believe you. Think hard about your decision. Think very hard." He released her arm. "The police might be interested in your methods." He stood then, picked up his glass and strolled across the room to join some others at another table.

She knew her ordeal wasn't over.

ဆာ ဆ

Tuesday, 26th April 1887

"Jamie. Jamie. Come quick." Laura barrelled into him, hands grasping at his jacket, and tried to pull him after her.

Jamie grabbed hold of her wrists. "Slow down, Laura. What's the matter?"

"You've got to come, Jamie. It's Maggie."

His heart sank. Not again! He knew what was happening, and it was becoming far too common for his liking. With barely an excuse to his boss, Jamie hurried Laura outside and headed towards their place.

Last month, he'd found Maggie unconscious on the floor of her cottage with little Jane sitting quietly beside her, smoothing her hair from her face. The child was as pale as a ghost and her blotchy, cried-out face was striped where the tears had washed the dirt away. Sally had helped him then. As he laid Maggie on Sally's bed, he had prayed for strength to stay away from Michael. Fortunately, Laura said he'd gone away again.

What upset Jamie most was that Maggie returned to the cottage once she had recovered sufficiently. "I have to Jamie. I don't have a choice. He's my brother, but I can't let him bash the girls like that."

Somewhere along the way, the flighty, half-baked, emotional Maggie he was used to had turned into a tigress since Michael had started taking his frustrations out on the girls, after being beaten in another fight. She was used to him hitting her when things went wrong, but until recently the girls had been safe.

Jamie had heard Michael was losing more fights – and money – than he won lately and was drinking heavily. He'd also been warned he would lose his job if he didn't shape up.

"I hid Jane so I could get here faster," Laura explained, "but I fear it's bad. Pa just wouldn't let up, but Maggie took to him." Despite being only ten, Laura was tough. There were no tears, just a fierce look on her face as she skipped and ran along beside him.

"What? What do you mean 'took to him'? How? With what?"

Jamie lengthened his stride and soon left Laura lagging behind. She tried to catch up and, between breaths, answer his questions.

"He slapped Jane ... she fell ... I tried to pick her up ... Kicked me ... Hit Maggie."

Jamie stopped in his tracks and turned to look at the girl. He gripped her by both arms but instantly let go when she winced. She had a cut above her eye, and her lip was cracked. She rubbed her lower back, and only then did Jamie see the bruises on her legs and guessed there were more under her clothes. His anger flared as he gingerly wrapped his arms around the girl and lifted her up.

"What happened next, *beag amháin*? Tell me, little one."

Head buried in his shoulder and arms wrapped around his neck, Laura murmured into his ear. "Maggie picked up the long poker and jabbed it at him to push him away. She told me to go, so I ran outside with Jane.

I could hear things breaking and falling over, and him shouting and her screaming. It was worse than the banshees at night."

Keeping his voice light, Jamie eased his arm slightly and tried to look at her face. "What, a big girl like you still believing in the banshees? Never!"

"But then it went all silent like, and I was even more scairt. I left Jane hid in the bushes and crept back to see. Maggie was lying on the floor. I couldn't see Pa."

Fear clutched Jamie's stomach. One day, he swore. One day he'd put paid to that monster. "Well. Let's go see how Maggie is, shall we? Sure all will be grand when we get there." He wasn't convinced, but he needed to give Laura hope.

Minutes later they arrived at the house and, wanting to go inside alone, Jamie told Laura, "Go and find Jane now, and make sure she is all right. Wash yer faces maybe and then come find me. Wait outside, though, till I give you the nod. Aye?"

Laura nodded and he lowered her to the ground and watched her pick her way across the long grass to find her sister.

The door was shut and he couldn't hear any movement from inside. He pushed it open. The squeak of the leather hinges sent a shiver up his spine. It took a moment for his eyes to adjust to the dimness of the interior until a dark shape in the middle of the room moved as the sunlight streamed in. A groan. Jamie's heart lifted. He darted forward, righting overturned furniture in the way. He knelt on one knee beside her and raised Maggie into a sitting position. "Maggie, love. I'm that glad to see you." He rested his head gently on top of hers and held her close.

"Michael," she croaked.

"Never mind him! I hope the bastard's gone for good this time."

Her hand fluttered, but her eyes closed as she passed out again.

Jamie put his other arm under her legs and lifted her up. He turned, stumbling, shocked by what he saw, and nearly lost his hold on her.

With his foot, he restored the wooden settle to its feet next to the fireplace and laid Maggie down. He knelt once more – this time beside the prone body of Michael. He could tell at a glance the man was dead. His forehead was split open, a pool of blood oozed over the wooden floor. Flies were already buzzing around the wound, but Jamie was certain the blood hadn't come from there.

He looked to and fro between Maggie and Michael, wondering how she had managed to hit him that hard. He had no doubt she had swung the blow and felt no remorse, he was glad. The problem now was how to get her away from there without getting the police involved. Murder was murder in their eyes, never mind the provocation.

He had to act quickly in case any neighbours began to get suspicious. He was up on his feet and back outside, pulling the door shut behind him, intent on finding the girls before they could see what he'd seen. He found them coming through the tangle of broken fences and bush into the back corner of the garden as he walked around the other side of the house.

"Ah, there you are, now. Don't cry, Jane. Everything is grand, aye. Maggie is sleeping right now." He turned to Laura, questions written in her eyes. "She's not hurt bad, so don't you be fretting none. All will be well, I promise, but I need you to do something for me. Will you do what I say?"

Laura nodded again.

"I need you to go to Sally. Tell her I'm with Maggie, ask her to come see me – and she's to come in the cart. Understand? But you two are to stay at the hotel. Do you hear me now? You are to stay. I'll be right vexed if you don't, and you don't like it when I'm vexed with ye, do you?"

Both girls shook their heads. Solemn. Silent. Trusting.

Jamie nearly scared the living wits out of Sally when he leapt out of his hiding place and jumped on the back of the cart.

"Christ Almighty! You great galoot. You gave me such a fright!" Sally didn't pull any punches when her dander was up. "What the blazes is going on, Jamie?"

"Sorry, I didn't want anyone to see me." He sat down, his feet dangling over the back as if they had been travelling together for some time. "We need to go visiting. Or rather look as though we are going visiting. I need your help."

Jamie explained what she would find when they got to Maggie's cottage and waited for her reply. If he'd read the situation right, Sally would support him and help Maggie. If not, they were on their way to the police station.

"And you're sure it was Maggie?"

"Aye, I am."

Sally didn't reply.

The cart bounced and swayed along the rutted roadway, kicking up a cloud of dust that soon had Jamie coughing.

While he'd waited for Sally, he sat watching Maggie, anger bubbling inside him at the sight of her. He had another go at cleaning up the bloodstain to make sure he left no trace. When Maggie stirred, he gave her some water and bathed her head and eventually managed to get her to sit up. She stared at Michael's body now covered with the only item Jamie had found that was large enough – the patchwork quilt off her bed.

Staring into a void only she could see, bit by bit she told him what she could remember. "When he kicked Laura like that, it was the last straw. I saw red. I grabbed the poker from the fire. It was still hot at the end, and one touch with it and he leapt back, which gave the girls time to run. Did I do it, Jamie? Did I really kill him?" Maggie sounded so forlorn it nearly broke his heart.

"I don't know for sure, *mo ghrá* ... Tell me your story, my love." Jamie held her hand and waited.

"I've seen him lose his temper before, but nothing like this. He hurled whatever he could lay his hands on at me and then started to throw the furniture around. I kept jabbing at him to keep him away from me. The stool hit me on the side of the head."

Maggie stopped and rubbed her temple. A frown creased her brow. She tilted her head to one side. "I don't remember much after that. Lots of noise ... Oh, I remember having a knife in my other hand at some stage, but I don't know how it got there or what I did with it. Did I stab him?"

Jamie shook his head, certain this time. "No. You didn't. You'd remember if you had. The crack over the head was enough. It laid him out, but I reckon hitting his head on the firebricks is what did him in in the end. Not you. Do you understand? He fell and banged his head."

Maggie nodded.

There had been a lot of blood, and wanting to clean it up as best he could while she was still asleep, he'd turned the head and saw a bloodied mess where Michael had hit the corner of a brick as he'd fallen. Not that that would matter to the police. While she hadn't meant to kill him, he was still dead.

"I don't know how long we edged around each other, but he started coming at me again, with something in his hand. The axe maybe, or the maul. I was sure I was done for, Jamie. The crazed look in his eyes really scared me. I must have dropped the knife then because I remember grasping the poker with two hands. I raised it above my head. I even heard the swish in the air as I brought it down. Then ... a terrible bellow, a jarring in my shoulders." Tears trickled unnoticed down her face and neck. "I don't know what happened after that. Not until I woke up and you were here."

Jamie nestled her into his shoulders and rocked her. "Hush now, my love. That's enough. I found you. That's all that matters."

He murmured his plans and made her lie down again and sleep while he went to talk to Sally. "I'll be back soon. Don't worry."

By the time Sally drew the reins back, halting the horse outside the cottage, Jamie was whistling songs from the old country and acting like he'd had too much to drink.

"Maggie. Are ye there, Maggie?" shouted Sally as she peeled off her gloves and strode towards the door. "I've brought someone to see you. You'll never guess who. It's our friend from the ship, it is. I thought we'd go for a picnic. Why don't you join us?"

178

She reached the door and knocked loudly, looking around to see if anyone in the street had seen her. The unusual and noisy arrival of the buggy up the narrow lane had attracted some attention from the house away to the right. The woman had come outside to see what the commotion was, and someone in the house over the back closed a window with a bang.

Satisfied, Sally nodded towards Jamie leaning against the wheel of the cart – hands in pockets, feet crossed, looking as relaxed as he could. She opened the door and disappeared inside.

"I've underestimated you, Jamie, me lad," she said, as she surveyed the mess inside. "How on earth did you come up with your plan so fast?"

"Maggie, wake up," Sally said quietly, as she shook Maggie by the shoulder. "Come on, wake up. We've got to go."

Maggie sat up slowly, ran her hands over her face and rubbed her eyes, trying to clear her head. She started to sweep the hair back from her face, but Sally stalled her. "Leave it loose."

"Now listen carefully," Sally continued. "Remember you are supposed to be sick. You've got the fever. So lean on me and I'll help you to the cart. Don't do too much yourself."

Maggie attempted a weak smile. "That won't be hard. My legs don't feel like they could hold me up anyway."

Sally put her finger to her lips to tell Maggie to be quiet and went to the door. "Paddy!" she cried, inventing a name, her voice shrill with alarm. "Paddy. Stop slouching and come and help me. There's sickness inside. We have to get them to a doctor."

Jamie straightened and pulled his hands from his

pockets but didn't move. He shouted back. "What is it? I don't want to catch nothing."

"Fever. But don't you argue with me, young man. Get in here and give me a hand. I'll help the woman, she's still on her feet – just – but you'll have to carry the bloke."

"Carry him!" Jamie sounded indignant.

"Well, if you don't think you are capable of doing it, then go get someone who is." She slammed the door shut.

"Are you saying I'm not up to it," he shouted. "I'll show you. I'll show you what I'm ... cab-apple ..." He pretended to stagger. "Um, cab-a-bul ... What I can do. You'll see."

Moments later, he too had entered the house.

He righted the rest of the furniture, and between them they returned the place to some semblance of order. Broken bits of furniture he threw on the fire and fanned the blaze. Sally swept up the broken china and stowed it in her carry bag. "Jamie," she said partway through the sweeping, "I've not found a knife or the poker." She turned to Maggie. "Are you sure about what you did?"

"Aye. No. At least, I'm sure I had the poker. But I have no memory of what I did with it."

"The fire axe and maul aren't here either," added Jamie, searching the fire surround and floor.

Sally put her broom away, and cast her eye about the room. "It'll do. Some mess should be expected if they've been sick, and we haven't time to worry about anything else for now. We have to get these two out of here before the nosy neighbours start asking questions."

She gathered her bag and put her gloves on again before helping Maggie to her feet. "Let's go."

Jamie wrapped a shawl around Maggie's shoulders and Sally guided her out the door and along the earthen track to the cart. "There there, dear. Not far now." She spoke loudly. "That's it. One step at a time. I'm here."

Once there, Sally climbed into the cart first and then pulled Maggie up. "I'll just get your hat. Won't be long," she said and jumped down again, hurrying back inside.

Jamie had managed to pull Michael over his shoulder where he hung like a slab of meat, arms and legs dangling on either side. Sally breathed a sigh of relief that no fresh blood oozed, and draped a jacket over Jamie's shoulders to hide Michael's head. She picked up the patchwork quilt, took Maggie's hat from its peg and followed Jamie out the door.

Slipping back into her persona as the loud and bossy woman who had arrived at the cottage ready for a picnic, she berated Jamie all the way to the cart. "Be careful, you great clod. Fancy carrying the poor man like that. He's ill, I tell you. Ill. Let me put the quilt over him. It'll help stop the shivering."

As soon as Jamie lowered Michael onto the cart Sally flicked the cover over him. Jamie jumped on the back again, in the same position as he'd arrived, and with a snap of the reins, Sally turned the horse in the direction of town.

Once they were out of sight of any of the neighbouring houses, Sally turned the buggy north, then west, and headed inland away from civilisation. For a while, at least, they would look as if they were going on an outing, but once they turned off the thoroughfare onto a byway, their progress soon became precarious.

"The horse is having a hard time of it already, and the cart's not built for this sort of terrain, Jamie," said

Sally as they bucked around on the hard, uneven surface littered with stones. "What'll we do now?"

"The horse will manage, just take it slow. Let him choose his path. There's been a bullock wagon up here at some stage so we should be able to get further along yet. We need to get a little higher, but not too far. Keep your eyes peeled for a ravine or crevice in some rocks."

Maggie had not spoken a word since they'd left the cottage. Sally glanced at her and saw her eyes widen at Jamie's words, but otherwise she showed no sign of having heard, let alone having any interest in what they were doing.

The torrential rains and high temperatures of January and February had gone and lessened with each passing month. The late April day held promise for a pleasant month ahead, weather-wise, much cooler and far less wet than anything else they'd experienced so far. The tussock grass looked fresh and was dotted with green shrubbery. Numerous gum trees wavered in the current of air. It would have been a perfect day for a picnic if they hadn't been carrying such a burden.

Wildlife scattered as they advanced, the vibrations of the bush the only sounds they heard. A kookaburra laughed, and parrots and galahs squawked. No human eyes followed. They let the horse meander where it could find a path, alongside a stream and small lake until a rocky outcrop appeared.

Sally and Jamie clambered down from the cart and climbed the hill to the side of the rock face until they came to a plateau. The view was astonishing. The expanse of red and gold, dotted with dusky greens and browns went on as far as the eye could see. In the distance, vague wisps in the sky indicated where Townsville would be.

"I hadn't realised we'd come so far," said Sally. "It'll be nigh on dark when we get back."

"All the better. We can say we got lost, if we're asked."

Maggie, who had not moved when Sally had invited her to come with them, now appeared by her side. She seemed drawn to the majestic wilderness and moved closer and closer to the edge.

"Don't go any nearer, Maggie. Maggie! Stop. Please." Sally tried to keep the panic from her voice. "You're making my stomach tingle." She inched towards Maggie and gently took her arm, tugging her back safely from the edge. They stood arm in arm in awe of their surroundings.

Meanwhile, Jamie fossicked for a place where, if a person were to fall, the body would tumble against the rocks on its way down. He'd not told Maggie what he intended, but Sally had guessed. Jamie needed to make this look like an accident, should anyone ever find the body. The task wasn't easy – but the man was already dead, so he could do him no further harm.

As quietly as possible, but whistling to cover any sounds, Jamie dragged Michael's body off the cart. His whistle rang in the vast openness, but he kept going. Out of sight of the two women, he rolled the corpse towards the edge where the slag was loose and it would be possible to lose your footing. About to push him over the edge, he stopped. Maggie and Sally shouldn't hear it. Not up close anyway – and even he couldn't do it without saying at least some sort of prayer first.

Dear Lord, help me. Time was running out. How long could Sally keep Maggie up there? Maybe it would be better to get the two of them to start back ahead of him. They'd still hear it, but less so from further away.

He ripped a few small branches off the nearby bush and laid them on top of Michael lying in the shadow of the rocks – partly to obscure the body, and partly to make it appear as if the man might have grabbed at them to save himself as he fell.

"Sally. It's getting late. I think we should be getting back now. Turn the buggy around, will you, and move down the track a-ways. I'll help Maggie."

A look passed between them. Sally did as she was bid while Jamie took Maggie's arm and walked beside her towards the cart, talking all the while.

"Now you go with Sally, there's a love. You should be getting back to the girls now. They'll be sore worried, and Sally will take real good care of you. I'll be right behind you, that I will. I can walk faster than the horse can pull its load on this ground. So don't you be fretting now."

With her eyes firmly fixed on the treetops, Maggie appeared unaware of anything Jamie had said, or of the risk he was taking to save her.

"There. Right as rain now, you are." Maggie was once again seated on the cart, and he hoped she wouldn't look behind. "Off you go now, both of you. Let the horse do the work, Sally. I'll catch up."

Sally's eyes were like balls of glass, shiny, knowing. She nodded, unable to raise a smile.

Jamie slapped the horse's rump. "Hup. Get along now." He watched as they jiggled and bounced along the track.

He climbed back up the hill and stood on the plateau, staring into the vastness, hat held against his chest. Prayers for the dead, from childhood, came back to him, and he silently mouthed them into the sky. When he was convinced the women would be far enough away, he crossed himself, shoved his hat on and scooted down to where he'd left Michael's body. Without hesitation, he pushed it over the edge. He didn't stop to watch it fall. He ran.

Above the clump-clump of his footfall, he could hear the sounds of stones rattling, branches snapping, birds squawking as they took flight, and the thuds as Michael crashed and bounced against rocks and trees. The echo rebounded around him and in his head. His blood pounded and his breath came in gasps as he tried to escape the inescapable images in his mind.

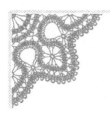

10

The Tide Turns

Brisbane
April 1887

"Why won't you listen to reason, Pa?" Philip was seething with anger. Nothing he said made the slightest difference to his father's high-handed and stubborn viewpoint.

"Because you have no idea what you are talking about. We lost nearly everything. How will setting up a new branch fix that problem, I ask you?"

Keen to restore his business as soon as possible after the flood, Harrison Browne II wanted to purchase newer premises near Eagle Street, which had its own wharf and where the warehouse and shop would be housed together.

Philip still believed they should establish a branch outside of Brisbane that would offset the risk and still bring in money should such a flood happen again.

"The river will flood again," he'd argued. "It has before and it will in the future. Will you survive another complete washout?"

Brisbane had already suffered two devastating floods in a little over twenty years and several smaller ones in between. There were no guarantees but plenty of risks.

"I'm the one taking the risks, young man, so I make the decisions."

"No. You're the one giving orders. The rest of us have to cope as best we can with your inflexible pronouncements."

Father and son faced each other squarely in the eye, neither prepared to give an inch.

"And I'll continue 'making pronouncements', as you so rudely put it," roared Harrison Browne. "We'll do it my way. Is that clear? Anyway, your mother tells me this girl you wanted to use is too valuable to her these days to allow her to fit with any of your foolish notions. So get all that rubbish out of your head."

The way his father flapped his hand airily when he talked about Brigid riled him to the point of defeat. And his father had called him foolish once too often.

"Fine! If you think me and my ideas so utterly foolish, then I'll remove the nemesis from your presence. Permanently."

He strode from his father's office, slamming the door behind him. Racing down the stairs two at a time, he was out in the street and marching towards The Queensland Club before he realised he'd left his hat behind. "Damn and blast!" he shouted aloud, attracting looks from passers-by, but he couldn't have cared less what people thought at that moment. He didn't have the faintest idea what he could or should do next. His father governed his allowance, his father provided a roof over his head, his father controlled everything he did and everywhere he went. He wanted out, but how was he going to escape those paternal clutches when he was thwarted at every turn. Brigid was supposed to be *his* meal ticket – his goose to lay the golden egg. If she was under his control,

Philip knew he could make his plans work.

The effects of the flood were still being felt, even now, three months later. Many were suffering great hardship after losing their homes or livelihood. Sheep losses were high, a shipment of wool loaded onto a ship ready for export was destroyed, several people were killed and often families were seen sleeping in the open or wherever they could find shelter.

The town was a mess, with many homes, streets and gardens in disrepair. Mud, silt and debris lay trapped in tangled swathes in every nook and cranny when the water receded. Only the business area and wharves showed any signs of industry as workers strove to get the commercial district operating again as soon as possible.

His mother was in her element working with both the Lady Musgrave Committee, which normally helped educated young immigrant women get settled, and the Anglican Girls' Friendly Society, which gave young maids and domestic staff a place of social interaction and religious guidance. After the flood, accommodation was difficult to obtain, and the ladies of these societies stepped outside their standard procedures to help those in need, especially women with young children. Beatrice had commandeered Brigid to assist her as soon as the girl was fit enough.

As he got closer to the club, he thought about the night of the flood – and Brigid, the woman who was, unwittingly, the source of all his ambitions and fascination and the woman who would be the ruin of him if he couldn't bring her round to his way of thinking.

He'd never forget that night.

Full of good intentions, Philip had made his way directly to the shop in Queen Street to see how it had fared and whether his father was there. Reassured by the two department managers that so far all was well, and that they had everything under control – with sandbags at the ready should they be needed – he'd been uneasy when they said no, Mr Browne was not with them. With their commitment to stay and protect the store should the water reach them, Philip had fought his way circuitously around to the warehouse.

The closer he'd got, the more he knew the story would not end well. The floodwaters collided as the river rose and the raging torrents raced towards each other. The whole of lower Brisbane and the south side were under water.

He'd doubted he could get close enough to be of any help, the floodwater was too deep. He could only hope his father – and Alf – would have the sense to stay upstairs and not try to do anything stupid to save the stock. They were insured.

Urging his mare, Meg, forward he'd positioned himself where he should have been able to see the building. Between the wind and the rain, he'd had trouble keeping the horse steady and his hat on his head, and the pitch-black sky hadn't helped. He could see a lamp burning in a window but couldn't be certain he had the right building. Nevertheless, he'd felt comforted by the warm glow and sent a prayer to the heavens that his father would be safe.

Having satisfied his mother's wish, he could now turn his attention to Brigid. It had been more luck than judgment that Philip had found her when he did. Even after all this time, he couldn't bear to think about the possibilities if she hadn't literally walked out of the murk in front of him and collapsed almost at his feet.

As soon as he saw her, he urged his horse forward creating a wash that ebbed and flowed against everything it collided with. Screaming her name, he'd leapt from the saddle and hauled her out of the water and into a sitting position, relieved she was still alive.

"Brigid." He wasn't sure she knew who he was. "Brigid."

Her eyes had opened briefly, but there was no recognition in them. They closed again. How she'd got there, so far away from the markets, he had no idea.

In the darkness, the floodwaters streamed past, but they had been relatively safe where they were. He had skirted the worst of it and they were now on the edge, not in the centre, where the warehouse was. Lifting Brigid in his arms like a rag doll, water streaming from her sodden clothes, he forced his way against the relentless wind towards his mount. Dear, faithful Meg. Capable of hauling wagons up and down the steep hills, she was his favourite of the big shire horses. The animal had whickered at his approach. He draped Brigid over the saddle until he regained his seat, then he pulled her upright until her head rested on his shoulder and he could wrap his arm around her to keep her from sliding off.

"Home, Meg."

But it was not to be. Their way was blocked.

The club had been his saviour that night. He'd found himself trapped in the flood zone east of the central business area with no way through to his home in the western hills. The distance may have been less than two miles in a straight line, but since the Breakfast Creek tributary to the north that fed the Brisbane River had burst its banks, the route was impassable. People had been trapped inside their homes by the speed of the rising floodwater, and bridges and houses were swept away in its path. The railway at Sandgate was submerged, and the force of the current had lifted the tracks. People clung to trees for their lives as police and firefighters valiantly attempted to rescue them. Their only means of transport and communication was by boat.

Thankful for the sturdiness of the animal he rode, Philip carefully forged a route towards the club. Floodwaters surrounded the building, but since the ground floor was raised above ground level, it seemed a safe enough haven. He'd kicked Meg hard, urging her up the steps to the portico entrance.

"Sir, sir. You can't bring your horse up here." The concierge of The Queensland Club burst through the doors.

"Shut up, man, and help me." Philip wasted no time in lowering Brigid into the arms of the uniformed man.

"What am I supposed to do with the, um, the ... person?" The man looked askance at the muddy, semiconscious body of what looked like a street urchin and almost shuddered with revulsion.

Philip dismounted and loosened the girth on the saddle and looped the stirrups to give Meg some comfort. "Take her inside, you idiot, before she dies from exposure."

"Women are not allowed in the club, sir." The man radiated defiance and continued to stand where he was.

"Go on. Get. I'll decide what's allowed and what's not."

The muscles of the man's jaw ballooned with the effort of controlling his temper. "If you would care to open the door, that would be most helpful. *Sir*." His surly emphasis was not lost on Philip.

He patted Meg. "Stay, girl." Swinging the door wide, he shoved the concierge on the shoulder. "And arrange a blanket and some food for my horse," Philip called after him.

"This is The Queensland Club! Not some home for animals and waifs," answered the affronted man. "And I am not a stable boy."

"I don't care who you are, just do as you are told if you value your job." Philip's temper had reached boiling and he didn't care what sort of scene he was creating, or what impression he was giving. "Now take her up to a suitable room. And see if any of the maids have a spare dress for her. Hurry up."

The man stood his ground until Blake, the maître d', approached to see what the noise was about. "Excuse me, sir. Can I be of assistance?"

"Yes. Tell your man here to take care of my guest – and my horse. Now."

He knew his father's standing there would ensure his orders were followed. There would be hell to pay later, but for now his only concern was Brigid.

With a nod from the maître d', and instructions to a fellow porter on duty in the foyer, the man started to mount the stairs with his burden.

The sound of Philip's raised voice had roused Brigid. When she opened her eyes to find a strange man carrying her like a baby, she panicked. "Help. Help. Put me down. Where are you taking me? Help!" Pummelling her fists against his chest was the last straw for the porter.

"With pleasure." He promptly sat her on the stair, turned on his heel and left. The heels of his shoes clattered on the parquet floor as he disappeared in haste down the corridor.

"It's all right, Miss O'Brien. You're safe," Philip reassured the girl. "I've brought you to my club for shelter from the storm."

Alarm sprang into her eyes. "That's kind of you, but I think I'll be going now." Brigid tried to stand but found her legs too weak. "Ah. No. Maybe I'll sit a while longer." She wrapped her arms around herself as her teeth started to chatter.

The maître d' and the porter were still watching the action as if frozen. "For goodness' sake," snapped Philip. "Get her a blanket. Can't you see she needs help?"

Stirred into action by Philip's bad temper, the maître d' ensured his orders were carried out.

Settling the blanket around Brigid's shoulder, he said. "You can't go anywhere, any way. There is floodwater surrounding us. Don't you remember?"

She nodded. "Aye, I do. Thank you for saving me." She reached for his hand and held it against her face.

A maid appeared and led Brigid away. Philip had booked a room and ordered a bottle of whisky and some food. Soon after, the maître d' returned with his order and information.

"The young miss is sleeping, and I can assure you Mrs Holdaway, the house matron, is taking care of her. Her clothes are beyond repair apparently, so if you could arrange for something suitable to be delivered, it would be appreciated. You realise she can't stay here once the flood has receded."

Philip acknowledged Blake's comment. "I do. And I will arrange for her to be taken home as soon as it is passable. Is my horse all right?"

Blake assured him Meg had also been cared for and wished him goodnight.

Now here he was, a few months later, back at The Queensland Club, and in a state of anxiety akin to the worst he'd experienced that night in January. Only now the misery was his. His father had made him pay for his manners that night – with a written apology to the board of the club and a personal apology to Blake, along with a hefty bribe – before he was allowed to return.

Yet, after swearing to extradite himself from his father's authority, he was again accepting his father's position for his own benefit.

Philip punched the wall several times in despair, which brought Blake to his door, knocking tactfully. "Is everything all right, sir?"

"What? Oh, yes. Thank you, Blake," he replied through the closed door. "Bring me a bottle of whisky, there's a good chap."

"Very good, sir."

The whisky duly arrived, and Philip set about getting drunk while he tried to pluck up courage to do what he knew he must – leave. Leave his home, the firm, everything, and strike out on his own. Or accept his father's wishes and abandon his ambitions.

ಬಿ ಲ

Sunday, 15th May 1887

So much had happened in the last few months Brigid could hardly believe it – had she not lived it all.

After the January flood, she had taken sick with a fever. For weeks, Mrs Browne and Mavis had cared for her, but she was left weakened and unable to help in the kitchen or around the house. Instead, she made lace.

Lying in bed she often heard raised voices coming from below but couldn't hear the words. Brigid knew Philip was arguing with his father, his mother torn between the two, and she blamed herself for all of it. Shame ate her soul. Father and son would not be arguing like they were, if not for her. She made sure she was nowhere to be seen when either of the men were at home.

Once she had recovered, Mrs Browne had taken Brigid under her wing. She was now visiting halls and meeting houses, going to the Industrial Home and the Lady Musgrave Lodge, and attending the Girls' Friendly Society - even if they were Anglican. She often went on her own, but sometimes she worked alongside Mrs Browne helping to rehome and retrain girls and young women, or showing newcomers around the town, and even providing comfort to those who needed it.

Brigid's job had been to teach them to sew, and those who showed some aptitude she taught to embroider and crochet as well. She had so little time to herself these days, she hadn't been able to write to Sally or keep up with her diary for many months.

She had written home once since arriving and received a short reply, not that long ago. But the news was sad. Granda Michael had taken sick with lung fever over the winter and had passed on. She was rare grieved to hear the news, and it hurt her even more that she couldn't talk to Jamie about it. The one bright spot was that the rest of her family were well. The men were working again, even if they were still sharing whatever cottage and space they could find, and the blight had stayed away this year.

"Brigid," said Mrs Browne as they walked home at a brisk pace after another round of visits. "I am very pleased with your work of late. You have excelled yourself with the girls. The standard of work is very high, given how little time you've had."

"Thank you, Mrs Browne. I really enjoy stitching and needlework, and I'm glad I can show the others."

"You certainly have a way with them. They all adore you. Now, something else I've been meaning to talk to you about. I know you blame yourself for the events that took place in January – but don't."

Surprised by the change of topic to something so personal, Brigid started to object. "But Mrs B ..."

"Don't interrupt, please, Brigid. You have to understand. Women too often take the blame for something that is not of their doing. Getting caught in the flood was bad luck and nearly a tragedy, and being found by Philip was good luck. Neither of those situations was under your control. Neither was suffering the fever, and neither is what is currently going on between my husband and son. They are behaving like wild creatures staking out their territory."

Brigid bit her lip and waited. She'd never heard Mrs Browne criticise her husband before. Working together as they had, Brigid's admiration for the lady had grown daily. Her energy was remarkable, even if her manner was sometimes a little too bullish. She could goad people into bending to her will, which sometimes provoked a caustic comment in response, but she still got done whatever she wanted.

Obviously displeased with something, Mrs Browne

said no more until they arrived home. She removed her bonnet and gloves and set them on the hall table.

"Put away the mercery, dear. Ask Mavis to bring me some tea in the drawing room and when you have completed your other chores, come and see me."

"Yes, Mrs Browne. But can you tell me, please, are the threads and things we use for sewing and lace and such what you call mercery?"

"Yes, my dear. They are. Well done. You are a quick learner. And it's important to know the proper names for such items. Now off you go."

Brigid was reminded what Maggie had once said about the need to learn to speak correctly and know the right words to say to get on in this world.

An hour later, Brigid knocked discreetly on the drawing room door. "You wanted to see me, Mrs B?" She closed the door behind her and stood in front of her mistress.

"Ah, Brigid. Yes. There is something important I need to talk to you about." Beatrice perched on the edge of the wingback chair. She appeared nervous, smoothing her skirts and fiddling with the lace cloth on the side table. "Ah, it's time ... that is, the time has nearly come for you to leave us."

"Leave?" Brigid's stomach did a back flip.

"Yes. Your six months' tenure is nearly over. Next month, you are free to choose what you wish to do next."

Beatrice raised her head and watched Brigid as she took in the significance of what she'd been told. She could leave – just like that. Like she and Sally had talked about on the ship.

"Do I have to?" whispered Brigid. Now the time had come, she wasn't sure she wanted to leave.

Mrs Browne ignored the question. "I have great admiration for your skills as a lacemaker, and I believe you would make an excellent dressmaker too. Philip has ideas to use your skills to his advantage in the store; Mr Browne has other ideas. I'm sure Philip will, one day, get around to telling you his plans. Don't let yourself be caught between the two of them. Do you hear me?"

"Yes, Mrs Browne." Brigid was totally confused. She couldn't imagine for one moment what use she could be to Mr Browne's store, or Philip for that matter, other than as a maid.

"You decide what you want from life. You're a clever little thing. Use those skills to better yourself, and don't let anyone dictate what that should be. Meanwhile, if you are happy to stay on, I am happy for you to remain – for now. Only one day, you must move on."

Brigid's eyes watered. "Oh thank you, Mrs B. Thank you. I don't know what to say."

Beatrice stood and took Brigid's hands in her own. "My dear, I have grown fond of you, and I will be sorry to lose you. But you have much to offer – far more than being a housemaid. I want you to take this time to search within yourself for what you'd like to achieve. When you've made up your mind, will you let me help you accomplish those dreams? If only to thwart those silly men of mine."

"Do you really think I could make something of myself as a needlewoman?"

"Yes, I do. But you will have to get away from here to do it. You may go now. Think about it, and we'll talk further."

Oh, Dear Lord, Brigid prayed as she took her leave of Mrs Browne. *Whatever do You want from me?*

Since the night of the flood when she started talking to God, she'd found greater comfort in talking than in writing her diary. She also found it easier to talk when she was working around the house or out on errands. Not always out loud, of course – people might think she was a little lost in the head if she was seen talking to herself in the street – but in her mind, or sometimes a low mutter – like when she was out in the garden collecting vegetables, or when she was doing the dishes. But right now, she needed to talk out loud. She headed for the big trees at the back of the garden.

"You're testing me something sore, You are, God. I've never had to do this much t'inking or make so many decisions in my whole life."

Her thoughts had to be put into words; she was too confused and too agitated to make sense of anything otherwise.

"If I make the wrong choice, will I be forever doomed to be what I don't want to be? What if I choose to leave and I can't get anyone else to believe in me? What happens to me then? Dear God. I know I've asked You for a sign before, and You sent me one. I know You did. You guided my feet so I'd be rescued from the flood. You also showed me how to be with people and to share the skills You gave me. But God, can I ask Ye to help me again? Show me the way. Send me a sign that tells me what you have destined for me."

"Who's that you're talking to, Miss Brigid?" Coming from behind her, Philip's voice was light-hearted and teasing.

Brigid jumped as she turned around, a small squeal

escaping her lips. "Oh, dear Lord. It's you." Brigid put her hand to her mouth. She'd asked for guidance once before only to have Philip rescue her. Now here he was again, moments after she'd asked for another sign.

"Tut-tut. I hardly think that's the way to greet a friend. We are friends, are we not? Despite our current positions."

"I can't say as we are, Master Philip. In truth, I think we could have been once, but things have changed, they have." Brigid's back was hard up against the tree trunk and she had no way of getting past Philip without pushing him aside.

"You've been avoiding me. I know you have." He moved closer to her, a tentative smile pulling at one cheek. "I've not seen you much since the flood."

"I've been busy, sir. With your mother, helping people and teaching sewing and that."

"So I heard." He turned away from her then and stared through the branches of the tree into nothingness.

Something about the tone of his voice stirred Brigid. He sounded depleted in some way, the tenor of which she recognised from home when the pratie crop had failed: the sound of broken dreams and tapped out lives.

Concern got the better of her and she had to ask, "Are you keeping well?"

He turned back to face her then with another attempt at a smile. "Oh, I'm well enough. Just at a bit of a loose end really."

"Surely not. There is so much cleaning up to do after the flood, and so many poor souls in need of encouragement. Mrs Browne is fair rushed off her feet. Mr Browne must sorely need you in the store."

"Oh, Brigid. You are a delight. And so innocent."

She didn't quite understand what he meant. Innocent of what?

"I have a proposition to put to you."

In all the time she'd known him, Philip had never made improper advances and, given her place in the household, she couldn't consider such an advance now.

"Proposition? Ah, no. I don't think it would be right for you to do that. Not right at all. Your mother wouldn't approve and I'd lose my job."

Philip laughed, a little too loudly. He looked about to see if anyone had heard him – but no one else was in the garden, or anyone at the window, that she could see.

He lowered his voice. "Not that sort of proposition – a business proposition." Philip extended his arm against the tree near her head. "I just don't know how I'm going to pull it off." Again Brigid heard that defeated tone, but he soon brightened. "When I came out to the stables, I heard you talking to someone. Who was it?"

Brigid dropped her head as she coloured from her neck up. "You'll think me foolish, maybe. But when I'm troubled, I talk to God. It helps me get my thoughts in order."

"I supposed it might be something like that. Well, I'm not much good at that sort of thing. But would you mind if I talked to you instead, to put my mind in order?"

Brigid nodded mutely, wondering how much longer she could stay in the garden before she was missed indoors.

"Not here. Come with me." He led the way into the cool, splintered light of the stables where the two carriage horses, Meg and another draught horse, and two riding horses were kept. Speaking softly to a couple of them, he stroked their muzzles as he passed.

He swept some straw off a bench seat fitted against the stable wall so they could both sit.

"Remember on the ship I said I'd take you around town to art galleries and museums and we could attend galas together? Well, I've still got plans for something like that."

"That's very kind of you, but I don't think it's possible. Not now I work for your mother. It wouldn't be fitting."

"That's what everyone says, including my father, which is why I'm at a loose end. He won't listen to me, and I don't agree with him. Australia is a new country. It's time to make our own rules and do things our way."

Thoughts of Jamie filled her mind. He'd said the same thing: a new life, a new country, new ways. Maybe such a life was possible.

Animated now, Philip spoke quickly, trying to get all his ideas out in one go. "Your needlework skills are outstanding. I've never seen anything like it – and I've seen lots of lacework. I want you to work for me at Harrison Browne Drapers, but I need to build up a mystique about you first – an allure, like you have secrets that are only revealed through your lace designs, if anyone can decode them.

"I'd planned for a new tailoring and dressmaking department where we would sell made-to-measure gowns and accessories utilising your lace. Later we could expand, employ more staff, do napery and bed linens – ready-made items, rather than just selling goods for people to make their own. Your lace would be the drawcard."

Brigid's unrealised craving for such an opportunity began to course through her. She turned towards him, to be sure to catch every word.

"I've invented a history for you – either as a descendant of Irish aristocracy or of French descent. I even made up some pseudonyms for you: Lady Catherine Ravenscraft – combining your dark hair and craftsmanship – or possibly Madame Brigitte le Mercier, the French word for haberdasher."

He raised his arm and swept his hand from left to right as if seeing a banner. "Can't you see the headline in the papers?" He lowered his hand, dropped it between his knees and bent his head. "Unfortunately, my father has pooh-poohed the idea, and I don't have the wherewithal to stand alone."

Brigid listened, astounded by his lofty plans. A thread of hope had flickered within her as he'd put her dreams into words, but reality soon took over. The pretence he considered necessary sat uncomfortably with her. She remembered all the rows she'd overheard, and what Mrs B had said just an hour ago.

"They sound grand, and I wish you well with them. I truly do, but I don't think it's honest to ask me to pretend to be something other than what I am. I'm not rich, or famous, or important. You can't cheat people like that. And I'd get found out. Sure as eggs is eggs, and it would be bad for you when that happened. If you build something on a bed of lies, it will fall down."

Philip looked at her, disappointment etched on his face. "But don't you find it a bit exciting? The thought of trying something original?"

"Aye, I do," she reassured him, momentarily putting her hand over his. "It would be my dream to have a wee shop to sell my handcraft. But the likes of me don't get chances like that. Anyway, if your father says nay, then it isn't possible. Is it?"

Philip's shoulders drooped. The months of wrangling with his father had taken its toll, and he was close to admitting defeat. The only bright spot in the whole scheme was Sam. He'd agreed to invest in the expansion if Philip's father allowed him to use the Harrison Browne brand as a starting point. Once he'd built up a reputation and clientele, they could talk more about other branches elsewhere. Sam had given him hope. His father killed it.

"No, it isn't," he conceded. "Without the company name, I have no starting point. No money, no influence, and no credentials."

"Brigid?" Mavis's voice drifted to the pair who sat silently inside the stable not knowing what more to say to one another.

There seemed no way forward, but Brigid had not wanted to leave him alone while he looked so dejected.

"Where is that girl?" Mavis said, her voice coming closer. "Brigid."

"I'd better go. Don't look so glum. There's an old Irish saying:

May the wings of the butterfly kiss the sun.
And find your shoulder to light on.
To bring you luck, happiness and riches.
Today, tomorrow and beyond.

Don't despair, Master Philip. It takes time to build castles. I'm coming, Mavis."

And with a swish of her skirt she was gone.

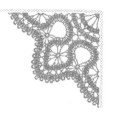

11

Consequences

Townsville
20th June 1887

"Are you James O'Brien?"

Jamie hoped his face would not betray him. The sight of the police constable had set his insides churning. "Aye, I am. What of it?" He continued loading the ice onto the wagon, certain any nervousness would be covered by physical exertion.

"I need to ask you some questions." The constable removed his notebook and pencil from his pocket.

"Oh aye? What about?" Jamie turned and headed back into the store for another block. Nearly two months had passed since the day he, Sally and Maggie had taken the trip into the hills. There'd been no talk that he'd heard of in that time, but he couldn't trust that someone hadn't seen something – but what, and who?

"Do you know a Miss Margaret O'Neill?" the man called after him.

Jamie swayed under the weight of the block of ice. He rested it against the side of the wagon and looked at the constable. "What's it to you?"

Should he admit to knowing her?

"It seems she's gone missing."

Now that was an odd thing to say. Maggie was no more missing than he was. She was still with Sally at the hotel. Mrs Emily was being ever so helpful.

"Missing?" he echoed, as he lifted the ice into place and got another.

"Yes, missing." The man trotted after him, obviously getting irritated. "Do you have to repeat everything I say?"

Jamie found it difficult to talk with the weight of the ice. "I'm just making sure I understand what it is that you're asking me, officer," replied Jamie as smoothly as he could.

"Do you know anything about her whereabouts?"

"Why?"

"Just answer the question." The man turned red in the face and shifted his weight from foot to foot.

"Not unless you tell me why you want to know. Where she is is her business, is it not?" He hoped he was right.

"Not when we've had a report."

"Report about what?" He was stalling for time, and he knew it. So did the prickly copper.

"This is getting us nowhere. If you don't answer me I shall have to take you down to the station where you will be forced to speak to the sergeant."

"Don't go actin' like a cur chewing a wasp over a little t'ing now. I'm only asking so I know how best to help. Now, is there anything wrong with that, I ask ye?"

By this time, the constable was behaving exactly as Jamie had described and almost spluttered with indignation. "You are supposed to be helping the police with their enquiries. Not helping someone escape the law."

"Is that what she's doing? Escaping the law?" Jamie grinned. He knew he'd gained the upper hand. This little pipsqueak knew nothing.

The constable admitted, "Well, no, not exactly. But we do need to find her."

"Aye. Well, tell me why and I'll see if I know anything. Otherwise, can ye let me go about my business? I've deliveries to do."

Huffing and puffing, the constable stepped in front of Jamie, blocking his way. "We believe something untoward may have happened to her," he said in a voice barely above a whisper. "It's come to our attention that Michael O'Neill may have left the area since he's not shown up for work for several weeks. Or been home either, it seems. The place is deserted. About the same time, neighbours reported seeing Miss O'Neill being helped into a buggy by a woman and drunken man. She hasn't been seen since. There is concern Mr O'Neill has taken her. Now, do you or do you not know anything about these incidents that can help with our enquiries?"

Jamie breathed in and out slowly. Their trick had worked.

"Don't care about the O'Neill man, but Maggie was sick. Miss Sally from Queens Hotel asked me to help take her there to get better – and I wasn't drunk. As far as I know she's still there safe and well. Along with the girls."

"Girls? What girls?"

"Laura and Jane, of course. Her nieces. They look after each other. Thick as thieves they are, the three of them – oh, pardon me. I meant no offence."

The man scribbled notes in his book and put it back into his pocket. "Thank you. You have been most helpful after all. I shall check on their welfare. Good-day."

Jamie climbed onto the wagon and clicked the reins to get the bullocks moving. He was shaking through and through and was glad of something to do with his hands. He needed to get a message to Sally, but he felt certain the police had nothing other than a missing person. And in this country a man could please himself when and where he went.

A few hours later he called into the pub to drop off the ice as usual. Sally came out as soon as he pulled the wagon to a stop.

"I got your message. Don't worry, Maggie and the girls are fine. Emily wouldn't let the constable speak to the girls at all. They were too scared anyway. Poor things. Their eyes were nearly bulging from their heads. Maggie was working in the kitchen, and Emily insisted on being with her so he wouldn't interrupt her work for too long. I told him the same as you did. I asked you to help me bring Maggie here because she was sick. Emily backed me up."

Jamie hugged Sally and swung her around, relief surging through him. He dropped a quick kiss on her forehead. "You are an angel, Sally Forsythe. Now let me unload this ice and you can tell me what else was said."

After Jamie had installed the block into the icebox, they talked in lowered voices in the cool room.

"Maggie hardly said a thing – but then she hasn't for weeks. When asked a question, if she could answer with a nod or a shake of her head, she did. She admitted she and her brother had had a fight; she had no memory of anything else that happened that day, and she had no idea where her brother was now."

Jamie held Sally's upper arm, anxious again. "And did he believe her?"

"He did," Sally reassured him. "Especially when I told him the girls had come running to me for help, and when I got there I found her unconscious on the floor, burning up with fever. I never mentioned O'Neill, and the copper didn't ask me if I'd seen him. I got to tell you though, Jamie, I'm worried about your Maggie."

Jamie nodded. Maggie had become increasingly withdrawn as the weeks passed. She never spoke of anything that happened that day. She worked stolidly in the kitchen in exchange for their bed and board, and a whole day could pass without her speaking. Some days she just got up and walked out the door, and didn't return for hours. When she did, she didn't seem able to tell them where she'd been.

The girls continued to go to school as usual and regained some of their youthful exuberance, but even they couldn't seem to bring Maggie out of her shell. Jamie couldn't either.

They'd sit together on the back porch, or go for short walks, since her strength had left her, but she hardly spoke even then.

He did all the talking, full of ideas for the future. Where they would live, him and Maggie and the girls all together, and how happy they would be. "Imagine it, Maggie. Would you like that, aye?"

She nodded. "Aye. 'Twould be nice for the girls," was all she said, her voice flat and distant. Often she would sit staring off into space, never once letting on what was in her thoughts, never mind how much prodding Jamie did.

He wasn't sure why she was so weakened. She'd not had the fever like they were telling everyone, but only

Sally and he knew that, and maybe the girls, if they understood it all. The fight had taken it out of her, and she had taken days to recover. The bruises turned many shades of blue, purple and yellow before she could walk properly again.

The story they'd told Emily McKendrick was as close to the truth as they dared yet still remain credible. She had believed them. She knew Michael O'Neill was a violent bully, and was prepared to shelter the woman and the girls, if only to get them away from him for as long as was needed.

Jamie sighed. "Aye. You're right to be worried, I think, Sally. I had hoped Maggie would regain her spirits and we could marry, but time's passing and little's changed. Maybe I should get her away from here. What do you think? Should we go see Brigid?"

At the mention of Brigid's name, Sally felt a load lift off her shoulders. *How strange.* On the ship, she'd considered herself the stronger of the two, but Brigid had a way with her that might bring Maggie out of her apathy. "Aye, Jamie. I think you might be right there. Brigid could be the answer to your prayers."

ജ്ഞ   ന്ദ

Townsville
17th July 1887

Sunday was Sally's least favourite day of the week. The bar was closed, and not being much of a churchgoer like the others, she spent the day idly wasting away the hours. A walk through the Queens Gardens among the palms, figs and frangipani in the cooler months after the

210

unbearable heat of summer often filled a pleasant hour or so. She found it refreshing.

On this particular Sunday, she'd intended to write to Brigid, but found the task laborious, and she wasn't quite sure what she would say anyway. She'd failed to come up with anything definite in the six months she'd promised Brigid it would take; Jamie was in trouble and needed help, but she couldn't bring herself to write about that sequence of events; and she was fretting about Mr Carruthers, who had not let up. Despite the fact she had deliberately let him win a few card games to restore his standing with his colleagues, his advances towards Sally had become more pressing. She'd bluffed, cajoled and hinted, all to little avail. A walk would be a reprieve.

The distant crunch of shoes on the shingle path went unnoticed until they were nearly upon her. A fleeting thought – men walking, not ladies – and a man appeared on either side of her.

Her startled gasp was cut short when one of the men linked his arm through hers and muttered, "Keep your mouth shut or you'll get this in your side." A sharp pinprick pierced her dress midway down her ribs.

The other man raised his Derby hat briefly. "Good day to you, Miss Forsythe. If you would care to accompany us, there is someone who wishes to speak with you."

"What if I don't want to go with you?" Her voice faltered, belying her haughty look and body language. The knife – at least she assumed it was a knife; she hadn't dared look – pressed harder against her skin.

"I think you will. Let's take things nice and easy, shall we?"

Sally agreed.

"Wise decision. We shall continue to the end of the path and pick up the carriage waiting for us." His voice was cordial as he clasped his hands behind his back and began to promenade. He looked casually around as if he was simply enjoying the fresh air and scenery with two friends, but she heeded his instruction.

"Where are you taking me?"

"I told you, someone wants to speak with you." His tone didn't change. Anyone observing from a distance, but unable to discern his words, would not have taken any notice of the trio enjoying a Sunday walk.

"Which someone? And why the need for these means?"

"It seems you've been less than co-operative. Stop asking questions and do as you are told."

They boarded the barouche – the man with the knife sat beside her, while the other man sat opposite, wearing a smug smile – and the driver set off at a steady clip towards the slopes of Castle Hill. They travelled in silence until the vehicle turned onto a long lane bounded by an avenue of trees. The circular driveway led to a grand, single-level house with shaded verandahs, latticework and several sets of steps, set in the middle of a large expanse of lawn. It spoke of money and power.

She knew immediately who had summoned her.

They alighted and the man who had spoken escorted her up one set of steps, through the French doors, open to the fresh air, and into an elegant library.

She decided to go on the attack. "What is the meaning of this, Mr Carruthers? I'm not partial to being kidnapped and brought here against my will. I wish to leave. Please instruct your man to take me back to the hotel immediately."

The portly, but elegantly attired dignitary casually dismissed the man who stood behind her. He rose from his wingback chair, came around from behind his desk and coolly approached her. "When I am good and ready, I will be only too happy to oblige, Miss Forsythe. But there is something I wish to say to you first." He hooked his thumbs into his fob pockets and rocked on his heels. "I've been a patient man, very patient, but I will not put up with your ridicule any longer. You will become my mistress or you will suffer the consequences. Do you understand me?"

A flutter of fear flapped its wings inside her. "Why me? Why choose an unwilling companion when I'm sure you could find many more agreeable partners?"

He stared at her for a few moments, rubbing his chin and pursed his lips as if weighing up his answer. "I like a challenge. That's why. You humiliated me, so I intend to return the favour."

"It wasn't intentional and have I not rectified my error of judgment of late?" She could almost hear the begging tone in her voice.

"Of course, but that doesn't change anything. And that is why you are here with me, instead of with my man who accompanied you here. He can be very persuasive."

An icy chill ran up her spine as she gingerly touched her side where the man had held the knife.

His face creased into a fearsome grin. Stepping closer, he cupped her chin in his hand and turned her face from side to side. "It would be a pity to spoil that pretty face of yours."

Her skin crawled, and she fought to control the bile rising in her throat. The loathing in her eyes would have stopped a kinder man in his tracks. William Carruthers was not kind.

He let her go, wandered across the room and stood looking out over the garden, with his back towards her. "The choice is entirely yours, but I'll be generous. You are free to go – for now. But the next time I ask you to come to me, you will come. Not here, of course. This was convenient because my wife is away visiting, but you know how easy it was to bring you to me today. Do not think I wouldn't apply the same method next time."

He had ceased to be charming, and Sally had no illusions as to how dangerous this man could be.

"Jamie, Jamie. Where have you been?" Sally demanded, desperate to talk with him. "We've got to get away from here. All of us. Today. Now."

After a contrived late morning tea, the driver had returned Sally to within walking distance of the hotel. She'd insisted on getting out beforehand in case people recognised the carriage, although she suspected it had been hired for the day, rather than being Carruthers' own. She searched frantically for Jamie during the afternoon but couldn't find him. Even Maggie didn't know where he was, and Laura, who usually clung to his side, wasn't any help either.

"Hold tight, Sally. Don't go getting yourself worked up into a lather. What's all this about?" Jamie demanded, holding on to both her arms and bending down a little so he could see her face.

"It's a long story, Jamie. And I shoulda told you about my worries a long time ago, but I thought I could handle it. Mrs Emily will be that peeved with me about it, an' all."

Afraid she'd be overheard, Sally led Jamie to the

bench under the Moreton Bay fig at the back of the hotel. She quickly related all that had taken place with William Carruthers from the first night she beat him at cards. "Mrs McKendrick doesn't know – I didn't want to embarrass her or risk losing my job. She said no men, but she didn't say anything about no cards."

Telling him about how she was abducted and menaced put her into shock. She started to tremble from head to toe and couldn't sit still. She talked faster and faster with each breath. "I'm that scared, Jamie. I am. And in such a dither." It never entered her head to become Carruthers' mistress. She didn't think she could ever willingly go with a man. Her flesh cringed at the memory of those other unwelcome hands and forced couplings. But more than that, she understood his sort. Once he was finished with her, he was just as likely to carry out his threat anyway, for revenge. To make sure no one else ever looked at her the same way. "The man is evil. He will do what he threatens. I have to get away. Oh, poor Emily. She's been good to me – to us – but I canna stay. Neither should you. Come with me, Jamie, please. Come with me. Let's go find Brigid and, and ..."

She didn't know what the 'and' could be. Finding Brigid seemed a good idea at first, but she would need to get further away than that. He would look for her and he would find her.

"Whisht now, lass. Don't fret. We'll think o' something."

Jamie sounded distracted, which came as a jolt to her, given what she'd just told him. "Well, what's up with you, ye numpty? I tell you my life's in danger, and you tell me not to fret!" Giving him a quizzical eye, she repeated her question. "Where have you been?"

He turned his face away and started pacing around. "The police have been back asking questions again about Michael. They don't know anything, but someone gave them that story about a woman and bloke picking them up in a wagon. It's only a matter of time, I fear."

Sally's heart dropped into her stomach. "All the more reason for us to get out of here then."

Jamie nodded. "I was thinking the same thing on my way back from the ravine."

Other people may have been rendered speechless by his recklessness, but Sally wasn't. "You went up there again? What a dang fool thing to do. Do you want to get found out? Right, that settles it. We're leaving – all of us. Have you told Maggie where you went?" Jamie shook his head. "No? Good. Well, don't say anything yet. We have to think about this."

"What do you think I've been doing all day?" Jamie sounded angry, desperate. "I can't make four people, five if you come with us, just disappear, now can I? And if we up and leave, the police will get even more suspicious. Maybe you should take Maggie to Brisbane. Say we thought she needed medical help and you knew someone."

Sally weighed up the possibilities, but her own worries that Carruthers would find her, never mind where she was, surfaced again. "And then what? I told you, 'twouldn't be safe. And what about Laura and Jane? What's going to happen to them? And you, for that matter?"

"The girls will be fine. They do more of the looking-after than Maggie does anyway. And it'll look better if the girls are still around."

"And you? What if ...?"

Jamie spun to face her. "Enough with the questions. How am I supposed to think with you boithering at me all the time?"

Both had fiery tempers, and under stress they flared in a flash. "So it's my fault now, is it? You got me into this shite in the first place. You and that nincompoop you've fallen for. But it looks like it's up to me to get us out of it. You can't seem to think straight. What did you think you were doing, going up to the ravine?"

"Why don't you just go your own way and leave us be, if that's what you think? You're not so canny yourself. Look at the mess you've made of things."

"Jamie. Sally," cried Laura running up to Jamie and wrapping her arms around him. "Stop it. What are you screeching and yelling at each other about? It's got me fair spooked."

Chagrined, Jamie and Sally looked at each other, nodded and silently agreed to drop their argument – for now, at least. They still hadn't solved the problem.

"It's all right, lass. There's nothing for you to worry your wee head about. Sally and me were just trying to sort out what's best."

"What's best for what, Jamie? Are you in trouble?"

Discomforted that Laura should pick up on the cause of their to-do, Sally squatted next to the child. She rested her hand on the girl's shoulder and spoke softly to her. "Like Jamie said, sweet pea, no need for you to worry about a thing." But with a quick glance at Jamie, she added, "There's no trouble exactly, but I'll be moving away soon."

Laura suddenly let go of Jamie and wrapped her arms around Sally's neck, nearly knocking her over. "No. You can't leave us. I wouldn't know what to do without you."

Sally's arms reached around the girl to comfort her. "There there, lass. I've been thinking about that too. Maybe we should all go – you and Jane, Jamie here, and Maggie and me – and find another place to live. Would you like that?"

Laura thought about it for a moment. "I think so, especially if we can all be together. I don't like it here. But where will we go?"

The girl's gaze followed her as Sally untangled Laura's arms and stood up.

"That's what we was on about," said Jamie. "Sally and me, well, we just couldn't agree on the where and how. We will. Don't you grieve none, little one. Now off you run."

Laura hesitated. "The police've been to see Maggie again. They were asking more questions about the day of the fight between her and Pa."

"When was this?" demanded Jamie, looking at Sally with horror as she turned several shades of ashen.

"A few days back."

Jamie bit back his annoyance she hadn't told him earlier. "What did Maggie say, Laura? It's important you tell me everything."

"Nothing. Like last time, Maggie sat and stared at the wall. It was like she was under a spell or something. He didn't get cross with her or anything, but I could tell he wasn't happy. He said he'd be back."

"Ah, well, that's good. All's well after all. And thank you for telling me. But Laura, can you remember to tell me these things when they happen, so I know. I can't take care of Maggie properly if I don't know."

Laura nodded but scuffed her shoe, making an arc in the dust, obviously unwilling to leave until she shared another fear. "That day ..." she began and stopped.

"Go on."

"That day I hid Jane in the bushes. I didn't tell you everything. Um ... Should I?"

Jamie led them back to the bench, sat down and lifted Laura onto his knee. Sally sat beside them, her nerves tingling with dread.

"That you should, lass. Come on, tell me now, there's a good girl."

Laura wrapped her arm around Jamie's neck. "When I went back to find Maggie, I didn't tell you the whole truth. I did see Pa lying there. I knew he was dead soon as I saw him."

Sally inhaled deeply, grasping how traumatic that would have been for the girl. Jamie closed his eyes as if in prayer. When he opened them again, he took a deep breath and let it go again. "I'm right sorry to hear that, Laura. It's not a thing a young one should see."

"What happened to him?"

"Some people came and took him away, and he was buried right proper, lass." Jamie crossed his fingers and hoped his lie would go undetected. He didn't want Laura to know the truth – not ever.

"That's good." Laura didn't appear perturbed by the news. "Pa wasn't a nice person, was he?"

"Don't think unkindly of your Pa," said Sally, thinking about her long ago dead father who she blamed for the troubles in her life. Only pain lay that way. "He had his problems, and we shouldn't judge people when we don't know what drives them. Pray for him."

Again, Laura just nodded. Wounds like hers would take a lifetime to heal, if ever. "Should I tell the policeman where I hid the poker?"

Sally had believed nothing more could shock her.

Jamie winced.

"No!" They both breathed, trying not to shout so they didn't scare the child.

"I don't t'ink that's a very good idea at all," said Jamie. "But maybe you should tell me and Sally the whole story. Aye?"

Laura laid her head on Jamie's shoulder and began to cry, something she rarely did. It tore at Sally's insides, and she could only imagine how Jamie felt. Hesitantly, Laura told him what she'd found. "I thought Pa would kill our Maggie. He was in such a temper, like nothing I'd seen before. I think he would've if Maggie hadn't fought him."

"You've already told me this bit. What did you do with the poker, pet?"

"There's a pit at the back of the house – beyond the hedge, but before you get to the wild bush. It's hidden by long grass. Jane nearly fell in it one day when we were out exploring. That's why I know it's there."

"Did you throw the poker down the pit?" prompted Sally, convinced the girl wasn't telling her everything, but trying to ease the telling.

Laura nodded.

"There were blood on it. And I thought ..." Laura didn't finish saying what she thought.

Sally pushed her for more information. "Did you throw anything else down the pit?"

The girl bit her lip, dropped her chin and looked guiltily at Sally. "I think you did. I think you threw several things down that pit. Am I right?"

Laura flicked her eyes up and down, watching Sally. Her chin wobbled and her head scarcely moved, but Sally took it to mean yes. Over the top of the girl's head, she put her finger against her lips to stop Jamie from saying anything. He wiped the tears from Laura's face with his sleeve instead.

Sally pressed on. "Maggie said there was a knife on the bench. Did you see it? Is it down the pit too?"

Again Laura barely moved her head, but simply flicked her eyes. "Axe," whispered the girl.

"The fire-axe? Did you throw that away too?" Jamie checked. "And the maul?"

Satisfied that all four of the missing tools had been disposed of somewhere no one would ever find them, unless they were told, she could hear Jamie's sigh of relief.

Sally was so light-headed she almost believed she would float away. "Why did you hide them?"

Laura shrugged, her eyes glued to the floor.

Jamie hugged the girl tightly. "You did well, pet. *Cailin maith.* Good girl. Now go see what your sister is up to. Sally and I need to talk." He placed Laura on the ground but she didn't run off straight away.

"Will Maggie come back to us, do you think?" she whispered.

Both Sally and Jamie understood her unease. Maggie had been so withdrawn, and so silent, that she was no comfort to the girls.

"I hope so. I truly hope so. We just have to be patient with her, aye?" said Jamie.

"Aye," Laura agreed, then, after giving Sally a quick hug, she raced off, outwardly a happy child again.

"Does Jane know, I wonder?" said Sally.

A look of unbearable sorrow crumpled Jamie's face. "I hope not. It's bad enough Laura has to carry the burden of such memories, but I suspect nothing Laura does escapes Jane."

221

"I think you're right. Poor child."

They sat wordlessly for a few minutes as each of them digested the news Laura had provided.

"Does that help or hinder our cause?" asked Sally.

"Helps, I think. Without a weapon or any evidence, who's to say what happened and who struck the first blow. Still, does it matter either way? Without a body, there's nothing to prove he hasn't just up and left."

Memory urged her to demand, "Is that why you went to the ravine? To see if you could see the body?"

Jamie didn't answer, but Sally was sure she was right. "And ...?"

"Nothing. Even the bush where I broke the branches has grown back. There's not a footprint or wagon track I could see."

"Except what you left behind today, eejit." Sally was cross with him again. "So, what do we do now?"

"We leave. Somehow."

Somehow.

That somehow was easier said than done.

It had sounded simple enough – they'd take passage with one of the vessels heading south – but nothing was that simple.

While demand for supplies and deliveries meant ships plying their trade along the eastern coastline sailed daily with the tide, Jamie failed to persuade any of the captains to take the women and girls along. He asked several, becoming more insistent each time, but the answer was always the same: "We can take you, if you're prepared to work the passage, and maybe one other. But a coaster is no place for women and children. I'll not take four."

Jamie trudged back to the hotel in the early evening, simmering about the delay. "No luck again, Sal. Looks like we'll have to take the regular passenger vessel after all."

Discouraged, but wildly anxious to get away, Sally's retort was sharper than intended. "But that's not going to work. They want names, and if we give them our names, it'll easy to track us down. You know that."

"You try then. See if you can persuade any of them. The captains just won't let women and children on board." Jamie ran his fingers through his hair and clasped his hands behind his head.

"Sorry, Jamie. I didna mean to snap your head off. I'm just upset, aye. The rail line's not all the way through yet. It would take weeks of toing and froing, and Maggie's not up to that. What other option is there? The mail coach?"

Just then, Laura stuck her head around the door. "Are there any more murphys, Sally? Maggie says there's enough for tonight's dinner, but we've nearly run out."

"What you asking me for? Ask cook. She's the one who does the ordering."

"Can't. It's her day off."

"Isn't there a sack in the store room?"

Laura shrugged. "Dunno. What you both looking so glum about?"

"Not glum, lass, just trying to sort out the best way to take a wee break from the questions and worries for a while. But we have to give our names to get the tickets and that'd make it too easy for the police to find us again. Maggie needs a complete rest."

"So give them a made-up name. Jane and I do it all the time. It's fun."

After the initial shock at the simplicity of the girl's plan, Sally started to laugh, which set Jamie off too.

"See, told you it was fun."

"Aye, you could well be right, an' all," said Jamie. "And what name would you suggest?"

The girl wavered for a minute. "Murphys – that's what I came to ask you about. How about Murphy?"

"A potato?" Jamie was aghast, but Sally said, "It's perfect. Plain. Common. Irish. What more could you want?"

And so they agreed. The Murphy family would board the next steamer bound for Brisbane. Sally gave him the money she had put aside and sent him off to the harbourmaster's office.

Jamie returned a short while later with five tickets. "That was easier than I thought it'd be. We sail on the early morning tide."

Next she sent him to hand in his notice at work and tell them his cousin had taken sick up north and he had to go see him. He'd be back when he could. Then he was to take some of his things, but not all, from his lodgings at Mrs Hoskins' boarding house and leave a few coins to cover his board. It wouldn't pay for him to vanish without reason.

Thankfully, Sunday evenings were quiet affairs since the bar was shut. After dinner, Sally packed up Maggie's and the girls' few belongings into carry bags – most of their possessions had been left in the cottage and no one wanted to go back there – and made the girls go to bed early. She promised she would wake them in plenty of time.

She and Jamie had agreed not to write to Brigid and tell her what they intended. They'd have to take the chance she was at the address they had for her, but they couldn't take the risk the postmaster would remember one of them posting a letter. The address would be a giveaway, should the police start asking questions. They had to disappear.

Even so, Sally couldn't leave Emily McKendrick without saying something. She didn't want to tell Emily about Carruthers and his threats. He was a good customer, and she deserved his patronage, but if she knew what he'd done, Emily would kick up a right fuss. This way they could all go on as normal.

In the end, Sally decided to leave a letter for her to find after they'd gone.

Dear Mrs Emily,

Yer've bin gud to me, and I thank ye for all yer've dun. I'm really sorry I've got to leave without a gud by or to tell ye why. Things hav gon bad for me and I need to go away where a man won't find me. Please don't tell any one. I will write one day when things get better. Yer've bin a gud friend. I won't forget you.

Sally

It would have to do. It wasn't the best letter, she knew, but she didn't have the strength to write what she really wanted to say.

Now all she could do was wait for the tide.

ᘓ ᘒ

"Mrs B, I don't know what to say." Brigid clutched the newspaper advertisement Beatrice Browne had given her, reading it through again, trying to grasp what her employer was offering.

In the weeks since Mrs Browne had told Brigid to take control of her life and not get caught up in the clash between her husband and her son, tempers had escalated. Frequent outbursts between the two men could be heard ringing around the house. Mr Browne wanted Philip to travel to England again to buy more stock. Philip had refused unless his father gave in and allowed him a say in the way the business was run, and the right to use the brand in his expansion ideas. They reached an impasse. But that didn't stop them yelling at one another at every opportunity. Beatrice was at her wits' end.

She decided to take action.

"You say yes, of course."

The advert was from a New Zealand paper. How Mrs Browne found it was anyone's guess, but a Mr A Munro, Draper of Auckland was quitting the business and offering the goodwill and stock at a ridiculously low price.

"I'd love the chance. But how? I've not got any money and wouldn't know how to go about all that business stuff."

"I do. Despite what my husband thinks, I know a few things about business. I know what women want, and how they want to dress themselves and their houses. I have money of my own – and ideas, too. Not that Philip would notice me either. But I can't be seen to interfere.

I'm prepared to purchase the building and the stock, if you are willing to go to New Zealand and ..."

"On my own?" Brigid was aghast at the notion.

"You came here on your own. Why should going to New Zealand be any different? It's only a few days by sea. I'd be sorry to lose you, but you'd be doing me a far larger service by going."

Beatrice had planned it all. She'd even talked to her bank manager. She had the means, the determination and the opportunity to bypass her husband's pig-headedness and meant to take it. "The shop is small, but it has passing foot traffic and rooms above it. All you have to do is give the customers what they want."

With accommodation sorted, stock on hand and an existing clientele, Beatrice couldn't see how they could go wrong.

Brigid wasn't so convinced. "How will I know what that is? I've never ..."

"Brigid. Stop arguing. You do know. You sew, design and make lace, and lots more besides, and you teach it, for goodness' sake! You've chosen fabrics and threads, and all the notions and trims. You know what is needed."

In spite of her reservations, Brigid had to admit her employer was right.

Mrs Browne continued without a pause: "All I'm asking you to do is open the doors in the morning, sit in the shop making your lace and let the customers come to you. When they come in, sell them what they want and write down the amount in a book."

Beatrice and Brigid talked about how she would price the stock, based on what they paid for retail stock here, and how she would replenish it.

"Hopefully, I'd have sorted those men out by then, and I'll allocate a share from the store here," answered Beatrice confidently.

Brigid thought of another problem. "What shall you call the shop? Not Harrison Browne, I'm guessing."

"Not yet, anyway. I can't openly oppose my husband, but Philip's ideas are the way of the future. Now, let me think ... how about 'Miss Brigid's, Ladies' Mercer'?"

Brigid was shocked and embarrassed. It would look like she was reaching above her station – she was a simple country girl, not a bigwig. "Oh, no, Mrs B, I couldn't. It's not mine, it's yours."

"Not until I get my way. I don't want to be seen to be involved. This way it looks like you up and left us for a chance in New Zealand that just happens to be exactly what Philip wanted but couldn't have. Don't worry, my dear. Your future will be secure."

Brigid raised her eyes heavenward. *What do You say, Lord? Is this Your Will for me? Every time I ask for a sign, Master Philip appears in some way. Now it's Mrs Browne offering me the same thing. Is my destiny tied to them?*

Beatrice continued to talk about the details, excited with her plans, while Brigid debated the alternatives.

She could stay on as Mrs Browne's housemaid. But that would put her in close proximity to Philip and, despite their initial fanciful affinity, nothing more could come of it. There couldn't be anything romantic between them, and Philip's father had made certain there wouldn't be any work for her in his store. She couldn't bear to be reminded of the lost possibilities every day.

She could leave and try to find other employment, but where? She didn't want to be a maid for the rest of her life, but since she couldn't imagine why anyone would employ her to be anything other than a maid, that was the least appealing choice.

Briefly, she considered Mrs Janet Walker, Brisbane's largest ladies' costumier, who employed over a hundred girls. Could she earn her living as a seamstress? While she knew her skills were as good as, if not better than, much of what she'd seen, why would Mrs Walker take on someone new when she employed so many already? She'd heard they worked long, long hours for little reward and even less recognition, so she'd certainly be no better off. And where would she live? And when would she make her lace?

She could go to Sally in Townsville, but Sally had promised to write with some ideas about what they could do together to earn a living, and hadn't. Brigid didn't know what that meant. Had Sally forgotten her? She didn't think so, they'd been close on the ship, but Sally had said little in the few letters she'd written, and nothing for some time.

But if she was thinking of leaving Mrs B, and Brisbane, then ... She could accept the offer, except it scared her to death.

Oh Lord, help me. I am riddled with doubt. What is Your plan? I keep asking for Your guidance, but everything that comes my way seems too lofty for a girl like me. I can't believe You want me to reach so high. Tell me what to do.

"Why me?" Brigid's voice broke and she couldn't explain her doubts.

The older woman looked intently at her, clearly weighing up her words. Brigid tried to fathom what she was thinking from her expression, but the longer her employer took to answer, the more frightened she became.

"Because you have special gifts. But you are also the most maddening of creatures. You are smart and talented but so meek and humble that I despair of you." Mrs Browne's exasperated tone of voice and manner sent Brigid's heart racing. "But you are also the most genuine person I've met in some time."

Is that really how Mrs Browne saw her? Brigid saw herself entirely differently, but she felt something shift inside her.

"Listen to me, Brigid. I have told you this before, but you obviously haven't listened properly. So listen now. I am not offering you anything I consider beyond your abilities. I would not ask you to join me in this venture if I thought you weren't worthy of it. When I say you have special gifts, I mean it. You have a way with people I find astonishing. You can't see it yourself because it's a natural part of you, but you draw people to you. You instinctively know how to help them feel better about themselves, but you seem incapable of feeling good about yourself. You are more skilled with a needle than I've ever seen – including the gowns from Mrs Walker's, which are superb – but your embroidery, your lacework and your crochet work is of superior standard. Why do you think I've never suggested you could work for her?"

Elated by the praise and amazed Mrs Browne had read her thoughts, Brigid stammered, "I ... I don't know. I didn't know you'd considered it."

"Well, I had. But I wanted to keep you for myself. Everyone admires the shawl you made. It is so soft it can be threaded through my ring, as you well know. Philip told me you could make something finer than the one I had – and you did. Mrs Walker asked me who had made the lace bodice on my gown, and who had embroidered the sleeves of my jacket. She wanted that girl. I refused to tell her."

"Truly?" Brigid struggled to believe what she was hearing.

"Yes. Truly. And you would have thought of it yourself if you had an ounce of ambition, but you are so lacking in conceit that you fail to see your own qualities. You are far too kind, generous and willing for your own good. That is what I see in you, and that is why I want you to be the face to my enterprise. Understood?"

Brigid had flushed every shade of pink to scarlet and back again during Beatrice's homily, but deep inside her the words started to feel real. Everything Mrs Browne had said was true, but she'd always felt it boastful to admit she was good at what she did and blasphemous to take advantage of the gifts she'd been given for her sole betterment.

Looking back over the last seven months since she had disembarked the ship with her head held high, determined to do something with her life, she had somehow failed to live up to her promises. In the aftermath of the flood, finding Philip was not who she thought he was, and feeling safe under Mrs Browne's patronage, she'd almost forgotten those promises and the goals she'd set herself. She'd allowed herself to slip back into the dutiful servant she and her family had been for generations. After all, she'd been born to it.

"In this country," continued Mrs Browne, "people make of their lives what they are capable of doing, not what they were born to."

There she goes again, reading my mind. Brigid opened and shut her mouth, not quite able to say anything as Mrs B mirrored Jamie's thinking. How are you, Jamie? Are you making the life you dreamt about? I wish I knew.

"Get that outdated notion out of your head, girl, and look forward. I believe you can make a success of this New Zealand idea. Now, what do you say?"

The warm glow she'd started to feel while Mrs Browne laid a bucket of accolades at her feet mushroomed. If Mrs B believed in her, then in duty, she should believe in herself too. "I think I'd like to try. That is – if it's what you want for me to do – then maybe ..."

Brigid wrung her hands in trepidation, but for the first time she truly believed the course of her life was about to change for the better.

"Pardon me, Mrs B," Mavis interrupted, as she entered the conservatory. She smiled when she saw the excited look on Brigid's face and the satisfied expression on her employer's. "Persuaded her then, did you?"

"Yes, Mavis. I believe I did."

"I'm that pleased for you, girl. Take what is offered, and honour the gift by being successful."

Brigid was astounded Mavis knew anything about the offer, but if Mrs B had confided in and discussed the matter with Mavis, it just went to show how much thought Mrs Browne had given the situation – and how serious she was.

Mavis started to leave.

"Did you want something, Mavis?"

"Oh, yes. Sorry, sometimes I'd forget my brain. There's some people at the door asking for Brigid. What would you like me to do with them?"

The arrival of Jamie, Sally, Maggie and the girls created quite a commotion. Mavis had shown them into the house through the front door and settled everyone around the table in the kitchen with tea and scones, and lemonade for the girls. Delighted at seeing one another again, friends and cousins talked over one another trying to get a word in.

But after the initial emotion had worn off, quietness descended over them. Sally and Jamie cautiously answered Brigid's questions but were plainly reluctant to give details about why they were here while Mavis and Mrs Browne were in the room.

Beatrice Browne was the first to make her exit, leaving Brigid with time to catch up with her visitors. "You'll have to excuse me, Brigid, I'll be going out now. I have some charity work to do. There are still poor souls in need of help after the flood. You are welcome to entertain your guests as long as you wish, and they are welcome to stay for the evening meal."

"Thank you, Mrs Browne." Brigid started to bob a curtsy until she caught the woman's eye and refrained.

Mavis took the hint. "Brigid, if you don't mind, I'll leave you to get dinner started. I've got errands to run, so I must be away now." She bustled out of the room to collect her hat and coat, and on her return picked up a basket and headed out the kitchen door. "Cheery bye. Enjoy your company."

Brigid was beside herself with joy at seeing those who mattered to her most on this far side of the world. Even Maggie – for all her faults and the separation from Jamie that Brigid blamed on her – but she seemed quieter and more remote than she remembered. "Are you well, Maggie? I hope that cousin of mine is treating you proper."

233

"I'm well enough. Jamie's been a great strength to me."

"Aye, well. I'm glad to hear it. That I am."

Brigid noticed how much the girls looked to Jamie, and even to Sally, for approval to take food, or answer a question, rather than to their aunt. They were far more subdued than they had been on the journey, but then much had happened to her in the last seven months, and she suspected a great deal had occurred to change them too. She would ask in time, but for the moment knowing Jamie could comfort them was both a surprise and a blessing.

"Aye, Breeda. Townsville didn't offer the chances I'd hoped for, and since Michael was still against me, he and Maggie ... well, ah ... let's say they didn't live comfortably together. We hoped maybe you could help us settle here in Brisbane, near you. Or if you know of work elsewhere, I'd be happy to look. Can ye help us, our Breeda?"

The looks that passed between Jamie and Maggie, and Jamie and Sally, were not lost on Brigid. Her heart cried out. Something was amiss. "I'll ask around, Jamie, that I will. But as you can see, I live in and can't offer you a place right now. Mrs Browne is a good woman. And generous. I'll tell you all about it when the time's right, but for now, let's see what she can suggest as a place for you to stay in the meantime – until you find your feet. She knows lots of people, does Mrs Browne. I'll ask as soon as she comes home."

Their conversation was genial but superficial. Each in their own way was assessing the other, and re-establishing the rapport they'd once had.

Listening to the talk, Brigid wondered where they were headed. They all wanted to believe Australia would be a good move and the living easier, but she wasn't so sure the reality was stacking up for Jamie and Sally.

As soon as Brigid started preparing the vegetables for dinner, the girls jumped to their feet, eager to help. Maggie shook herself out of her little world and quietly went to help as well. While busy hands made light work of the job, it soon became clear that busy hands also reduced the tension, and talk became easier.

"I'm right glad to see you again, our Breeda," Jamie said at the same time as Sally spoke.

"Brigid, you've no idea how frightened I've been."

"I've missed you," finished Jamie, and the warmth in his voice brought a lump to her throat, but Sally made it worse.

"I need your help," she whispered.

An awkward laugh followed while Brigid looked at the two of them. They had secrets, these two. For a moment, she felt left out but only briefly. They would tell her in their own good time. That's why they were here.

She wiped her hands dry and sat down again, leaving the girls and Maggie to finish.

"Tell me what's happened," urged Brigid.

Sally took her hands and softly rubbed her thumbs across Brigid's knuckles. "Here was I thinking I had my future planned, but it all fell apart," said Sally. "I got it wrong, Brigid. I hate to admit it, and it's been a long time since I got it so wrong, but there it is. There's a man determined to do me harm. I have to get away."

"Me too, Bree. Michael's dead and the police are asking questions."

Whatever Brigid had been expecting, nothing like that had entered her head.

Word by word, sentence by sentence, Brigid listened to their tale – sensing more could be said, but not in front of the children. Knowing that little ears took everything in, Brigid suspected Laura knew a lot more than anyone gave her credit for.

She could hardly believe her own ears, but she understood. Not only was it possible, it had happened, and they were scared. It put all Brigid's fears into perspective. In comparison, her doubts and insecurities were shallow and internal. Theirs were real and external – and beyond their control.

Within minutes of Mrs Browne's return, messages had been sent and accommodation arranged for Sally, Maggie and the girls. Jamie was offered quarters in the stable if he was prepared to rough it for a few days.

Around the kitchen table over the evening meal a sense of togetherness cloaked them, and a bond was created that Brigid hoped would never be broken again.

Thank You, Lord. You answered my prayers.

There were short-term plans to be put in place, but looking ahead, Brigid was no longer in doubt about what her purpose was or what she would do. They needed a haven to keep them safe and someone to care for them until they healed.

She would gather her clan around her and take them to New Zealand.

⋈　⋊

Brisbane
23rd July 1887

"I've sent her to New Zealand."

"What? Mother! How could you?"

"Now Philip, stop behaving like a two-year-old. You

236

will never win your father's approval with that attitude. Sit down."

"But ..." Philip was lost for words. With his insides in such turmoil, he couldn't even stand still, let alone sit, nor could he gather his wits to put together a coherent argument. All he wanted to do was roar. He could almost understand why women resorted to tears when they couldn't control their feelings. He was close to them himself.

"I know this has come as a shock to you," continued his mother, "but you must see it was the only option – and an unmissable opportunity."

"But the idea was mine. I found Brigid. I could have changed the face of Harrison Browne and dragged it into the present. Now you've taken all that away from me."

His mother took a sip of tea from her favourite tea service elegantly laid out on the table by the conservatory window. She offered him a plate of biscuits. He shook his head.

"No, Philip. I haven't. What I've done is establish a branch in New Zealand away from your father's control, and when he comes to term with your ideas – and he will in time – 'Miss Brigid's' is already a viable business. Isn't that what you wanted?"

A niggle in the back of his mind admitted his mother was right, but to do it without consulting him was too much to take. "Why couldn't you talk to me about it first?"

The exasperated sigh that escaped his mother's lips sent him straight back to his childhood. "Be reasonable, Philip. If I'd told you what I wanted to do, your father would have found out – because you would have bragged to him. You know you would, just to show him up – and then what?"

Damn it. He punched his fist into the other hand. "He would have stopped it."

"I know your father better than you. He is a proud man. Proud of his achievements, and so he should be, given the way life began for him in this country, but he is too old to change his ways. You handled it wrong from the start. You challenged him, and like a creature protecting his territory, he fought back."

Philip sat down, calming himself with deep breaths.

His mother refreshed her tea and poured one for him.

"What should I do then? I told you Sam is still prepared to back me, but only with the store's brand." He took a sip of tea and carefully placed the cup back on its saucer, afraid he would break it with his ill humour.

"Be patient. The flood was a major setback, and your father is still reeling from its impact. He nearly lost everything. And he has to cope with the staff who lost people or homes or possessions and have their own problems. You can't expect him to hand over all he has worked for and let you try new ways when he is trying to save what he has. One step at a time, Philip. Make him think he is still the kingpin, and he'll allow 'the boy', as he often calls you, to test the waters soon enough."

Philip nearly exploded with resentment. "Boy! I'm not his lackey. Even though he treats me like one."

How could his mother sit there so calmly and serenely, with that knowing smile pleating the side of her mouth, when his life was falling apart?

"Your father has run a successful business for forty years. Did you ever think that by sending you to England he was teaching you the fundamentals of how to run that business?"

Philip stretched his legs out in front of him, crossed his feet and shoved his hands in his pockets. "I hate those trips. They are tiresome and it's all the same. I'm not learning anything new; I'm just following orders."

"For now, maybe." Beatrice Browne tutted and tapped him on the knee. "Stop being petulant and sit up properly." Philip did as he was told, picked up a biscuit to chew on, and swallowed his tea. "Of course he wants his son to take over the company. But he wants you to work your way to the top knowing it inside out. Branching out now is beyond him."

He considered what his mother had said. She could be right for now, and as long as he mastered Brigid in the end, that was all that mattered.

"How did you get away with it?"

A calculating smile reached her eyes. "I haven't told him."

He roared with laughter, his bad mood dissipating in one swoop. He might win his battle after all.

PART THREE

New Zealand

12

New Beginnings

Auckland
Friday, 29th July 1887

The group of six weary travellers stood outside the wooden building jammed between two much taller stone buildings halfway up Queen Street. Here lay their future, but the frontage was far more timeworn than anyone expected. The air was chilly after Brisbane, and the light rain dampened their spirits even further.

Sally spoke first. "I bet your Mrs Browne didn't know what state the place was in. Not much to look at, is it?"

Secretly, Brigid agreed, but she had to think of something good to say, and quickly. Tired, and still catching her breath after the whirlwind preparations and departure, Brigid knew her charges were more exhausted by their even longer ordeal, than she.

"Maybe not." Brigid jangled the keys they'd collected from the agents' office. "But we're here now, and this is home. So we have to make the best of it. We've known worse back in Ireland, haven't we, Jamie me boy?"

"That we have." Jamie let his eyes wander over the crooked boards above the verandah, a lopsided upper window and the unpainted timber. "That we have. But at least with the front doors being set back like that, you've got grand front windows. Aye, nothing a hammer and a few nails and a lick of whitewash won't fix, though I've not seen a building like it."

Buoyed by Jamie's apparent confidence, Brigid strode forward and unlocked the door. The smell of dust and decay made her cough as she stepped across the threshold. *No wonder the business failed! Oh, dear Lord.*

Brigid was thankful Mrs Browne had not been in the least put out by the extra cost for Brigid's newfound family to travel with her.

"In fact, my dear," said Mrs Browne, "I think it will be an advantage and a blessing." Even knowing Jamie was the only true family member, everyone accepted the six of them couldn't be separated: Jamie would never leave Maggie, Laura and Jane needed Sally, and Sally needed Brigid. Now it seemed, she'd need *them* – all of them.

"This place hasn't seen daylight for a long time," muttered Sally as they toured the ground floor.

"Aye, but it's not damp." Jamie sniffed the air. "That's a good thing."

Laura ran her fingers over the leadlight pattern framing each window with an arch. "The windows are pretty."

Brigid eyed the shelves on either side behind the counters, still stacked with fabrics, with reluctant approval; at least they had dust covers. She was more pleased to see the small drawers for the notions, as well as the glass-topped display drawers for larger items. The deeper into the store they walked, the gloomier it became.

Brigid squinted into the shadows. "We'll need to find some lamps before we can see everything properly, that we will."

"Aye. We will." Sally stuck her head into a large storage cupboard under the narrow staircase in the middle of the building and sneezed. "There's boxes of something in here, but it's too dark to see."

To one side, an anteroom with a grimy window overlooked the backyard. Brigid found a treasure hidden in the corner, buried under piles of discarded junk. "Look. There's a treadle sewing machine in here under everything."

Sally watched as Maggie looked inside the Shacklock coal range, opened cupboards and drawers, and peered into the scullery on the other side. "Kitchen's not bad, and it's big enough. Maggie seems at home."

Jamie prised the back door open and investigated the lean-to, woodshed and backyard. "There's a good rain barrel that's full, and I've seen worse outhouses."

Back inside, Jamie led the way up the creaky staircase, testing each tread as the others followed him in single file. The top of the stairs opened out into a living room running the length of the building with a window at either end. Jamie had to tilt his head to one side as he edged his way along the passage next to the stair banister until he could get to the middle where the roof beams were higher. Two armchairs, a table and four chairs, a couple of stools and a dresser filled the space towards the front.

By now Jane was shivering. "Can we light the fire?" She sat in front of the small wood stove built into the brick chimney breast from the kitchen below and looked up at Jamie.

"Soon, but I'd better check it first." Jamie put his hand reassuringly on the girl's shoulder. "It'll probably need a clean."

"The sooner the better, then. It's right chilly," said Sally, leaving Jamie to open the stove door and prod around with the poker.

Under the lower part of the high-pitched roof, on either side of the larger room, were two more rooms. The ones at the front were obviously bedrooms. Each had a sash window and held a small, double-sized wire-framed bed, wardrobe and washstand. One of the two rooms at the back leading off the narrow passageway had been used as a sort of office. Boxes, folders and papers lay everywhere. The other was another storeroom. They were small, but both had a window.

Brigid sighed with relief. "Looks like there is plenty of room for us all anyway, if we make a few changes."

"Are we really going to stay here?" asked Laura, putting her hand over her mouth and nose. Behind her, Jane sneezed.

Dust and cobwebs coated everything, but apart from that, the place seemed sound. Mr Munro, whoever he was, had abandoned the store, leaving behind furniture and chattels and the trappings of a drapery business not well managed.

Taking off her coat, the ever-silent Maggie, her voice croaky from lack of use, answered Laura. "There's nothing a bucket of hot water and some hard work won't fix, girl. Let's get started."

Brigid looked at her in amazement. Of all the people she'd come across in her travels, Maggie would have been the last one she thought willing to tackle what looked like an almost insurmountable task. The chameleon Maggie she'd distrusted on the ship was still as changeable as ever.

"Like Maggie says, Laura, once we clean the place up, it'll look different. Today's Friday. We have three days to get this place clean and ready for business. What say you – shall we see what we can do with it?"

At nine o'clock on Monday morning, Brigid opened the door to the shop and stepped outside onto the footpath. She looked up at their handiwork, framed by weak sunshine and an almost cloudless blue sky.

"I thank you from the bottom of my heart, our Jamie. Aye, but the place looks grand all washed white."

Jamie looked as if he'd painted himself as well, but the satisfied grin he wore showed how pleased he was with the result. "Aye, well. 'Tis only one coat, but I made it up thick and strong. It'll have to be done again afore long to make it last. But aye, it looks grand."

Inside, the three women had cleaned the place from top to bottom.

Maggie excelled herself, directing the work methodically, with a bucket of hot water constantly in her hands. She washed and scrubbed, boiled all the linen and towels, and somehow cobbled together meals for them all.

As soon as one room was clean enough, Jamie whitewashed the walls with a large brush. Beds were made, furniture and rugs beaten, and the girls helped by sweeping, and washing anything that needed it in the large butler's sink.

By Sunday evening, only the anteroom still required attention and a whitewash. Despite the long hours and the hard work, they felt optimistic for the first time in a long while. One or other of them often hummed a tune, the girls' laughter came easily, and Brigid hoped the Maggie she'd seen in the last three days would replace the silent, morose Maggie of before – the one Jamie and Sally had told her about.

In between their upstairs renovations, Sally helped Brigid clean the shelves and sort the bolts of fabrics, removing the dust sheets and restacking them. She then set about displaying the finished work Brigid had brought over in her trunk, alongside extra supplies of fabrics and threads packed in another trunk from Mrs B. If her lacework was to be a draw card, Brigid needed to have all her tools at her fingertips.

"Sally, come join us," said Brigid as her friend appeared in the doorway. Brigid linked her arm through Sally's as the three of them stood side by side looking at the window display. "It's beautiful. You have such a flair for display. I never knew. "

"Neither did I," laughed Sally. "But when I started to lay things out, ideas just came to me."

"Well, I think it's grand. It'll be sure to stop the ladies as they pass to take a look. And, hopefully, come inside and buy something."

"Yes. Lots of somethings," added Sally.

Mrs Browne had warned that while she had the capital to make the purchase and meet other necessary set-up costs, she would not be able to supplement Brigid's income. She didn't want Mr Browne finding out about her undertaking before she was ready to tell him. The shop would have to stand alone.

Brigid would worry about all that later. Right now, she was elated with their achievements. "Mrs Browne said she'd arranged for a signwriter to call and put up the new signage. When that's finished, 'Miss Brigid's' will definitely be open for business."

A week passed, then a month and another. Brigid's delight with the elaborate signage, which could be seen from the other side of the street, stayed with her. She could barely take the smile off her face. Sally changed one of the window displays each day, putting together fabrics and colours not normally associated with each other.

In the mornings, Brigid sat in her chair near the window and set her fingers in motion. Thread flashed back and forth in a blur as she crocheted her traditional designs or tackled the slower-paced Carrickmacross lace. After applying the organdie to the net backing, she painstakingly cut away the net within the design to create the openwork pattern. Sometimes she did fine tatting, other times, Kenmare needlepoint lace.

A steady stream of ladies oohing and aahing over the new window displays filled the shop, and many stopped simply to watch Brigid's mastery.

"Can I tempt you with a few yards of this elegant satin, or maybe this lighter weight cotton?" coaxed Sally, taking advantage of the moment. "With summer only a matter of weeks away, maybe now is the time to consider a new dress?"

Sometimes they were so busy Brigid was forced to put aside her lacework and serve the customers. Trade was brisk, and as their customer list grew, so did her confidence.

It had come as a bit of a shock when she'd walked up the other end of Queen Street to discover Smith & Caughey, Drapers and Clothiers were doing a roaring trade. But she was pleased to see their stock was different to hers. They had a range of ready-to-put-on clothing, and Brigid had no intention of getting into millinery or men's tailoring. Still, her hopes remained high that there would be room for her little shop too.

Every month Brigid reported how well they were doing. Mrs Browne was delighted to see her plans come to fruition.

"I will come and visit you. I promise," she wrote. "I just need to pick my time. The town appears to have recovered from the flood, and new stock is arriving with each ship, but I fear business is not picking up the way Mr Browne had hoped. I'm comforted that at least he and Philip seem a little more reconciled, for now."

At the mention of Philip's name, a wave of loss coursed through her. She remembered the Philip of the ship: chivalrous, charming, exciting, as opposed to the Philip in Brisbane: a dreamer, disheartened, insecure and angry. For a short while, she'd allowed herself to believe in the impossible – a future with Philip – but within a short time it became obvious such a future would never have worked. Still, she yearned for the man who had sparked her ambition.

More difficult to believe was the quirk of fate that took her to the Browne household in the first place, knowing she wouldn't be where she was now if not for her benefactor. She would miss the people from Spring Hill this Christmas. Mavis had been her rock, helping her transition and learn about her new country, and they had parted tearfully. Here in Auckland, she was the cornerstone of her little family. Sometimes it scared her.

If she stopped to think about it, a part of her still wanted a home that was hers, a man to love and children of her own, but time was passing – she'd be nineteen soon and had responsibilities no man would want to take on. Still, she was content.

More than content – she was happy.

The feeling had come slowly, but her unusual family had blended together better than she had hoped. As they continued shaping the store and living quarters to their liking, life settled into a pattern.

Laura and Jane blossomed at the school at the top of Wellesley Street East, opposite Albert Park, a short distance up the hill behind them. They still looked to Jamie first for approval, then Sally, but increasingly they were turning to her. Especially since she'd started to teach them to sew and crochet. Both girls showed ability, particularly Laura.

Maggie had claimed the kitchen as her domain and seemed content in the role of housekeeper and cook looking after their material needs. Although she was still often quiet and aloof, she no longer sat staring at walls, lost in her own world.

Jamie – she wasn't sure about Jamie. He wasn't the same cousin she remembered from back home, or the one who'd jumped on a cargo net to chase Maggie. He had plenty of male companionship and went off cheerfully to whatever work was on offer, and which seemed to change every week. But he also stayed out late sometimes and was starting to drink heavily again.

Sally loved everything about the shop, which had come as a surprise to Brigid. Sally had been an opportunist, taking what chances were necessary to earn a living, and she needed to be around people. The shop had allowed a latent talent to flourish, and her head for numbers was a great help.

Yes, Brigid was happy. Auckland was a different town to Brisbane, smaller, with a beautiful harbour – once you passed the foul-smelling stream oozing from the pipes at the foot of Queen Street – and the people were friendlier. Nobody seemed concerned with where you came from, only what you were doing. She liked a society that judged people on their ability.

The climate was kinder too. The sun shone most days, but not nearly so hot, and she'd thrived in the freshness of the spring winds and rain. Either she, Maggie or Sally would walk with the girls through the park to school in the mornings. Not that they needed to, and often the girls objected, but the women enjoyed the park. The trees offered shade and a pleasant place to walk, to meet and greet people and admire the fountain. Everything appeared greener and brighter than in Brisbane, and the park became a haven, when time permitted.

Her biggest concern was still Jamie – and Maggie. Where was it all leading?

Still, now wasn't the time to worry about that, she chided herself. There were more important things to think about: the new range of lacework still to be made, expanding her clientele, and where her next shipment of fabric and threads was coming from.

And Christmas. They had to celebrate Christmas – even if everything was all upside down in the middle of summer, in this topsy-turvy world.

Life was good.

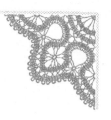

13

Double Jeopardy

Saturday, 10th December 1887

Jamie kicked the rubbish bin as he staggered past, a bottle swinging from his hand. A small rebellion when likened to the fights he usually got into, but helpful nevertheless. Where was this better life he was supposed to be coming to? He'd thought he'd found it on the ship. He thought he'd found his future in Maggie, the tall, brown-haired girl from the north who had captured his heart, but so far it hadn't been much of a new life. He couldn't even find decent work.

He and Maggie still took evening walks, but less frequently, and all the fire had gone out of her since ... well, since that day. Michael deserved what he got, but even in death he had succeeded in destroying her life, and Jamie's with it. They'd had dreams, the two of them – bold dreams with goals he had to measure up to – but none of it mattered any more. It seemed as if Maggie had accepted a lesser place in life as punishment for what she'd done.

"I'm at ease here, tending for Brigid and the girls, I am. And I do still need you, Jamie, but not like before.

253

I need your strength to know I did right – for the girls. Whatever happens to me now doesn't matter. But the girls ..." She drifted off to her inner world again, leaving Jamie bereft. Nothing he said made any difference.

His fear of being followed had abated as time passed, but with Maggie as a constant reminder of what could have been, he was eaten up with doubts. He still worried that some clue might lead the police to them, even though there were no names on any passenger lists coming to New Zealand. But what if they did find them? Then what?

He stared up at the strange night sky, wishing for something worthwhile to cling to. Twelve months to the day since he'd jumped ship, full of hope, and now he felt as though he was back in Ireland twelve months before that, knowing life was leading him nowhere. He felt trapped.

Oh, for sure, he had Brigid, whom he adored, and the girls reminded him of his little sisters and cousins, but a man needed more than cousins and sisters to sustain him. A man needed a woman.

Slowly, he'd come to the realisation that he hated city life. He hated the routine. He hated the hard surfaces, the noise, and expectations. He was a country person. It had taken a journey of many thousands of miles and many months for him to come to the decision that the good parts of Ireland – clean fresh air, animals, crops and a family – were what he wanted here. He didn't want the hardships and poverty that had gone with it, people starving and the English landlords taking everything – that's why he'd left. He wanted a just life where hard work brought wellbeing and pride.

A man needed his pride.

Sitting around the table after dinner one evening later that week, with the girls playing happily at some game, the adults chatted amiably.

Christmas, and how they would celebrate this year, was high on the agenda.

"I can make us a spiced beef roast, just like from home," offered Maggie quietly.

Laura jumped up and down and clapped her hands. "Can we make cards to give our friends at school?"

"Aye. We can do that." Stirrings of gaiety tickled Brigid's insides. "We can decorate the room too. And I'll teach you to make paper chains. Jamie, can you find us some greenery to use instead of the holly we had at home? Oh, and we must light a candle in the window on Christmas Eve to guide Mary and Jesus to us."

Jamie wasn't the slightest bit interested in any celebrations. "Ach, don't waste your money. I tell you, Brigid, t'ings is not looking good. I hear about men being put out of work for the slightest of notions. And there's endless talk about the recession, and it's getting worse. Folks are worried."

While Brisbane had been having a building boom in the few years before Brigid and the others arrived, it seemed New Zealand had not enjoyed the same prosperity.

"I wonder if Mrs Browne knew about the slowdown?" asked Sally.

Jamie shook his head. "I doubt it. She wouldn't have risked her money if she had."

Brigid wanted nothing to dampen her spirits. "We're doing well enough for now, so don't fret, Jamie. We'll just have to come up with some other ideas to attract customers. I am determined to make a go of it. I like it here, and I want to stay."

"Me too," said Sally.

Jamie remained silent.

He'd made up his mind. He was leaving – as soon as the New Year was in. He'd go. Somewhere. Anywhere. He couldn't stand the guilt any longer.

14

Make or Break

Monday, 2nd April 1888

"Something's not adding up," Sally said to Brigid, after totting up the takings. "We should be doing better than this, what with all the interest you've created. There's lots of customers, and word is getting around. I can tell, 'cos I know the regulars and can spot the new ones. But they're spending less each time they come in."

"But we've been doing so well," said Brigid. "Surely you must be mistaken?"

"Nay lass, I wish I were." The small shipment Mrs Browne sent across had met the Christmas market, but Sally was aware of how low the stock was getting again. "And there's more on tick than you realise."

Sally had never had to keep books before as she'd been able to account for her card winnings and tips in her head. Her newfound ability with figures surprised them all, including herself, and keeping a ledger had come naturally to her. But she was worried. Brigid had said she needed a lot more for the winter season coming up. "We'll have to ask people to pay their accounts sooner, that's all."

Brigid bit her lip. "Is that a good idea?"

Sally knew Mrs B had been guarded about how much more stock she could provide. Mr Browne was asking too many questions and ongoing shipments would be difficult. The matter between Philip and Mr Browne had still not been resolved either, and until Mr Browne could be persuaded around to their way of thinking, she suggested it would be better if Brigid found a local source.

To do that, they needed money.

"I wish I didn't have to do this to you, hen," said Sally. "You've enough worries on your plate."

The household was still reeling from the shock of Jamie leaving. Sally had been through some terrible days, but that day was one to match them all.

As the months passed without any sinister knock at the door, Sally began to believe she had escaped the clutches of that Carruthers maniac, and convinced herself the police in New Zealand would have no interest in old events in Townsville. She thought the fear had gone, but it hadn't. She was tied to Jamie and Maggie in ways she couldn't break, whether she liked it or not.

Brigid had pleaded with Jamie to stay, distraught at the notion she had failed him – that she would lose him again – and alarmed at the heartache he was inflicting on them all.

But the look in the girls' eyes was what tore at Sally's heart. She could have killed him herself for the pain he was causing them, let alone what he was doing to the rest of them. She didn't think she would ever forgive him for that, nor for abandoning Brigid and leaving her to pick up the pieces of his failure. But he wasn't listening.

Maggie had retreated further into herself, if that were at all possible, although no one could fault her work. She maintained the house to an exacting standard, but the girls turned to Brigid for comfort. Brigid was the one who talked with them, played with them, taught them.

Laura's eleventh birthday in February had been a solemn affair, even with Brigid's frantic attempts to make the girls laugh. Only after, had Sally found out Brigid's birthday had passed without anyone noticing.

Brigid deserved better.

Sally had stacked some savings away, and Maggie was a canny one with the household budget, but it wouldn't last long if the takings dropped. Most of their clients were working girls and wives. What they needed was for upper-class ladies to buy from them.

"We're going to need credit from somewhere. What happened with that last bloke after you talked with him?"

Brigid had approached a local importer, but he'd been less than helpful. "Don't come to me asking for credit. If you bring cash, I'll sell you goods to match, but I'm not dealing with a chit of a girl who knows nothing about business."

Sally had done her best to reassure Brigid she was a knowledgeable merchant on the brink of great things but never mind what she said, sometimes the unassuming Brigid of old returned.

"I couldn't go back there. He was right. I don't know anything about running a store."

"Maybe not, but you're learning – we both are. For goodness' sake, trust your gut. You've come a long way. You know more than I ever realised about fabrics and threads, and you've learnt all the proper words. I've got the head for figures, and you've got the skills. What more do we need?"

Sally knew the answer to that – a man. Ridiculous as it seemed, a man would never encounter the problems Brigid was having. Despite the burgeoning women's suffrage movement, which was trying to get a bill through parliament to allow women to vote, men still ruled the world, and especially the world of money.

Sally paid little heed to those women. They were against alcohol of any form or quantity, and Sally still liked her tot of gin now and then. But, if it stopped men like Jamie doing dumb things, she supposed they had a point.

She sighed. She didn't miss the falseness of deference and coquetry, knowing what men were capable of, but an all-female house was a curse sometimes. She'd known some mighty strong women who'd been successful in what they'd done – Emily McKendrick and Beatrice Browne were two such women, but both had a man with money behind them. After working with Emily and Brigid, she knew which she preferred.

"I tell you what. I'll go see the bank manager. If I take along the figures and show him what we've been doing so far, and outline our plans ..."

"What plans?" said Brigid. "None of our plans have quite worked the way we wanted, have they?"

"For pity's sake, girl. What's with all this gloom? You've done a grand job. Times are tough and you have to spend money to make money. I learnt that in the back alleys and at the card games. Bluff, girl. Bluff."

The Sally who emerged from the shop a few days later was the Sally who had fronted up to the bar in the Queens Hotel in Townsville. Dressed in her best finery and exuding confidence, she was determined to achieve her goal. Brigid deserved it; the girls needed it; and Maggie – well, she didn't really care about her, but Maggie wasn't going anywhere. Poor Brigid, lumbered with that encumbrance. And Sally had to admit this was as much for her as for anyone else. Her future rested on Brigid's success.

"Mr Fortesque," trilled Sally, extending her hand. She had checked all the banks, their reputations and their managers. She chose one of the longest standing, whose manager was reputed to be an educated and progressive man, and whose wife was known in the right social circles. "I'm so grateful you could see me."

Mr Fortesque led her into his office and showed her a seat. "Now, Miss ... um," he checked the papers before him, "Forsythe. How can I help you?"

"It's not what you can do for me, exactly, but what I can offer you. I believe I can offer your bank an opportunity too good to miss."

A flicker of a smile crinkled his face. He folded his hands on the desk and leant forward. "And how are you going to do that?"

Sally settled to her story. "'Miss Brigid's Ladies Mercer' is the newest enterprise in town. In a matter of a few months, it has grown beyond all expectations, and we wish to expand. To do that we need to employ more people and purchase more stock. And better still, from an investment point of view, by doing that we will gain prominence by dressing the notable ladies of Auckland in the finest and latest fashions. Would that not gladden your wife's heart, Mr Fortesque?"

Sally fluttered her eyelids and looked at him impishly. "You do have a wife, Mr Fortesque, don't you? After all, I feel sure a man as charming and astute as yourself would have been snatched up long ago."

He fluffed and puffed for a moment and adjusted his necktie. "Mrs Fortesque would indeed wish to be considered the best-dressed lady about town, but she already has a dressmaker."

"I'm sure she has, and I'm sure the lady in question is capable, but only a select few have had the privilege of applying Miss Brigid's accomplishments to their benefit. And it's not the making of the gown that makes the difference, it's the design and accoutrements."

Brigid had learnt that word from Mrs Browne, and Sally had practised it over and over to make sure she said it correctly, hoping to sound knowledgeable.

"I'll need more information than simply your opinion, of course. I'll need figures."

"Of course." Sally reached into her handbag, removed a set of papers and handed them across the desk. "I think you'll find these are what you want."

"How did you do it?" Brigid grasped Sally's arm to steady herself.

"This time, apart from a bit of flattery, I told the truth. I told him your plans, I gave him my figures, and he decided to help us."

Brigid stared in disbelief at the bank contract in front of her. She'd never known such money existed, and it almost scared her into refusing it.

"Seems his daughter, who is not one of the best dressed of ladies around town, is heavily involved with the suffragettes. She's pushing for women's rights, and people acknowledging women are intelligent, talented and – um, now what was the other word he said ... courageous, that's it – and deserving of equal opportunities."

"He said that?"

Brigid looked at her disbelievingly, knowing Sally was capable of making a rotten potato sound edible when she wanted to.

"Well. No. He didn't exactly. He said that's what these suffragettes want, and since his daughter is so convincing and my figures backed up our expectations, he believed 'Miss Brigid's' worthy of support."

But Mr Fortesque's support came with conditions, and a warning associated with several factors: the country had been in an economic depression for some time, fewer people were arriving, and many more were leaving to go to Australia; and the wool industry had virtually dropped out of existence.

"I can't remember all he said now," said Sally, "but he reckons people are struggling. Wages are down, and customs duties are up, thanks to Atkinson's new government. He says too many women work in terrible sweatshop conditions, to make ends meet. And he won't support a business that uses sweat labour.

"But he says change is coming. He thinks the refrigerated meat and dairy industry will bring more trade in the long term. And the Liberals are making headway – they'll be the government at the next election, he reckons, and we are to mark his words. He likes it that the unions are gaining strength and helping to protect workers, and he thinks these suffragettes have a point.

"The next twelve months aren't going to be easy, hen. We'll have to work hard and do some careful budgeting. But we got the money!"

Mr Fortesque also wanted to inspect the books each month, the figures needed to show growth – and would Miss Brigid kindly invite Mrs Fortesque to view her wares.

Brigid listened to the warnings and conditions with mixed feelings. "But from what you told me, we're showing a loss. Why would he expect growth?"

Bother. She'd hoped Brigid wouldn't notice. "I told him," she admitted. "I embroidered the figures a bit."

"You did what?" Brigid thrust the papers towards Sally. "Take them back. Go on, go back to him and tell him I can't meet his conditions. I can't tell lies, Sally. I can't."

"Oh, stop being a fusspot. I only altered them a little bit – just to get us started. Do you want new fabrics and stuff or not? Pander to his dear old Mrs and word will get around, and before you know it, business will have picked up and my figures will be telling the truth anyway."

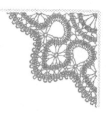

15

Making an Impression

Wednesday, 10th October 1888

"Sally. Sally, come quickly." Brigid scanned the letter as fast as she could, then reread it more slowly.

"What is it? What's the matter?" Sally hurried into the newly refurbished anteroom where Brigid was working. "You sound upset."

"I am that." Brigid passed the letter to her friend. "There's been a fire – a huge one." Tears welled as she imagined the scene. "It's destroyed the Harrison Browne Drapery store, it has."

Sally put her arm around Brigid's shoulder, as she wiped away a tear. "What? Oh, that's terrible news."

"Mrs B says her husband has had a stroke and is confined to his bed. Master Philip has taken over the clean-up, but she says the losses are huge. Between the floods last year and now this, she doesn't think Harrison Browne's will recover. I hope that doesn't mean bad news for us here."

But what would she do without Mrs Browne as her guiding hand? She hoped Philip wouldn't try to take it all away from her.

265

"Don't worry. Surely it can't be that bad. You always said young Mr Harrison-Browne would modernise the place as soon as his father would let him. Looks like his poor old dad has no option now, and the young man will have his chance."

Would this mean Philip coming back into her life? She didn't know how she felt about that possibility. She had put him completely out of her mind – most of the time. Especially since she'd met ... no, she mustn't think about *him* right now.

"Perhaps you're right. You were right about this place."

Over the last six months, 'Miss Brigid's' had exceeded the growth expectations Sally had predicted. Delighted that Mrs Fortesque had accepted her invitation, their first step had been to redecorate the anteroom and turn it into a comfortable, if not quite elegant salon in which to greet her estimable guest. On the day, Brigid was even more delighted her slim-built attractive customer was as stylish as she'd hoped.

Brigid eagerly indulged her visitor with tea and Maggie's best baking. Sally had rushed to and fro bringing examples of laces, trims and fabrics from the shop, while Brigid demonstrated her craft and explained her ideas. "Your costume is beautifully made and looks grand on you."

Mrs Fortesque simpered at Brigid's compliment.

"And I don't plan to compete with your seamstress, I want to add to her work – with lacework made just for you. I'm sure a woman of taste, such as yourself, likes to be distinctive."

Brigid's assessment had been correct, and she was thankful to Mrs Browne, yet again, for teaching her better words to use. A smile lit the face of her client.

"I've noticed there is a current trend to mass production, and I'm not happy seeing fabrics in shop windows the same as those my dressmaker is offering."

Perfect, thought Brigid, in full agreement, taking note to look into where to get better quality fabrics than those she'd found in the shop when they arrived.

"I know I could be a dressmaker if I wanted to. But I t'ink I can give people better service through my traditional lacework. Each piece I make is unique to its owner. Don't you agree?"

Lacemaking took time, and in Ireland the girls received little for their efforts since machine-made lace was quicker and cheaper to make, and much more profitable. It undermined the market for the genuine article, and it had taken Brigid a long time to accept that her lace was not only beautiful but also rare and valuable.

A nod from her visitor encouraged Brigid to keep talking. She picked up a roll of lace Sally had left on the table for her. "Like this machine lace, here. It comes to me by the yard, it does. And, aye, I can sell it cheaply to anyone with the skills to sew it onto a blouse or jacket. But you'll find similar laces at your dressmaker's. You might even see a sales girl, or a secretary, or a housewife, wearing the same lace you have on your visiting and evening gowns. I can guarantee every piece of my lace is a one-off that no one else has. I'm sure you would prefer that."

By the end of the afternoon, Mrs Fortesque had agreed to order several pieces of lace to enhance dress designs Brigid had sketched, along with others seen in the fashion catalogues Mrs Browne had ordered from London and Paris to be sent to her.

But, more importantly, Mrs Fortesque intended to tell all her friends and advise her dressmaker that, from now on, all the materials required for her gowns were to be purchased through 'Miss Brigid's'.

The tide had turned that day, in more ways than one.

The bell over the door tinkled. Sally got up to answer it but stopped when a voice called out.

"Are you there, Brigid? I've got some new samples to show ye."

Still flustered by the news of the fire, Brigid jumped at the familiar but unexpected Welsh accent. She straightened her shoulders and wiped any remaining trace of tears from her face before making her way into the shop. "Thomas Price. What brings you back so soon? I thought you'd gone travelling."

The jaunty, dapper young man standing before her was an entrepreneur before the word had come into fashion. Sometimes he sailed the oceans, returning with hand-picked stock, sometimes he brokered deals with importers for top-of-the-line small runs, all of which he on-sold to shops like hers.

"You." He winked and grinned that cheeky grin she'd come to prize. "I've been and gone and now I'm back."

Brigid's spirits lifted. He might always be on the move and she never knew when he'd appear next, but she liked him. She'd found him trustworthy ever since he'd first arrived on her doorstep the day after Mrs Fortesque's visit, as if destiny had sent him.

"You'll never guess what I've got." Tom was a sweet-talker – Brigid had no doubts about that – but he knew his trade and she was the beneficiary.

"Now how can I guess if you won't give me any clues?"

With a flourish, he withdrew a short length of peacock coloured silk from his bag. "Look what I've brought my favourite girl."

Individuality had become her mark of difference. She dealt with exclusive, quality products, but this piece was outstanding. Brigid put her hands on her face, her mouth opened, eyes widened. Then she reached out to touch smooth, soft and unbelievably luxurious fabric. "Where did you get it?"

She could feel Tom's eyes on her as she held the fabric up this way and that to the light, seeing how it draped. Of all her patrons, she would offer this fabric to Mrs Fortesque as a thank you for all the new clients she had sent her way. Dressmakers, milliners and cloak makers were now buying their fabrics and wares from 'Miss Brigid's' and she was sometimes stretched to meet demand.

"Now that would be telling, wouldn't it." He wiggled both eyebrows and made her laugh.

"I don't want to know your trade secrets, Tommy. I want to know where it was made. This didn't come from Britain."

"You are right on there, lass. It comes from the Far East, does that."

No amount of persuasion and cajolery would make him tell her how he'd got hold of it. 'Influential businessman' was all he'd say. "But this much I can tell you. There's not a lot of it, but I've laid me hands on a bolt just for you. Can you use it?"

"Of course I can! I know just the person – but what's it going to cost me, Tommy? The customs tariffs have just gone up again and everything is so expensive now."

"A kiss?" He tapped his finger against the side of his face and beamed.

She put both hands on her side of the counter, lifted herself up and dropped a brief kiss on his cheek.

Tommy was so surprised he staggered back and, grinning from ear to ear, put his hand over his heart and patted his chest.

Brigid blushed and then giggled. She hadn't giggled like that in such a long time, not since Philip made her giggle on the ship. Goodness, that was two years ago, she realised as she registered the date. Two years since she'd boarded the ship in London looking for a new life, and what a new life she'd found. Full of ups and downs, heartaches and triumphs, successes and failures, but she'd come a long way, in so many ways.

They negotiated a price that suited both of them, and Brigid ordered other stock from his range of notions and threads.

He gathered up his samples, put his bowler hat on top of his curls and prepared to leave. "One day, Miss Brigid, I'm going to come in here and ask you to step out with me. Would you do that? Would you come out with me?"

Brigid felt her legs go wobbly, and a tingling in the pit of her stomach guaranteed her answer. "Aye, Tommy. I would." She dropped her chin and tilted her head coyly to one side. "When you ask me proper."

He crossed one foot over the other and spun around on the spot. "Until next time, Miss Brigid."

As soon as he stepped outside and the door closed behind him, Sally emerged from where she'd been hiding, listening. "Well, well. Looks like you've made a conquest there."

Brigid's gaze remained on the door, but her mind had walked a mile or two further. "Maybe. But I thought I had a future with Mr Harrison-Browne once, and look where that got me."

Sally snorted. "Yes, look where it got you. In this thriving establishment, living in New Zealand surrounded by people who love you, and a man knocking on your door. No more doubts, Brigid O'Brien. The world has arrived at your doorstep. Enjoy it."

In spite of Sally's assertions, Brigid couldn't quite get rid of all her doubts. Jamie's silence and prolonged absence weighed heavily on her, and Maggie had become stranger as time had passed. She could often hear the woman talking to herself, and she'd started to twist her hair in her fingers so much she pulled some out, then more and more until her hair looked like string rather than the luxuriant locks she'd once sported. Her interest in the girls had completely waned to the point they were nervous of being around her, which troubled Brigid greatly. Laura and Jane were Maggie's blood nieces, but their welfare had fallen to Sally and herself.

Brigid couldn't deny she enjoyed their company and it felt like having little sisters again, but their free spirit was so distant from her life at that age. Not for them the uncertainty of where the next meal was coming from, or whether the bailiffs would take their house from them. They would be the educated, well-fed, adventurous ladies of tomorrow.

From time to time she wondered what her parents and siblings were doing back home. Their letters were brief and infrequent, and did not always hold welcome news. Máire was away working in the town as a kitchen maid, and the babby Katie was growing into a pretty wee thing, but there'd been more evictions. The papers were full of it, they said. Things weren't getting any easier.

She prayed for them and lit candles.

Laura was already asking about the suffragettes and what it all meant. She was a clever one was Laura, and little Jane, coming up ten soon, was the quiet one. Laura's stitching was exceedingly accomplished for her age, and Jane had Sally's eye for colour and shape. And she loved to draw.

While high-society ladies were sticking to the fashion dictates of Britain, fashions for the emerging class of women, working as professionals in shops or offices and who rode bicycles and played sport, were changing. Brigid saw a bright future in dress design for Jane.

And as for Sally, well, sometimes, she was at a loss about her friend.

Watching Sally change the window display while she sat in her habitual early-morning spot making lace, Brigid guessed it as good a time as any to broach the subject. "Have you ever considered what you want to do for the rest of your life?"

Sally stopped what she was doing and removed the pins from her mouth. "What are you talking about?"

Brigid covertly glanced up at her friend as she worked the hook and thread between her fingers. "You told me I should enjoy the rewards of what I've done, but what about you? What do you want that you don't have?"

Sally bent to pin another length of trim to the flounce she'd created. "I have what I want."

"I don't believe you. You didn't leave the old country to go to Australia, or come here to New Zealand for that matter, to work in a shop."

Lifting her skirt, Sally clambered down from the window and went in search of something to add to the display. "Why not? It's a better job than anything I had back home. I've a roof over my head, food in my belly and the best clothes I've ever had." She turned to stare at Brigid, one hand on her hip, the other still holding the open button drawer. "Why are you asking?"

"No reason." Brigid dropped her head to her work. "I thought you might want to find something more exciting. That's all."

"Damn and blast it."

Startled by the noise of the drawer falling out, and surprised at Sally's cursing, Brigid put her lacework aside and started to help pick up the scattered buttons.

"Do you want me to leave?" Sally kept her head down, but her voice sounded close to panic.

Side by side on their knees, their hands touched briefly as they both reached out at the same time to drop the retrieved buttons back into the drawer. Their eyes met. Sally's were brimming.

Standing up, Brigid took her friend's wrist and pulled her close. She wrapped her arms around the other woman. "Of course not."

Sally sobbed into her shoulder. "Don't send me away, Bree. Please don't send me away."

"Whatever happened to you, Sally? Where did the woman I met on the ship disappear to?"

For a long time Brigid failed to convince Sally that Carruthers would not find her in New Zealand. They'd left no trace anywhere, on any paperwork, to show she'd left the country, but more importantly than that, with her gone from Townsville he had no need to look for her. She was no longer a temptation or a problem.

"Are you haunted by Maggie's brother, is that it?" For some time after hearing the rest of the story, Brigid had struggled to get it out of her mind. The whole episode went against everything she believed in. She'd even talked to God about it, but she'd received no answer, no guidance. The problem was not hers to solve. Did Jamie struggle? Was that why he left?

"No. I hardly knew him, and after what he did to Maggie and the girls, he deserved everything he got." Brigid crossed herself at this godless thought but said nothing, wanting Sally to say what plagued her. "Jamie was the brave one. He took all our troubles on his shoulders and now he's gone. I feel bad that Maggie rejected him after all he'd done for her."

Brigid had known on the ship that Maggie would cause Jamie heartache, and she'd been proved right. "Aye, I am too, but it's not Jamie I'm asking about – it's you. Are you still frightened of that fella?"

Most of the time Sally's accent was only slight, but under stress it became exaggerated. "I dinna think so. We've been here all of twelvemonth now. The life I had in Townsville's all past, just like the life I had back home. But summat's gone from in here." Sally placed her hand over her rib cage. "The hollow feeling I used to have and tried to fill has gone. I canna explain it. But I'm no troubled any more. Do you ken?"

Brigid knew only too well what she meant, but could three women continue to live together, raising two girls, forever? Or rather, two women and one who was slowly losing her mind.

"Did you ever write to your friend at the hotel – what was her name? Emily?"

Sally shook her head. "I was too scared she might

let something slip and the police or ... or ... he would come looking for me. Like I said – it's in the past. Leave it where it belongs."

"All right, I will. If you're sure you are happy here. You're my dearest friend, but I don't want you to stay with me if there is something in life you want to do. You used to like to sing, to party, even to risk a game of cards. Where's that Sally?"

"She's grown up and got some sense."

"But you never go out. Don't you want a husband and family of your own?"

"Nay, lass. Never."

"But why ever not? You're always trying to hook me up with someone. Tom's your latest target."

A dark cloud veiled Sally's eyes, and her face paled. "There's one last secret you should know ..." Between long pauses and deep breaths, Sally spoke of her hidden past for the first time. "I were not much older than Laura when it started. My stepfather and ..." she shuddered but put her hand out to stop Brigid from comforting her as the tale unfolded. "It all came back to me when that man started pawing me. I can never let a man touch me. Never."

Sally shook her head as if coming out of a trance. "Now don't speak of it. Put it out of your head. I'm here because I want to be, not because I'm obliged. I treasure our friendship. And I've learnt a new trade. That yon bank manager is impressed with my bookkeeping. You do what you're good at, and I'll do my part, and 'Miss Brigid's' will prosper and keep all of us in style."

Whatever Brigid thought would come from the conversation, it certainly wasn't that, but reassured Sally was here to stay, she smiled.

"And don't forget your window dressing talents." Brigid had been delighted when Sally had been invited to dress windows for other merchants. "Now, let's open the doors and see if we can conjure up some new customers."

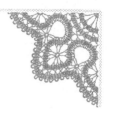

16

The Proposition

Thursday, 15th November 1888

"Your fella's back again." Sally recognised the jaunty walk of Tom Price the instant he came into view. Bowler hat slightly tilted back on his head, cigar in hand and wearing a beautiful, well-tied cravat and pin, he looked the essence of an up-and-coming dandy about town.

"He's not my fella, I tell you. He's a friend, 'tis all." Brigid always denied the obvious, but Sally knew otherwise. Thomas Price was now a regular visitor, and Brigid had indeed accepted his invitation to walk out with him on occasions. If Brigid wasn't smitten, Tom certainly was.

"If you say so." Sally shrugged her shoulders. "I'll look after the shop while you take him into the salon if you like. Just call if you need me, which I doubt."

The once dirty anteroom had become a favourite place of theirs since its refurbishment back in April, and the more elegant furnishings they'd added since then. Brigid entertained all the society ladies in the salon, where she could show the fabrics and laces to their best advantage on the long table, and in private.

With natural light pouring in through the rear window, off-white walls and drapes, a chaise longue and two chairs with cabriole legs, the room was as elegant and modern as you'd find anywhere. Since Brigid had started selecting exclusive lengths of fabrics for preferred customers, she was able to guarantee the exclusivity she'd staked her reputation on. Dressmakers now flocked to her for materials demanded by their clients.

On warm sunny days, such as today, the women opened the doors wide, thinking them more welcoming. Tom strode on in, tossing the snub of his cigar into the street. "*Bore da*. And a fine good morning to you, Miss Brigid and to you, Miss Sally."

"Good morning, Mr Price," said Sally, lifting the hinged section of the counter top. "Come on through."

"Will you join me? I'm about to have a cup of tea." Brigid extended her arm towards the salon.

"Would I ever say no to anything you ask of me, Miss Brigid?" Tom's infectious grin lit up his face, and Brigid smiled in response.

Sally tittered quietly and turned to Brigid pointedly. "What did I tell you?" she whispered.

"Thank you, Sally." Brigid tried but failed to sound severe. "I'll leave you to the shop, I will. I believe Mrs Armstrong will pick up her parcel this morning."

In jest, Sally poked her tongue out at Brigid as she turned her back and retreated to the salon, leaving the door open, as usual, for propriety's sake.

An hour or more passed. Sally could hear voices in the background, but they were muted and no laughter had erupted to startle the steady stream of customers.

"I'm sorry, Mrs Dufresne, Miss Brigid is tied up for the moment. Would you like me to make an appointment for you? Say, tomorrow?"

At a time when Sally was trying to serve three customers at once, a man walked into the shop. Voices stilled and, as one, they turned to look at him. A man in a ladies' shop was a rarity, but a fashionable gentleman with an arrogant tilt of his head was unheard of. Sally recognised him instantly, even though she hadn't seen him for more than two years. Her spirits plummeted.

"I'll be with you in a moment, sir. Now Mrs Smith ... your parcel. Ah, yes. You've chosen well, Mrs Sedgely."

As quickly and efficiently as possible, Sally completed the sales for the women still hovering around the counter, watching the man who was inspecting the place from top to bottom, peering intently into each of the glass-topped display drawers. Moving from behind the counter, Sally guided the ladies to the door. As soon as they'd stepped onto the footpath, she closed the doors and slid the bolt home.

She gathered her breath and pasted a smile on her face before she turned towards him. "Mr Harrison-Browne. It's been a long time. What brings you to 'Miss Brigid's'?"

The man flinched slightly at the inference Sally made as to who owned the shop. He inclined his head slightly but did not remove his hat. He carried gloves in the hand that held his cane, his shoes were the latest fashion and he looked prosperous, and indifferent. For a man whose father had just lost everything, he seemed remarkably assured. "Miss Forsythe, I believe? If my memory serves me."

Sally said nothing. In the silence, a murmur of voices could be heard, and she immediately attempted to cover the sound with a cough. "Pardon me," she apologised.

"This is a surprise. Can I help you?" Retreating behind the counter, she bustled about tidying up the laces.

"No, I don't think you can. I wish to see Brigid. Will you fetch her for me? That is, if it's not too much trouble for such a busy person."

Rude creature, thought Sally, standing her ground. "Ah, but Miss Brigid is tied up at the moment. Can I ask you to come back in about an hour?"

Philip raised his chin and sneered. "You could, but as it is not convenient for me to do so, I will ask you again to fetch her." He took two paces forward and stood immediately in front of her. She was grateful the counter was between them. "Or I will find her myself." His threat was not a hollow one.

Without warning, his hand flashed across the counter, and he caught her chin between his thumb and forefinger. "You always were a pretty little thing."

Instinctively, she batted his hand away. "Take your hand off me."

"Fiery too. Mm, I like what I see." He chuckled. "Now, will you get Brigid or will I?"

"Wait here," she ordered, and feeling distinctly nauseated, hurried to the back room. She shut the door behind her and leant against it, afraid she would fall down without its support.

"Sally. Whatever is the matter? You've gone a funny shade of green."

If the alarm in Brigid's face meant anything, at least she'd do as Sally asked without argument. "Come to the kitchen with me, will ye?"

Brigid looked at Tom. "I'll be back in a minute."

"I'll be here, waiting for you."

Sally made sure the salon door was securely closed

and pulled Brigid across the corridor into the kitchen. "It's Philip Harrison-Browne. He's out front," she hissed. Brigid's eyes widened with shock. "I tried to put him off until Mr Price has gone, but he's insisting on seeing you right now."

"Aye, well. I'd better speak with him, then." Brigid turned to leave.

Sally grabbed her arm and held her back. "Don't let him see Mr Price. He'll put two and two together and make it into something it's not." Sally didn't say that Philip had frightened her. She lowered her voice. "And you mustn't let him see Maggie either."

Comprehension registered in Brigid's eyes. She nodded. "Will ye see Mr Price out the back door then, will ye?"

"Where is she, by the way?" Sally looked around the kitchen expecting to see Maggie somewhere.

"Gone to the markets."

Brigid patted her hair and straightened her gown, and walked into the shop. Sally followed a few paces behind and hovered by the screen dividing the store to listen in and see what developed next.

"Mr Harrison-Browne." Brigid extended both her hands to take one of his in hers before releasing it again. "'Tis wonderful to see you, again."

Philip bowed and smiled, returning to the suave, charming person of old. "I am so pleased I have found you at last, Brigid. You have been elusive."

Sally detected the cold tone, despite his manners.

"We must talk at length, and you can tell me all that has been happening, that ye can. I especially want to hear about your mother," Brigid replied enthusiastically. "But for the moment, I must apologise I'm a bit tied up.

Could we meet again later? I know a delightful tearoom further up the street."

The smile fixed on his face never quite reached his eyes.

"I can wait for a few moments more while you finish whatever you consider more important than me. I have travelled a long way to find you, but I won't wait any longer."

Sally turned and rushed into the salon. "Mr Price ..."

"Isn't it about time you called me Tom, Miss Sally?" he grinned. In contrast to the menace she had felt not more than ten yards away, the natural, easy-going goodwill of this man was a tonic.

"Tom, then. But there's no time for questions. Come with me, quickly." She glanced around the room. "Bring your hat."

She stuck her head around the door and, content that Brigid was still chatting to Philip in the front, she beckoned to Tom and hurried him into the kitchen.

"What's going on?" A frown creased Tom's brow.

"Miss Brigid will tell you when she can, but right now can I ask you to leave? By the back way. It's important."

Tom shrugged, seemingly nonchalant again. "Anything to help. Tell Miss Brigid I'll be back later."

Sally sighed, relieved. "I'll send you a message. Are you staying at your usual boarding house?"

He confirmed he was and skipped down the three back steps into the yard and set off down the alleyway.

She had just shut the kitchen door behind her when Brigid appeared in the corridor, heading towards the salon. The question on Brigid's face was obvious. Sally nodded.

Brigid raised her voice slightly so Philip could hear.

"Aye. Miss Forsythe, will you unbolt the front door again, please. I would hate to turn customers away. And then I'd like you to join us in the salon. We'll hear the bell should anyone come in."

Sally went to do as she was bid, leaving Brigid to tidy up the two teacups.

Philip stood exactly where she'd left him, but his pose was belligerent. He meant trouble, if Sally's instinct was anything to go by. She reached up to unbolt the door, but he grabbed her wrist. She pulled away from him, but couldn't break his grasp. They glared at each other.

"Leave it. I don't want anyone interrupting our little tête-à-tête." His voice was icy smooth, and his face wore the slightest hint of a sneer.

Sally's mouth went dry. "What do you want?"

"What's owed me." He let her go and Sally rubbed her wrist where he'd left red finger marks. "What was taken away from me."

Sally didn't quite understand his meaning. Every penny Mrs Browne had spent on stock for the shop had been repaid, and they had started paying a small monthly rental. "We owe you nothing."

"Oh, but Miss Forsythe, I beg to differ."

At that moment, Brigid returned. She looked between the two of them, sensing the tension and animosity. "What's going on here?"

"Nothing, my dear Brigid." Philip removed his hat, flopped his gloves inside and held it out with his cane for Sally to take. "Miss Forsythe and I were reaching an accord, weren't we, my dear."

Sally forfeited the battle and took the proffered articles.

"Now, is there somewhere private we can talk? Behind

here, maybe?" Philip started to move behind the counter, but Brigid didn't budge or allow him to pass. She clearly wasn't convinced any accord had been reached. She smiled sweetly. "If you wish, the three of us can talk in my salon. Maybe it is better the doors stay shut for now. Come along, Sally."

Brigid extended her arm and Sally crossed in front of her to lead the way into the salon. She placed Philip's hat and cane on the hat stand and stood at the far side to watch Brigid and Philip come through the door.

Philip's face was thunderous, and his temper barely under control. "Brigid, is this really necessary? It's you I want to talk to."

Sally saw him flick his hair into place, a sign she remembered from the ship. She was sure he was up to something.

"I think it is, Mr Harrison-Browne." He squared his shoulders against Brigid's self-assurance. "If you want to talk business then, aye, I need her advice. Miss Forsythe is the clever one with the figures. Please take a seat."

Philip sat, flipping the tails of his coat. "Very well. Have it your way." He leant back in the chair, placed one foot on the other knee and hooked his fingers in his waistcoat pocket. "I've come to claim my property."

Brigid blanched. Sally knew it had been the one thing she'd dreaded ever since she'd heard about the fire.

"Forgive me, but I'm not sure I understand? Your property, did you say? What property is that?"

A wave of admiration washed over Sally. The timid girl who usually accepted authority was directly challenging him. She'd never seen Brigid like this, but then, maybe she had. Sally knew Brigid would fight to the death to protect those she loved.

He waved his hand around the room and pointed up to the ceiling. "This property. The shop, a showroom and accommodation, I believe."

"Ah, I see. Miss Forsythe. Can you explain the arrangements we came to with Mrs Browne, please?"

After Brigid had got the money from the bank to buy the stock she wanted, Mrs Browne had agreed to offer her the right to purchase the building once she had some capital.

Philip jumped to his feet. "I know all about your little arrangement with my mother, but she had no right. You ..." he pointed at Brigid, "you have no right. You were my idea. You were mine to say what happened and how it happened. How dare you go behind my back? And as for this harlot ..." Philip swished his hand towards Sally.

Brigid stood. "I'll thank ye to keep a civil tongue in your head. You forget your manners. I don't know what has upset you, but I will not have such language in my house."

Somehow, Sally managed to keep a straight face while she rejoiced for Brigid standing up to the man who once offered so much, but who had turned into a right bully.

Philip exploded. "It's not your house. Nor your shop. And your name should not be on the door. It should be mine!"

"It'll do you no good to get all hot and bothered, that it won't. I'm right sorry that what you'd hoped for didn't happen, but 'twas between you and your father. I had nothing to do with it."

Momentarily silenced by her insight, he looked at her more calmly, but his eyes were cold. "You are an employee and I require your services in Brisbane."

"I think you are wrong there. I don't work for you or your father. Anyway, I have responsibilities that prevent me from leaving."

"Responsibilities?" His dismissive harrumph troubled her.

"To my family, aye, and your mother. I was saddened to hear about the fire, and Mr Browne's affliction, I truly was. Are you finding your way? I hope you are." Brigid's voice softened, and she spoke as she would to an injured child, or Maggie.

No sooner had the thought of Maggie entered her head than a soft tap sounded on the door, and Sally saw it inch open. Maggie appeared carrying a tray of tea things, as was her habit when she knew Brigid had company.

Philip stared at the woman and then looked back and forth between herself and Brigid. Sally didn't think he would recognise Maggie from the ship, but Maggie knew who he was. She dropped the tray with a clatter, tea splattered over the floor and china shattered. She stood trembling in the middle of the room, staring.

Brigid went to her and, with a gentleness only Brigid could achieve, eased her from the room. Sally bent to clear up the mess, keeping a wary eye on Philip who had sat down again.

He was watching her. "Who was that woman?"

"A maid."

"Have you known her long?"

"She was on the ship with us." The words were hardly out of her mouth, and she knew she'd made a big mistake, but thankfully, Philip didn't seem to have noticed.

"How can you afford a maid?"

Sally didn't like the inference she detected in the

question. "You'll have to talk to Miss O'Brien about that when she comes back."

Having collected all the broken china and put it on the tray, Sally stood up. "Excuse me while I take this away."

"You have to get rid of him!" Sally whispered, as soon as she entered the kitchen.

Brigid was seated beside Maggie on the kitchen bench, still trying to comfort the terror-stricken woman. She got up and crossed the room to speak softly with Sally without Maggie overhearing.

"I know, but how? I've been trying to think of a plausible reason for him to leave, but I don't think he'd fall for any of them."

"We'd better come up with something quick, before he takes it into his head to go causing mischief." Sally tipped her head at Maggie. "How's she?"

Brigid shook her head. "Not good. Although why he particularly scared her, I don't know. She hardly knew him on the ship and I doubt she's seen him since. It doesn't make sense."

Sally bit the side of her thumb, trying to think of a connection. "Didn't she go outside for a while when we were all at the Browne house in Brisbane? Could she have seen him there?"

"It's possible, aye. I didn't know he was there that day, but that might explain it. If she thinks he's followed her and found her here then others could too."

Following Brigid's logic, Sally began to panic. "Maybe she's right. I just admitted we knew her on the ship. What if the police or that madman from up north find us? Then what?"

"They won't even be looking." Brigid had already

been through all the arguments. "Pull yourself together, Sal. We've more important things to worry about."

Sally took a few deep breaths. "Well if he's not after her, he's certainly after you. My God, but he's as crazy as a loon. What's all this talk about taking back what he's owed?"

"He's always had the silly belief I was the key to making his dreams come true. He said without me they wouldn't work. He's convinced himself the only way to get Harrison Browne's back on its feet again after the fire is for me to go back to Brisbane with him and work in the store."

"How is that going to work? You've got your own business here."

"I know that. But if he thinks his ma and I have ignored him and stolen his ideas he'll want me to pay, tit for tat."

"You can't let him get away with that. What's he got himself so twisted about all of a sudden?" Sally was indignant on Brigid's behalf.

"It's not so sudden, Sally. I've felt for a while he could be nasty when things don't go his way. He'll pay his father back for not believing in him, by some means or other. But listen. I think I've an idea that might work."

Philip was nowhere to be seen when Brigid re-entered the salon. His hat and gloves were gone, but his cane was still there. When she went through to the shop she found the door swinging wide open. Alarm bells jangled but, for now, at least, she could do nothing more until he returned.

She checked the appointment book and was relieved she had no more clients booked for that day. Given it was now well into the afternoon, and worried she had missed a lot of the lunchtime passing trade, she clipped the doors back hoping those who had found her closed would return later. As long as she'd not offended a regular client, all would be well, but with three ladies scheduled for the next morning, she had to prepare.

Returning to the kitchen, she asked Sally to tend the shop while she tried to rouse Maggie who had not moved or spoken since Brigid had sat her down. The girls would be home from school soon, and seeing Maggie in this state always upset them.

Still getting no response, Brigid collected her notebooks from the salon and returned to the kitchen. She would work at the table next to Maggie for the afternoon and hope her presence and a stream of inconsequential chatter might help the woman relax. Voices drifted through from the shop occasionally, and Brigid was content that business had returned to normal. Laura and Jane returned from school and while Maggie flinched at the noise they made, she remained inert.

Brigid poured them each a glass of Maggie's homemade ginger beer and gave them an oatmeal biscuit. She had just finished asking them to do their chores when the sound of heavy feet stomping on wooden boards and Sally's high-pitched warning coming from the shop reached her ears.

"What is it, Sally?" Standing by the kitchen door, she stuck her head into the corridor. The sight that greeted her turned her feet to lead and her stomach to jelly.

Two policemen, followed by Philip, and Sally in the rear, were heading towards her.

"Miss Brigid O'Brien?" The older officer with several braids on his uniform spoke first. "If you would be so good as to answer a few questions."

Taking another step forward he as good as forced Brigid to move out of his way.

With Maggie, the two girls and three men, as well as herself and Sally, the kitchen was crowded.

Sally looked terrified and Philip looked pompous and self-righteous.

"I believe you may be able to help me locate the whereabouts of one James O'Brien, or a Miss Margaret O'Neill."

Brigid placed herself on the other side of the table, her back against the stove, near Maggie. She held herself upright, even though her knees wobbled dangerously, and prayed for strength.

"This gentleman here ..." He indicated Philip who now leaned against the wall, arms folded, one foot resting on the toe of his shoe. Philip flicked his hair back when he saw Brigid look at him. "... he tells me O'Brien is a relative of yours, and Miss O'Neill was entangled with him in some way."

"And why are you looking for Mr O'Brien?" Brigid knew only too well, but if she hedged enough she might be able to protect Maggie from their clutches.

"We believe they can help us with our enquiries into a missing person." The policeman consulted his notebook. "A Mr Michael O'Neill."

At the sound of his name, Maggie began to wail. She covered her face with her apron and rocked madly back and forth. The noise was dreadful. Laura and Jane scuttled around the table, clamped their arms around Sally and hid their faces against her body. She wrapped one arm around each of them and comforted them, but said nothing.

Again the officer consulted his notebook. "He went missing from Townsville in Australia in April 1887. So did his sister."

Brigid forced herself to make light of the date. "Goodness, that's nearly eighteen month ago. He could be anywhere by now. Australia is a big country."

"Have any of you heard from him?"

"I have not. I don't believe I know anything about a Michael O'Neill." Brigid crossed her fingers behind her back at the partial lie, promising to say her prayers and take confession as soon as she could. "But I knew a Maggie O'Neill once. Aye, but that person is no longer with us, that she isn't."

"I see. And you, miss?" Sally shook her head. The girls edged further behind her, avoiding the man's gaze completely.

The younger policeman scribbled down notes, and a hidden message passed between the two officers. Maggie's wailing had shifted into a keening that was setting everyone's teeth on edge. Even the policemen were looking uncomfortable.

"Can't you stop her making that noise?"

Brigid shook her head. She placed her hand around Maggie's shoulder and pulled her against her skirt. "Not when she gets like this. Not until she wears herself out. Poor woman." Feeling utterly disloyal, but thinking it one way of getting out of this predicament, she twirled her finger near her temple to indicate Maggie was not quite sound of mind, which, in truth, she wasn't.

The questions continued as the officer established how long she'd been in New Zealand, who her companions were and how they fitted. More lies to tell, *forgive me, Lord.* She stared at Philip wondering how much he knew or guessed.

Sally and the girls were sisters, she explained. They'd met on the ship coming out from the old country but lost touch until they met up again here in New Zealand. Her other friend, quiet now she was resting against Brigid, had fallen on hard times, poor soul. Buried her children after a sickness and hasn't been right since.

"She's lying." Philip moved away from the wall and, placing both hands on the table, glowered at her across its surface. "I saw this one," he pointed to Sally, "and the two girls, although they were younger then, leave my house in Brisbane before they came to New Zealand. And I think you'll find that madwoman was there too along with O'Brien. That is Margaret O'Neill. Ask her."

Bile rose in her throat. Why did Philip hate her so much he would destroy everything she had?

"We're not likely to get any sense out of the woman, even if she is who you say she is," said the senior officer. Turning his attention back to Brigid, he repeated his question. "Do you know the whereabouts of James O'Brien?"

Brigid almost sighed with relief. This was one question she could answer truthfully. "No. I do not. I haven't seen him, or heard from him, since he sat at this table Christmas last. Does that make him a missing person too?"

"Thank you for your time, Miss O'Brien." The senior policeman nudged the other one to put his notebook away. "This is not really our jurisdiction, Mr Harrison-Browne, so we'll be on our way. We can't spend any more time on it." Turning again to Brigid, he said, "But if you do see or hear from Mr O'Brien, be sure to let us know."

Brigid forced a smile to her lips. "Allow me to show you out."

To her horror, she found Philip sitting comfortably in the salon.

"Why did you bring the police to my door?" Brigid was fuming but willed herself to stay calm. Losing her temper with Philip would only make it worse, and he would find it hard to fight with someone who didn't fight back. "What were you hoping to achieve?"

Philip's nonchalant shrug infuriated her more. "Control, of course. I have the power and since your sense of responsibility to your so-called family seems to be part of your reluctance to return to Brisbane, I decided to show you how difficult I can make things if you don't comply." He stood up suddenly, angry, and towered over Brigid. "I'm in charge now. You have become too brash for your own good, my girl. Some humility wouldn't go amiss. You had it once. I suggest you find it again."

Brigid was shocked that the man she had once admired, and had fallen just a little bit in love with, was so eaten up with bitterness that his only avenue was malice. "Mr Harrison-Browne. I am not your enemy. Your enemy is within."

Their eyes met, but he was the first to turn away.

Wanting to avoid any questions about Jamie or Maggie, and scared to ask how he knew anything about Michael's disappearance, Brigid changed the subject. She needed to come up with an idea where he could save the business without her and feel justified at the same time. She was small fry in the grander scheme of things.

He needed newer and bigger ideas.

"I've an idea or two. Will you let me help you?"

He flung around and took a couple of paces away from her, then turned on her. "What are you talking about? I am insisting you do your duty by me, and you offer me your help."

His tone was scathing, but Brigid knew she'd hit a nerve. "We can't go back to what was. Nor can we try to recreate your dreams as they once were, with what is."

Brigid saw through the little act Philip put on – his astounded look, opening and shutting his mouth as if unable to put his thoughts into words and turning his back on her. But seeing the habitual flick of his hair grieved her.

"I am right sorry to hear about your troubles, that I am. Your mother wrote to me and ..."

"I bet she did," he interrupted, resolutely keeping his back turned. "Gloating, no doubt."

Brigid could not and would not stand for the disrespectful inference, but she kept her voice and manner as calm as her churning belly would let her. "Mr Harrison-Browne! Be kind. Or are you not the man I once knew?"

Philip didn't respond.

She moved closer and took his arm. "Please, let me explain at least."

Leading him to the chaise longue, she nudged him to sit beside her. He rested his elbow on the back, turned his head away and propped up his chin.

"Tell me what's a-boithering you? What is making you so hurtful? Your mother believes in you, I know she does. It is not her fault that your father clung to his dreams for too long when he should have been respecting yours."

His detached pose abruptly changed, and he readjusted his position to sit back, once again placing one foot on the other knee, but he still didn't look at her. He looked at the ceiling.

"It's too late for your smarm," said Philip. "I decide what happens to the Harrison Browne brand from now on. And I want you in Brisbane."

Brigid took a deep breath and prayed for guidance. "Aye, I know that, but answer me this: how *can* I help? And forgive me if I am wrong, but I seem to remember much of the stock was lost at the warehouse after the flood. And a fire ravaged the shop, destroying everything – or nearly all – I believe. Do you have new premises? And new stock in want of selling?"

Again Philip didn't answer. She peered around to his half-hidden face and saw he was biting his knuckle. She took it to mean he didn't have either and was at a loss as to where to start.

"Well, then, what to do. Like I said, I have an idea ..." Brigid paused. Now was not the right time to tell him the details. He needed to be enthusiastic about the prospects before she could plant any seeds. "You once told me your father wanted new premises in Eagle Street, and you and he fought over it. Who won the argument?"

Suddenly Philip jumped to his feet. "What's with all the questions? I don't need you nagging at me as well."

Brigid looked up at him with reproving eyes, saying nothing. He held her gaze. In the past, she would have dropped her head and accepted his dominance, but not any more. She was her own woman now and had too many people relying on her to give in. She had to win him over if she was to keep her reality intact. She stared back.

Philip snapped. "He did, of course." The anger came pouring out of him. "He went ahead and signed up for the building behind my back. Now I'm lumbered with the cost and no stock to fill it. And the stupid old man is now laid up in his bed unable to do or say anything. All I get is his disapproving eyes following me."

A knock on the door, followed by Sally peering cautiously around the edge, halted any further exchange.

"Pardon me, Miss Brigid. I'm terribly sorry to interrupt, but there's a Mr Price wanting to see Mr Harrison-Browne. Urgently, he says."

How she managed to keep control of her poise was beyond Brigid. It seemed as if her heart leapt, her stomach fell and her head spun all at the same time. Would her ruse work?

"Mr Price, you say, for Mr Harrison-Browne?"

Feeling slightly panicked now, she wondered if she should keep the two of them apart after all, but the impish desire to find out how Tommy would carry it off won.

She bent her head to one side and looked at Philip with an innocent and baffled eye. "This is a surprise. Mr Price is an importer of some very fine fabrics. I wonder how he knew the well-known Mr Harrison-Browne from Brisbane was in town."

Brigid didn't dare look at Sally. It took all her control not to giggle.

"Shall I show him in, Miss Brigid?"

Brigid deferred to Philip, who in turn sought permission back from Brigid, but finally Mr Thomas Price was ushered into the salon.

"At your service," said Tommy, handing over his business card. "I couldn't believe my ears when I heard the renowned Mr Harrison-Browne, from Brisbane no less, was in Auckland. If you are looking to conduct business while you are here, sir, then I am the man for you."

Sally stood behind Brigid who remained seated on the chaise longue. They held hands over Brigid's shoulder and watched the theatrical performance going on before their eyes.

Tommy threw his arm around the taller man's shoulder and compelled him to keep in step and pace around the room. Since the area was not that large, they appeared to be going around in circles while Tommy kept up an endless stream of persuasive chatter.

During the course of their conversation, Brigid learned Philip's hands were tied until the bank and insurance company had finished their investigations and handled much of the recovery work. Two disasters within the space of eighteen months had been too much for them to leave uncontested.

Philip explained, "Gradually we increased the stock after the flood last year, but most of it had been moved from the warehouse to the store. Trade had increased tenfold, but the fire took just about everything we'd built up. One shipment is due next month that will tide us over the Christmas period, I hope, but after that, there's nothing. It's like starting out all over again."

Tommy had convinced Philip that not only could he procure fabrics for him, and many other goods exclusively for the Harrison Browne store, but he could also put business his way.

Money had talked. The two men shook hands.

"Thank you for the opportunity to do business with you, Mr Harrison-Browne. And thank you, Miss Brigid, for introducing me. Until tomorrow, then."

The more Brigid had watched and listened to Philip, the more resolute she became. The country girl from County Clare, who'd once been flustered by his attentions, was now the more fortunate of the two. She was fulfilling her dreams while his were wasting away. She had grown in stature while he was diminished.

After Tommy had left, Philip explained why he was in Auckland.

"Mother told me what she had done about setting you up here in New Zealand. It was to be the first of the Harrison Browne branches and it would be mine, she promised me – as soon as Father shared control. But the stubborn old fool wouldn't listen to anything she or I said. Still won't."

Because of his father's indisposition, the lawyers had not sorted out the tangle that would give Philip control, since his father was sole signatory and couldn't, or wouldn't, put his mark to anything. Alf had continued to be the Harrison Browne right-hand man, even under Philip's command. He was busy refitting the Eagle Street premises according to Harry's wishes so they could reopen the shop, leaving Philip with nothing to do. The only thing still in his favour was that his friend Sam Barton had stuck by his promise of financially supporting Philip as long as the Harrison Browne brand prevailed.

"I'm itching to diversify into other areas, so I decided to start work developing the one branch we had. Imagine my surprise when I discovered not only did it *not* carry the Harrison Browne name, but the stock no longer belonged to me either." He became angry and agitated again.

298

"My mother went behind my back and sold me out. But I still own the premises. Now I want it – and you – back."

"That's not quite the way it happened, and you are hardly being fair to your mother," Brigid argued, desperate to convince him her little enterprise was beneath his attention.

Mrs Browne had decided her idea had failed because of the downturn in Auckland, and she needed a return on her money. The shop was too small to succeed under the name of Harrison Browne but it suited Brigid.

"Brisbane was on the up, she said, and I had a choice. I could stay here if I could pay her back, or I could return to her employ, and she would sell."

"I don't believe you." But the habitual flick of his hair told Brigid he did. He knew, all right.

Even so, and mostly thanks to Tommy's reasoning, Philip agreed to meet Brigid on the corner of Queen and Wellesley streets the following day after she had attended to her morning clients. She wanted to show him around town.

The pair stood on the western side of Queen Street as people and carriages hurried past going about their business. Brigid pointed to a store across the road. "What do you see before you?"

Mrs Marianne Smith's Cheap Drapery Warehouse business had grown considerably since its humble beginnings in 1880. Based on 'the quick sixpence rather than a slow shilling' precept, she partnered with her husband William, and later with Andrew Caughey, to form Smith & Caughey. The firm had moved to these grander, larger premises in 1884.

"A large drapery store. What of it?"

Brigid was keen to give Philip ideas he could take back to Brisbane without it seeming as though they came from her.

"You'll see. The place has grown significantly in four years. It's not just a drapery store as you know it. Come with me."

They crossed the road and entered the building. Brigid took delight in pointing out the tailoring section, the milliner's department and the accessories division, which sold ladies crystal dressing-table sets, knick-knacks and perfumes, as well as gloves, handkerchiefs and men's grooming kits, among other things. Philip was interested in the haberdashery section and fabric area, but Brigid pulled him away to look at the handbags, parasols and shawls. She also took pains to ensure he saw the finished garments on display.

After a while, she tugged his arm. "We're not finished yet."

They strolled down Queen Street admiring the new buildings and discussing the state of some of the original buildings.

Fires had devastated Queen Street in the 1870s but had lessened since the advent of the fire brigade who had a newfangled water-throwing device called a 'hydropult', but building expansion had slowed since the 1886 stock market crash. Large businesses and banks were hurting and many small businesses closing down. Now was not a good time to be in business in Auckland, but shops that sold supplies were better off than those that sold services or handled money.

Their conversation was amiable enough, but not in the same the way they had talked on board the SS

Dorunda two years earlier. Brigid was nervous and Philip was withdrawn.

"I hear Brisbane is doing much better," she said.

Philip was forced to admit her sources were right. "Yes, business confidence is high now. The economy has lifted and people are spending."

Their conversation continued until Brigid came to a stop outside the elegant frontage of the troubled Bank of New Zealand. She was glad Sally had chosen another bank for their business.

Again, she pointed across the street. "Do you want to look inside?"

Philip took her arm and, once safely on the other side again, entered Court Brothers, Drapery and Clothiers. Smaller than the Smith & Caughey building and more traditional, Court Brothers was still impressive in size and dealt mostly in wools and velvets for clothing and curtains. They also had a tearoom.

A range of felts, blankets and upholstery fabrics caught Philip's eye, but while he found the layout and displays interesting, the diversification of Smith & Caughey interested him more, he said.

On their way down Queen Street towards the wharf Brigid had kept Philip talking so he didn't notice they had passed 'Miss Brigid's' on the other side of the street, a few doors down from the Victoria Street corner. Now they were on the same side of the street, Brigid directed them back the way they'd come. He almost walked past the shop barely a block further on, before he realised where he was. He stood looking up at the shop front as if noticing it for the first time.

Compared with what he'd just seen, the shop would appear small and old-fashioned. While it had a quaintness about it that would appeal to ladies, which was its sole purpose, it would never be in the same league as the other two stores Brigid had shown him, and she knew it. Her point of difference was the uniqueness of her product and the personal attention to detail ladies wanted.

"Would you care to buy me a cup of tea?"

Philip took her arm again, and she led him to the nearby tearooms and found a table away from the door where they could speak quietly.

After Brigid poured the tea, she approached the subject she most wanted to address. "I know it is not my place to tell you how to run your business, but can I offer you my opinion?"

Obviously deep in thought, he acceded without comment.

"The small scale operation that is 'Miss Brigid's' – and I have to tell you, your mother chose that name, not me – is not what you need right now."

"Never mind my mother. What do you know about what I need?"

Brigid bit back the retort on the tip of her tongue. They had been companionable throughout the morning; she didn't need his resentment resurfacing before she'd argued her case. "I don't mean to offend, that I don't. But in the year since I've been in Auckland I've seen changes, both good and bad. The good has been the growth and variety you saw today. Both of those stores have branches in other parts of Auckland."

Brigid took the pursed lip, a small hmm and a slight tilt of his head to mean he was impressed. "The bad has been the downturn in trade and small businesses closing up."

"So?" He looked at her over his teacup, his eyes joyless and distant and not giving anything away.

Brigid gathered her thoughts and took a deep breath. "You agreed to listen to my opinion – so here it is."

She reminded him about his dreams and fancies, the ones he'd outlined to her on the ship. All of them were extensions of what already existed, what his father had put in place over four decades. What he had seen today were examples of those new ideas, built on a solid base.

"You said yourself your father has lost the will and the ability to be in charge any more. You are the one to lead Harrison Browne into the future. You've always said that. Well, here's your chance. Take it. I think your future looks bright."

Her soft, lilting voice lulled Philip into the scene and he listened, sometimes making a comment, sometimes dismissing an idea. She tried not to hurry him or argue against any of his contrary thoughts, but slowly she built the store in his mind from the ground up.

"Harrison Browne already has a reputation for good-quality fabrics and household goods. The stock losses have been a setback, but they are not insurmountable. With Mr Price to source new products for you, you would have an edge over your competitors. You could have the most up-to-date, modern store selling the latest trends – even setting the trends. You could become Brisbane's answer to David Jones. Even Grace Brothers is growing. Look what they've achieved in the last three years. Those are the things you dreamed of."

"And why would 'Miss Brigid's' not fit into that scheme?" Philip might have emphasised the Miss Brigid name a bit too heavily for her liking, but at least he was discussing the options and not rejecting them entirely.

"Not that you need telling, but back then you wanted a little corner of your father's store to prove your worth – to test whether your ideas would work. You don't need to do that any longer."

He needed to think bigger. Little money could be made from a few buttons, ribbons and corset boning, and lacemaking was time-consuming and needed personal service. If the form of 'Miss Brigid's' was incorporated into a large, busy store, quality would be compromised. "Which would destroy your whole idea. I have enough trouble keeping up with the demand as it is, but it's enough for the likes of me."

After a few moments' silence, he seemed to accept her reasoning. He asked questions about what could be done: how many staff would he need, which departments to start with and which to grow into, and where to get the stock? Brigid could feel the excitement rising within her as she pictured the store they described between them. How could Philip not want such a place? And yet he still seemed unmoved by their discussion.

She knew she was blathering on and he was just as likely to get cross with her and tell her to stop, but she had to convince him. Everything he had ever wanted was there for the taking.

"Aye, that sounds grand, it does. Auckland is smaller and not so up to date, but you can offer something no one else in Brisbane has."

She saw no hint of any burning desire to get started or that glow of hope that came into people's eyes the moment they thought something better had come their way. She still had no idea what he was thinking.

Brigid laid her fingers on top of his hand, her eyes bright and eager. "You could make it work. I know you could. I fell for your ideas then because selling my lace to ladies was my dream, but it's too small to be your dream. Your dreams are out there waiting for you. Go and grab them with both hands."

17

Resolutions

Sunday, 16th December 1888

In the days after they'd parted company at the tearooms the previous month, Brigid had not seen nor heard from Philip. However, in the build-up to Christmas she barely had more than a few moments to herself to think about what that meant. Except at night, when worry gnawed at her. She had trouble sleeping and she was losing weight. She simply had no idea what he might do next.

A couple of weeks earlier, a note from Mrs Browne had eased her mind a little and put a smile on Sally's face. Philip had returned to Brisbane like a man possessed, she said, and the new store in Eagle Street was being redesigned.

Then this week, she received another note to say they were planning a big opening of the new Harrison Browne Department Store on Christmas Eve.

"She wants to know what I said to him."

Sally and Brigid sat in the living room upstairs, Sally working on the accounts while Brigid stitched. Laura, sitting beside her, worked at her embroidery, and Jane was sketching at the table.

Sally didn't take her eyes off the figures in front of her. "From what you told me, you never stopped talking."

Brigid chuckled. "Aye, but I haven't any idea what made the difference. He never said a word."

Secretly, Brigid thought the visits to the drapery stores had sparked his imagination. Although drawing a parallel between his vision and the department stores in Sydney and Melbourne hadn't done any harm either.

"Will he be back, do you think, hen?"

"I feared he would return, but maybe not any more – not from what Mrs Browne says. And Mr Price tells me he's as busy as a bumblebee, full of instructions and a sense of importance. But Tommy's right happy – Harrison Browne ordered a massive amount of fabric."

Speaking of Tommy had reminded them of those ghastly days of anguish after the visit from the police. Whilst the constable had seemed uninterested in a case from Australia, Brigid couldn't be certain. Would they be back? And how had Philip known anything?

"Don't you worry your pretty little head about it, Miss Brigid. Leave it all to Tommy Price here. I'll find out what the lay of the land is and let you know."

Without waiting for an invitation from Philip, Tom had taken ship for Brisbane only days later and turned up at the Eagle Street premises. She'd long considered Tommy could sell silk to a silkworm if he set his mind to it, and was not in the least bit surprised when Tommy told her the agreement they had come to.

"Looks like I won't be visiting you as much as I'd like to for a little while, my girl," he teased on his return. "I'll be away, I will, travelling the length and breadth of the globe to source and deliver the type and quantity of product that young mannie wants."

But Tommy's greatest revelation was yet to come. He'd made enquiries, both in Brisbane and Townsville. "You see; it's like this. There'd been these notices put in all the papers. A Mrs Emily McKendrick from the Queens Hotel had advertised for people knowing the whereabouts of Miss Sally Forsythe, or Miss Maggie O'Neill and two little girls, to get in touch. I bet that Harrison-Browne fella saw the notices and put two and two together. After all, he knew their names, if not what happened to them."

Tommy had talked to Mrs McKendrick. The police had initially connected their disappearance to that of Michael O'Neill, who was listed as a missing person, and questioned her. Mrs McKendrick had explained she'd had a farewell letter from Sally explaining her reasons for leaving, but not a forwarding address. She'd wanted to be in touch with her friend again. With no leads to follow and no reason to suspect anything untoward, the police dropped the matter.

"So you see, there's nothing to worry about. Mrs McKendrick says she put the advert in several times. One had gone in not long before he turned up here."

Sally was delighted and immediately wrote to her friend Emily. She would never return to Townsville, she was still scared of Carruthers, and she was happy in New Zealand, and could they still be friends. Emily's prompt reply followed and the two women continued their friendship by post.

With that matter off her shoulders, and with her mind at rest, Brigid's more pressing worries concerned Maggie. She had become totally reclusive and unresponsive after the police had been. She usually hid in her room, only emerging when some urge came on her, then she would clean the house from top to bottom and bake and cook until they had more food than people could eat. Spent, she'd retreat again.

She and Sally had talked about her when the girls weren't around but couldn't come to any conclusion. Laura and Jane avoided her and were even frightened by her. Brigid was the only one who could calm her or communicate with her in any way.

Christmas would be a strange event this year, with Maggie likely to hide herself away and Jamie still missing from her life. Brigid was glad to get a letter from home. Nellie's writing had improved a lot and the letter was longer than most.

> Our Breeda,
> I'm that excited, aye I am that. I sold my lace pieces, just like you used to, and I gave Ma a few coins. I'm learning dressmaking from the nuns and will be as good as you one day. Ma says she is well and to tell you Máire's still away working and has a boy now. She sends money home too. She'll wed next year.
>
> Norah's good at stitching an' all, but she still has some funny ways about her. She says she can talk wi' the faeries. John's talking a lot to the priest these days. I don't know what that's about.
>
> Da says the crop is better this year, and we have plenty of food. It's not as wet as most years. There are still evictions going on. Bad it is, but we are right as rain now.
>
> The grandparents are getting old. They are tired, they say. Granny Brigid's not the same since Granda

Michael went. She sits in the chair and spins, and sleeps a lot. Ma and me have to do all the work.

I wish you the blessings of the season. I miss you, Nellie

Brigid folded the letter and put it away safely in her drawer. A tear misted her eyes as she thought about home. *Aye, Dear Lord, I give thanks for all You have given me, and for the strength to cope with what You have taken away. But don't go anywhere, will You? I'll need You to guide me through this time ahead.*

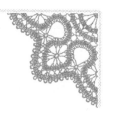

18

Coming of Age

Sunday, 10th February 1889

The next day would be Brigid's 21st birthday. She would officially come of age and could legally decide her own destiny – and control her own money without parental control. The situation seemed ludicrous since she'd been doing that for so long, but at least now she was officially grown-up.

Sally and the girls had insisted on a party and decorated the place with flowers and ferns. They'd set the table with the best of everything they owned, and Laura gave Brigid a special present of a matching cup, saucer and plate, which she begged Brigid to open so she could use it at the party.

In one of her bursts of energy, Maggie had baked a fruitcake, which Laura and Jane decorated, and made delicate sandwiches and other sweet goodies. She didn't say much, but Brigid felt she understood more of what was going on around her than she sometimes let on. But then she'd disappear into her lost world again.

Their surprise guest was Tom Price, returned only that morning from his journey.

"Mr Price, this is a pleasure to see you back so soon."

Tommy removed his hat and bowed low.

The girls giggled and he winked at them.

"And a pleasure it is to be here, Miss O'Brien. Those new steamships are so quick it fair takes one's breath away. But I would sail on the wind from anywhere to be at your birthday celebrations."

With a flourish and the return of the cheeky grin Brigid had missed, he pulled a small parcel from his pocket. "For you, fair lady, with my grateful thanks."

"Thanks for what exactly, Mr Price?" Brigid took the parcel from him but didn't immediately open it.

"For putting a fortune my way in the shape of Harrison Browne Drapers, of course."

Sally hovered around wanting to move the proceedings on. "Do sit down, Mr Price, and join us for some tea and sandwiches."

"And cake," said Jane, taking Tommy by the hand and leading him to a chair.

"Thank you, Miss Forsythe, I will. And later in the day, will you join me in a tipple, the two of you? You do still enjoy a glass or two, do you not, Miss Forsythe? And for you, Miss O'Brien, I've brought a small bottle of the best sherry from Spain."

Sally assured him she did enjoy a glass of spirit every now and then, and Brigid blushed. "Shush now. Not in front of the girls."

The parcel from Tommy sat on the table. Brigid itched to open it but manners dictated she wait until they had finished eating. They chatted amicably about the places Tom had journeyed to, and he teased the girls something awful about the scary things he'd seen.

In due course, Sally asked the girls to clear the table,

putting the plates to one side on the dresser.

"We'll take them downstairs to the kitchen in a wee while, but I think maybe Brigid should open her presents. What do you think, girls?"

"Oh, yes. Now, please."

Jane rushed off to her room and came back holding a small, flat parcel in her hands. Laura, already having given Brigid her present of matching crockery, hugged her, wished her a happy birthday and sat on the stool beside her.

Tommy moved his chair closer. "Open Jane's first," he said, seeing the girl's excited face.

Brigid inspected the handkerchief Jane had given her. "I made it myself; I did all the embroidery and hemmed it and crocheted the lace around the outside."

"And a beautiful job you did of it too, Jane, my love. You are a wonderful girl, and I thank you."

Then Jane gave her a sketch of a gown. "I thought it might be something you could make for yourself."

Sally looked over Brigid's shoulder as they studied the sketch together. "That is an amazing design, young miss. I am so proud of you. You have great ideas," said Brigid.

"Aye, lass you do too," agreed Sally. "I think Brigid should make it, and I know exactly which fabric she should use."

"Please, Brigid. Please," begged Jane.

"How can I say no?"

"You can't," they all chorused.

Sally pulled an envelope from her pocket. "This came for you."

Brigid turned the plain brown envelope over, but there was no return address, just a single stamp and a postmark from a place she'd never heard of. She ripped it open and took the flimsy sheet of paper out.

Turning it over she squealed, "It's Jamie. It's from our Jamie," then flipped back to the beginning.

Dear Breeda,

I am real sorry I have not written before, but I have been on the move a lot. I found work on a sheep farm down in the south island but then times got tough for the farmer and I had to move on. I found work in the mines for a while but couldn't stand it no longer, so I went and got work on a wee farm a half-day from Christchurch. It's been right grand it has. And I'll stay for as long as the farmer wants me. I like it down here, aye. The grass and the mountains and the clean air.

We had an earthquake at the beginning of September that scared everyone silly. I've never felt anything like it, Breeda. The ground shook and trembled under our feet, and buildings rattled and crumbled. There were a funny noise too. The new spire on the cathedral in Christchurch was damaged, and people are moaning something dreadful, that they are. The ground rumbled off and on after that for a time, but nothing more was damaged.

Anyways, I'm writing to tell you I met a girl from the neighbour's farm, and we are to be wed. Wish me a blessing from home, Breeda, for I miss you sorely. And wish me luck. You always were the lucky one, Breeda, but I think some of it has rubbed off on me at last. Write me news if you can. I hope you and the girls are safe and Sally keeps you company. I

*was verra sorry to have left you – and Maggie – but
I couldn't stand the jitters in my head no more. The
city crowded my thinking. All that's gone now.*

*Your cousin
Jamie*

PS: Tell Maggie I'll never forget her.

She scanned the page to check he was well, and
would read each word he'd written later. "Jamie's well.
He's got work and he's found a girl to wed."

Brigid was on her feet doing a little dance she was
that excited, when Maggie came shuffling out of her
room. She took Brigid's hand, put a screwed-up piece
of paper into it and folded her fingers over her palm.
Brigid looked down, wondering what it could be, and
then up at the haggard face hovering inches before her
own. Maggie took Brigid's face between her hands and
her eyes bored into Brigid's – tormented, pain-filled eyes
engraved with loss.

No one moved or said anything, in case they broke
the spell, or frightened Maggie, waiting to see what
would happen next.

Her lips moved and a croaking sound emitted from
her throat. "For you." The muscles of her neck bobbed
up and down and she swallowed. "Love you." Brigid read
her lips more than heard the words.

The burning in Brigid's throat prevented her from
saying anything either. She wrapped her arms around
Maggie and whispered a thank you into her ear. Just as
quickly as she came, Maggie scurried back to her room,
leaving everyone bewildered.

Brigid opened her palm and unfolded the paper. She could hardly believe her eyes. Covering her mouth with her hand to stop her lips from trembling, she tried in vain to hold back the tears that rolled down her cheeks.

In her hand lay a brooch: a simple, silver brooch, a common shawl pin of little value, in the shape of a Celtic cross – a St Brigid's cross – like sheaves of wheat woven together. Her great-grandmother's brooch, the one she'd lost on the ship so long ago. It didn't matter now why Maggie had taken it, only that she had returned it. Brigid couldn't decide whether to laugh or cry. She was happy and sad, full of pity and full of love, and more joyful than she'd ever been.

She looked around the room at the four beaming faces: Laura, Jane, Sally and Tommy. Jamie had reminded her that back home she was considered the lucky one but was too shy to accept it when others said she was accomplished, handsome and big-hearted: an angel in disguise. But whatever her reservations back then, she felt the luckiest girl in the world right now, surrounded by the people she loved and who loved her.

"Thank you," she whispered. "My heart is full and I can't tell ye how much you all mean to me. I couldn't have done any of it without your love."

A loud knocking on the door downstairs broke the moment.

"Who can that be – and on a Sunday? Don't they know we're closed?" said Sally. "I'll go."

Within a few moments voices carried up the stairs. Sally was angry and trying not to shout. The other voice Brigid recognised instantly. Dread replaced the elation she had felt only moments earlier.

Sally's head popped up at the top of the stairs first.

"Mr Harrison-Browne to see you, Miss O'Brien," she announced, formally introducing the unwanted guest. "He refuses to listen to me and insists he sees you now."

"Thank you, Miss Forsythe."

Brigid brushed the last of her tears from her face and straightened her spine, ready to greet Philip as soon as he turned to face her.

"Good afternoon to you."

She gave a quick nod of her head in greeting.

Philip removed his hat and flicked his hair back, which was enough to rouse her suspicions.

"However, as you can see I am entertaining guests and since this is my day of rest, I would ask you to be brief."

"I shan't disturb you more than necessary, Miss O'Brien. But I am here with news – favourable news, I hope." His eyes roved and stopped at Tommy. "Ah, Mr Price. You are the very person I have come to see. Can we discuss business later? Tomorrow, perhaps?"

"At your service, guv'ner." Tommy sat carelessly in one of the armchairs, legs crossed, a glass in one hand, a cigar in the other. "Tomorrow would suit me very well." He looked at home – a demeanour Philip could not fail to notice.

Laura and Jane retreated to the far corner near the window, and Sally took her place just behind Brigid's shoulder.

"I have come to offer you an arrangement." He reached into his inside coat pocket and pulled out a long document secured with wax seal. It looked important – and legal. Brigid held her breath.

"Don't you want to know what it is?" His voice was teasing and light-hearted, but she didn't trust him.

"I'm sure you'll tell me when you are ready."

He looked around the room again.

"You've made this place quite comfortable. I congratulate you. May I sit?"

Brigid nodded and he pulled out a chair at the table. Brigid and Sally remained standing. He set his hat and the papers down and tapped his fingers on them with an annoying rhythm that kept time with Brigid's heartbeat.

Moments passed.

"This document is courtesy of my mother. You will be satisfied with its contents, I feel sure, but I did take the liberty to ask my lawyer to prepare another document."

He flicked his hair back again, and Brigid's fear she would lose everything resurfaced.

"Aye, and will you tell me what the second set of papers says?"

Philip smiled, not quite confidently, but far more warmly than she'd seen him smile for a long time. "It's a contract, which I hope you will sign."

Feeling her knees go wobbly, she perched on the edge of the chair opposite. Sally stood behind with her hands on Brigid's shoulders.

"A contract, you say? What's it for?"

"It's simple really. It says you agree to attend the Harrison Browne Department Store to demonstrate lacemaking and give personal service to selected clients."

All of a sudden Brigid didn't feel so lucky anymore. It seemed her luck had changed. "And if I refuse?"

"Then you don't get this one." He pushed the larger sealed certificate towards her. "Open it."

Brigid broke the seal, unfolded the paper and started to read. She needed to rest her arm against the table end to stop herself from shaking. The more she read, the more she shook. Blood pounded in her ears. Sally gasped.

Brigid read to the bottom of the page, then folded it in three again. "Is this a joke?"

"Not at all, my dear Brigid, not at all. My mother insisted, and in light of your good sense and judgment last time we met, I could not, in all conscience, object."

"So what is the proviso should I accept?"

The second contract in question Philip held between his fingers. He waved it towards her. "Like I said, I want you to sign this contract with me to attend my store."

Brigid still couldn't understand what was going on. "How can I do both? Be here in New Zealand as per your mother's wishes, and in Brisbane at your command at the same time?"

"You'll find a way, I'm sure."

By this time, troubled by Brigid's obvious anxiety, Tommy sat forward. "Is that a threat, I'm hearing?"

Philip turned his head casually towards Tommy. "Not at all, dear chap. More like an opportunity."

"Doesn't sound like an opportunity to me. Sounds more like bullying."

Philip feigned shock. "Is that what you think of me? If that is so, Mr Price, then maybe you and I are not suited to do business with each other."

Clearly perturbed by the intended slight but prepared to do battle for Brigid nevertheless, Tommy stood up and leaned over the table. "All I'm asking is that you deal fair with Miss O'Brien. Stop the shilly-shallying and get on with it, man. It's enough to set a man's teeth on edge to see her so bothered."

Philip looked genuinely dismayed. "Why should you be bothered, Miss O'Brien? You've read the document from my mother – and do enlighten Mr Price here and then maybe he will think more kindly of me – so I fail to understand your concern. This ..." and with that he pushed the envelope holding the second document across the table, "... is a mere bagatelle in comparison."

Brigid gingerly retrieved the envelope, opened the unsealed flap and removed the contents. Her eyes scanned the document with trepidation. She reached the bottom of the page, and relief engulfed her. The overwhelming urge to laugh and cry at the same time returned.

Sally, reading it from behind, gripped Brigid's shoulder so tightly she flinched with the pain.

Brigid covered Sally's hand with her own while she gathered her composure. "Sit down, Mr Price, I beg you," she said at last. "Mr Harrison-Browne here has been playing games at my expense." She glared across the table at Philip but was unable to maintain the severe and ill-humoured facade.

Tommy, the only one not in on Philip's prank, still looked unhappy.

Brigid eased his discomfort. "As he said, Mr Harrison-Browne requires me to attend his department store in Brisbane – but only for one full week, twice a year. In return, Mrs Browne – and I presume it is with Mr Harrison-Browne's agreement – has gifted me the premises known as 'Miss Brigid's'."

"So will you accept?" laughed Philip.

"Under the circumstances, I believe I shall."

Tommy extended his hand to Philip. "Forgive me for my assumptions. I do apologise. Can I offer a wee drink as compensation?"

Tommy poured drinks all round. Sally and Brigid

hugged one another in disbelief and reassured the girls. What a grand birthday party after all!

Brigid moved towards Philip and placed her hand on his arm. "I cannot thank you enough. I, too, owe you an apology. I doubted you before I had heard your proposal."

"The pleasure is mine, Miss Brigid. And it is I who should apologise to you. My behaviour last time we met was unforgivable. My only excuse is that I was driven by despair and desperation. Circumstances have changed since then."

He turned to Sally and Tommy and included them in the rest of his little speech, raising his glass. "A toast to you all. Thanks to Miss O'Brien's inspired guidance, Mr Price's salesmanship and service, and Miss Forsythe's outstanding ability with the accounts, not only is 'Miss Brigid's' thriving but the new Harrison Browne Department Store is also a reality. I invite you all to join me – at your convenience, of course – to participate in its success."

Later that evening, after the girls had gone to bed, and the remains of supper had been cleared, Brigid, Sally and Tommy sat in relaxed comfort together, admiring the night sky through the windows. There seemed nothing left to say about Philip's appearance and astounding gifts.

Brigid fingered the St Brigid's Cross pin secured to the bodice of her gown. "I'm not sure Maggie remembers this was once mine. I can only assume she stole it in a jealous rage. She used to get them a lot. But I am that pleased to have it back."

"Aye, poor Maggie," said Sally. "She's a troubled soul, all right. I guess she thinks she was giving you something precious whether or not it was hers to give."

"I will thank her for it again when I think she understands, but I won't say it was once mine. I will leave her with her delusions."

"Do you think hearing Jamie's name again stirred her up?"

Brigid thought about Sally's suggestion. "Aye, maybe. But I'm right glad to know Jamie is grand and settled now. Makes me feel easier, it does."

They were talked out, the excitement of the day having sapped their energy and strength, and sat silently with their own thoughts, sharing a nightcap.

"I must take my leave, Miss Brigid," said Tommy into the quiet. "It's been a rewarding if unusual day, but one little matter, I believe, was overlooked."

"Are you sure, Tommy? I can't think what that might be. We checked and double-checked the contract before I signed. And I do believe Mr Harrison-Browne will be true to his word."

"Aye, so I do," agreed Sally. "This time. I think I'm even a little excited by the thought of seeing it myself, even if it does mean returning to Brisbane."

"So am I," said Tommy. "And he'll hold to his word. You will be amazed what he has achieved. But no, it's naught to do with that." He took the little parcel he had given Brigid many hours ago, which had lain forgotten and unopened in the furore caused by Philip's arrival. "It's this. Would you be so kind as to accept it?"

"Oh, Tommy. I am so sorry. How rude of me."

She took the parcel, untied the ribbon and unwrapped the paper. The plain black box gave no hint of its contents. Brigid lifted the lid and for the second time that day was propelled into confusion. She looked up to find Tommy at her side, on one knee. That wicked grin of his spread ear to ear, and he struggled to control his laughter. Sally was no better. She bounced up and down on the chair in a most unladylike fashion.

"You told me once you'd walk out with me if I asked you proper. So here I am, asking you proper like. Miss Brigid O'Brien, will you do me the honour of walking out with me?"

He took the Claddagh ring from its box and held it up to Brigid. She took it from him, slipped it on the ring finger of her right hand with the heart pointing inwards – to show her heart had been captured – and threw her arms around his neck, nearly knocking him over in her enthusiasm.

"Mr Thomas Price, I do believe I will."

THANK YOU

If you enjoyed this book, discover more unforgettable family heritage stories inspired by immigrants seeking a better life in a foreign land.

THE NEW ZEALAND IMMIGRANT COLLECTION
suspenseful family saga fiction about overcoming the odds.

The Cornish Knot
Portrait of a Man

Brigid The Girl from County Clare
Gwenna The Welsh Confectioner
The Costumier's Gift

The Disenchanted Soldier

* * *

Available at
Amazon.com/vickyadin
www.vickyadin.co.nz

Please consider leaving a customer review.
I'd be delighted if you would sign up for my newsletter on my website.

* * *

Look out for the upcoming series
THE ART OF SECRETS –
dual-timeline stories about discovering your roots.
First book *The Art of Secrets* available now.

Gwenna
The Welsh Confectioner

A powerful tale of family life amid Auckland's bustling Karangahape Road at the turn of the 20th century

Against overwhelming odds, can she save her legacy?

Counterpart to *Brigid The Girl from County Clare*
Prequel to *The Costumier's Gift*

Gwenna's life is about to change. Her father is dead, and the family business is on the brink of collapse. Thwarted by society, the plucky sweet maker refuses to accept defeat.

Gwenna promised her father she would fulfil his dreams and save her legacy. But thanks to her overbearing stepbrother, that legacy is at risk. Gwenna must fight for her rights if she is to keep her vow.

She falls in love with the cheeky and charming Johnno, but just when things are beginning to look up, disaster strikes. Throughout the twists and turns of love and tragedy, Gwenna is irrepressible. She refuses to relinquish her goal and lets nothing and no one stand in her way.

But blind to anything that could distract her, Gwenna overlooks the most important person in her life, putting her dreams, her family, and her chance at happiness in jeopardy.

Utter brilliance. Vicky really brings the characters to life and you can really engage with what it must have been like to be a young girl like Gwenna going into business at the turn of the century in a male dominated society. Every character contributed to make this a truly wonderful story; my only disappointment was when it ended. ***** 5-star Amazon review

THE NEW ZEALAND IMMIGRANT COLLECTION

The Costumier's Gift

An absorbing multigenerational dual-timeline family saga

Why does a stranger hold the key to untangling Katie's family secrets?

Continues the lives of *Brigid The Girl from County Clare* and *Gwenna The Welsh Confectioner*

Jane thrives in the one place where she can hide her pain and keep her skeletons to herself. As principal costumier at Auckland's Opera House in its Edwardian heyday, she is content – until the past comes back to haunt her.

Her beloved foster mother Brigid and her best friend Gwenna are anchors in her solitary yet rewarding life. When the burden of carrying secrets becomes too great, Jane surrenders her role as keeper of the untold.

Generations later Katie seeks refuge from her crumbling life with her Granna, who lives in the past with the people in her cherished photographs. Katie discovers she must identify the people behind the gentle smiles and reveal generations of secrets before she can claim her inheritance.

Through Jared, an intriguing new client, Katie revives her stalled career until she learns he holds the key to uncovering her past. Despite an increasing attraction, she shies away from any deeper involvement ... but without him she will never know the truth.

THE NEW ZEALAND IMMIGRANT COLLECTION

The Cornish Knot

One woman's emotional quest to discover her family roots

Can one woman's secrets change the life of another a century later?

Prequel to *Portrait of a Man*

A grieving widow, a century old journal, a missing portrait, and an engaging art historian. What will the secrets of the past reveal?

When Megan receives a journal written a century earlier, she sets out on an irresistible path. Following in the footsteps of the diary's author, Megan journeys from her home in New Zealand to Cornwall, France and Italy, uncovering an unsettling past. She meets a fellow countryman in Florence and is soon caught up in the aesthetic world of art where the truth lies hidden beneath the layers of paint.

Charmed by the man her daughter disapproves of, and captivated by a series of unknown paintings, Megan is drawn deeper into the mysteries and conflicts of long ago. As she unravels her family history and reveals its life-changing secrets, can she find love again?

An engaging tale of grief, loss, love and family intrigue ... wonderful story, and a real page-turner, which leads the reader through all the twists and turns of a well-constructed plot. I loved the insightful descriptions of family relationships, the fully realised characters and the various locations in which the action takes place. Seldom have I read such a poignant and faithful account of the effects of bereavement. I can't wait to read more. **** 4-star Amazon review

THE NEW ZEALAND IMMIGRANT COLLECTION

Portrait of a Man

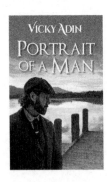

The gripping multigenerational tale of lies, lost chances and misplaced love.

Will the secrets of the past destroy an artist's legacy?

The soul-searching conclusion to *The Cornish Knot*

An Italian artist, a Cornish knot and a Māori koru lead to a shocking exposé. As World War One escalates, can he keep his secrets safe?

In 1863, Matteo Borgoni is a desperate man. If he is to free his beloved wife held captive by her father in Melbourne, his picture framing business must succeed. Haunted by the memory of failure, he has many obstacles to overcome before he can establish himself with the artists of Dunedin, New Zealand and be reunited with his love.

Fifty years on, Luciano, a rakish Italian portrait artist fleeing from a life of lies, turns up at Borgoni Picture Framers seeking refuge. As the ravages of World War One escalate, an unusual friendship and newfound rapport brings unforeseen repercussions. A terrifying pandemic is the last thing they need.

Over a century later, a man recognises a portrait in an Auckland gallery, and demands it back. Amid another global pandemic, a marriage on the brink of failure, and a life-and -death struggle, the portrait exposes generations of family secrets and deceptions with life-changing results.

Portrait of a Man is told over three timelines through the eyes of different generations.

THE NEW ZEALAND IMMIGRANT COLLECTION

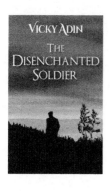

The Disenchanted Soldier

A heart-breaking dual-timeline family saga

From soldier to pacifist

In 1863, young Daniel Adin, a trained British soldier, embarks on an adventure of a lifetime. In pursuit of a new life and land to farm, he travels to New Zealand to fight an unknown enemy – the fearless Māori.

A hundred and thirty years later, Libby is fascinated by the stories of Daniel as he looks down at her from the aged black-and-white photos on the wall. Surrounded by four generations of his large family, she wants to know more, to know what he was really like.

As she researches his past, Daniel's story becomes so much more than she expected.

I loved this book and so will you if you like historical fiction and family sagas set somewhere you likely know little about. This is beautifully and sensitively written. The characters are terrific. The fascinating part to me was how Vicky was able to take us on the family's journey in a thoughtful and non-judgmental way.

***** 5-star Amazon review

THE NEW ZEALAND IMMIGRANT COLLECTION

The Art of Secrets

An uplifting tale of friendship, grief and lies.

Emma wants to forget; Charlotte never can. Together they remember.

First in the upcoming series THE ART OF SECRETS

A young journalist and an ageing author have little in common, until their secrets tear them apart.

Emma is an enterprising young journalist with a bright future, but her life and career are falling apart. In a last-ditch attempt to save her position, she accepts the assignment to interview the bestselling author, Charlotte Day.

The ageing Charlotte has a reputation for being cantankerous and is highly secretive about her past, one she considers too painful to relive and too shameful to share. Preferring her roses to people, she grudgingly agrees to meet this girl who gets through her defences, forcing her to confront her past.

As Charlotte and Emma's relationship deepens, they become enmeshed in a tangle of secrets that changes their lives.

The art of great writing! ... Adin keeps a tight rein on her leading characters, their actions and reactions credibly grounded in genuine emotions. The change of tone from Emma to Charlotte, from young to old, works, helps the reader see behind the lies and half-truths they tell each other. Their progress from antagonists to friends is seamless, as the layers of the story peel back like petals, exposing the truth at the flower's heart. Bev Robitai, author of *Sunstrike*

Book 1 of THE ART OF SECRETS series

330

About the Author

Vicky Adin is a family historian in love with the past. Like the characters in her stories, she too is an immigrant to New Zealand, arriving a century after her first protagonists, and ready to start a new life.

Born in Wales, she grew up in Cornwall until aged 12. Her family emigrated to New Zealand, a country she would call home. Vicky draws on her affinity for these places, in her writing. Fast forward a few years, and she marries a fourth-generation Kiwi bloke with Irish, Scottish and English ancestors and her passion for genealogy flourishes.

The further she digs into the past, the more she wants to record the lives of the people who were the foundations of her new country. Not just her own ancestors, but all those who braved the oceans and became pioneers in a raw new land. Her research into life as it was for those immigrants in the mid-to-late 1800s and early 1900s gave her enough material to write for many years about the land left behind and the birth of a new nation.

Her first book, *The Disenchanted Soldier*, is the most biographical of all her books, inspired by her husband's great-grandfather. For the rest, while the history of the time is accurate, the characters are fictionalised to fit with the events and happenings as they occurred.

Vicky holds an MA(Hons) in English, is a lover of art, antiques, gardens, good food and red wine. She and her husband travel throughout New Zealand in their caravan and travel the world when they can. She hopes younger generations get as much enjoyment learning about the past through her stories, as she did when writing about it.

Author's Note

The fortitude and resourcefulness of immigrants, especially the women who had hearts of lions, has always held a fascination for me. I enjoy researching their lives. I hope you have enjoyed reading about them.

While Brigid's story is fictional, it is based on a real family who immigrated to Australia in the late 1880s, one of whom later travelled to New Zealand. Brigid is a composite of several individuals. The story line has been adapted from various adventures and incidents, some of which are unrelated. Tailoring, dressmaking and lacemaking were common occupations, and drapery stores were alive and well.

In Part One, the 1886 voyage of the SS *Dorunda* follows newspaper articles of the time found on the website of the National Library of Australia Trove and the Papers Past website of the National Library of New Zealand. These amazingly detailed and lengthy reports covered the dates, route, weather, deaths and other misadventures, as well as providing the names of the captain, surgeon, matron and other officials – all of whom have been named and mentioned.

The SS *Dorunda* was, indeed, known as the 'Cholera Ship', after an outbreak in 1885. In December 1886, she was manned by twenty-six white (sic) officers and crew, and eighty-one lascars, and carried 401 passengers, with itemised lists of the numbers of males and females, married or single, and of which nationalities and occupations. It was easy to create characters with such specific information available.

Similarly, in Parts Two and Three, descriptions of life in Australia and New Zealand were found on Trove and Papers Past and other sites such as Brisbane History and the Australian Dictionary of Biography. The history of the settlement of Brisbane and Townsville, the buildings, schools, streets and other such specifics, are as accurate as I could make them. I spent several hours researching whether the drinks would be cold in 1887 in Townsville and was surprised to find an enterprising and active ice industry. And I didn't know Schweppes was available that long ago either.

The January 1887 flood in Brisbane is well recorded and was one of the most devastating at that time. The Great Flood of 1893 was worse. D L Brown & Sons Drapers of Eagle Street, Brisbane survived the 1887 flood, only to be destroyed by fire in 1888. The dressmaker mentioned in the story, Mrs Janet Walker (1882–1938) was a well-known and well-respected costumier employing 120 workers.

Shipping between Australia and New Zealand was common and frequent, similar to catching a long-distance bus or train today. Auckland was in the throes of a deep economic crisis commonly known as 'The Long Depression', at the same time as the suffrage movement was pushing for women's rights. We all know the suffragettes won their fight and New Zealand women were the first to be granted full rights to vote in parliamentary elections by a self-governing country. Brigid lived in interesting times.

The large department stores such as Smith & Caughey (established 1882), Grace Brothers (founded in 1885 and bought by Myer in 1983), David Jones (established 1838), and others since closed or amalgamated, like Court Brothers (1886) and, more recently, Kirkcaldie and Stains (established 1863), all began as drapery stores. 'Miss Brigid's' fitted the scene.

Australia and New Zealand are nations built by immigrants. Brigid's story is one of many and indicative of countless real characters who brought their skills, resourcefulness and resilience to our shores.

I salute them.

Acknowledgements

I offer my humble and grateful thanks to the many people who have listened to me talk endlessly about Brigid, have given me advice on words and design, and helped fix my mistakes. I am certain that in naming individuals I will miss some I should have included, so please take it as given – if you have supported and encouraged me in any way, I thank you.

I particularly wish to thank the members of the Mairangi Writers' Group who listened, critiqued and helped improve the story line and language. I am especially grateful to authors Jenny Harrison, Erin McKechnie and Stephanie Hammond, who as my beta-readers gave me invaluable feedback that helped mould the story.

I am indebted to Adrienne Charlton of AM Publishing New Zealand, who is my ever-faithful and ever-vigilant publisher, proofreader and editor. I praise her skills in ensuring this book is as flawless as humanly possible. Any remaining errors are mine and mine alone.

As a genealogist I pay tribute to the immigrant families – wherever they came from and wherever they live. They brought stories of triumph over hardship. *Brigid The Girl from County Clare* is one of those tales – a history of love and loss, of conflict and resolution, and of personal renewal.

Lastly, to my family – especially my wonderfully patient husband. I thank him for his constant support in so many little ways, and for his brilliant suggestions and insightful comments.